THE SYNDROME THAT SAVED US

ROBERTA KAGAN

TITLE PAGE

The Syndrome That Saved Us

By
USA Today Best-Selling Author
Roberta Kagan

PROLOGUE

T he room smelled of sweat and fear as Lory and Alma Bellinelli stood side by side in the long line to register at Rome's main synagogue. Lory cast a worried glance at Alma. But she returned his glance with a reassuring smile. *My sweet wife. She is always trying to make the best of everything.* Lory forced himself to return her smile, but his eyes were still narrowed with worry. And the wrinkle between his brows had deepened. As they stood waiting, they could hear the soft pitter-patter of rain on the roof outside.

"We should have worn our raincoats," Lory said, acknowledging the sound.

"Yes, we should have. But we didn't. Oh well, so we'll get wet," Alma whispered to him as she gently squeezed his arm. "Nothing like walking in the rain in the springtime."

"You're right. Even if it is still cold outside."

"We'll put our arms around each other, and that will keep us warm," she said.

"I can't help it, I still get a bad feeling about what is going on here, Alma." Lory was suddenly serious again. "Why would it be that all of a sudden, out of nowhere, Jews are forced to register and report everything they own?"

"I don't know. But look around you. Everyone else who lives in the Jewish Quarter is here with us. And we are at the Jewish synagogue. No one else seems concerned they are all reporting their assets. If all of the others think it is all right, then it must be."

"Ehhh, I just don't know," Lory said, shaking his head.

"We don't have that much, really, to worry about. Heaven knows we aren't rich. If the Nazis are looking to take valuable things from people, they will find that all we have is a small flat filled with secondhand furniture. It they want it that badly, they can have it," she said.

From across the room, a deep baritone voice called out, "Bellinelli, is that you?"

Lory let out a belly laugh when he saw the familiar face of his old friend. "Sacerdoti, I haven't seen you in years. How are you?" Lory walked across the room and put his arms around his old friend, taking him into a bear hug.

"I'm all right," Sacerdoti said, "but you sure look good."

"You look good too. What have you been doing with yourself these days?"

"I was working at the Civil Hospital Umberto 1 of Ancona, but they let me go because I am Jewish. Then my uncle introduced me to Dr. Borromeo, who offered me a job at the Roman Catholic hospital, Fatebenefratelli. It's on Tiber Island. Are you familiar with it?"

"Yes, of course," Lory said.

"Dr. Borromeo is a wonderful man. I wish you could meet him. You two would get along well. I know it. Anyway, I have been so busy that I hardly ever get out and see the light of day. And what are you doing these days?" Sacerdoti asked.

"I'm working at the Israelite Hospital. And . . . I got married. Come, follow me, I want you to meet my Alma."

The two men walked back to Alma, who was still in line.

"This beautiful woman is my wife, Alma. She works as a nurse at the Israelite Hospital, and we are also doing some private medical work in the ghetto. So many people need help, and they are unable to get to a hospital," Lory said, then he put his arm around Alma proudly.

"I'm Vittorio Sacerdoti. My friends call me Vito. It's a pleasure to meet you. Your husband and I have been friends for a long time. In fact, he kept my spirits up all through the time we spent at the University of Bologna together," Dr. Sacerdoti said, smiling, then he embraced Alma and kissed her on either cheek.

"It's nice to meet you too," Alma said.

Then Vito looked at Lory with a puzzled expression on his face and asked, "I don't mean to pry, but I never knew you were Jewish."

"I'm not Jewish; I'm Roman Catholic, but my Alma is Jewish, so we have come to register."

"Ahhh, all right. That makes sense. I think you knew that I am Jewish, so that's why I am here."

"I didn't remember, quite frankly. But it's so good to see you."

"When I first got out of school and came back to Rome, I thought about getting a job at the Jewish hospital. But then I got such a wonderful offer from the Roman Catholic hospital that I couldn't refuse it. They are a wonderful bunch of monks who run the place. And that's what I have always loved about Italy. Here we can all live together in peace. Not like in Germany where they are treating Jews worse than dogs. I think it is disgraceful."

Lory nodded, but then he added, "My wife's mother and her grandparents are from Berlin. They are still living in Germany."

"Oh, I am sorry. I hope I didn't offend you. I certainly didn't mean to," Vito said. Then not wanting to upset Alma, he changed the subject. "You and I have lost touch for far too long, Lorenzo, my friend. We must arrange to have dinner together soon. And, of course, you must bring your lovely wife," Vito said as Lory and Alma came up to the front of the line.

Lory took out a small book of paper and a pencil from the breast pocket of his shirt. He scribbled down his address, then he handed it to Vito. "Here is my address. Please come by. Alma and I would love to have you over for dinner. Our apartment is nothing fancy. But you are always welcome in our home."

"As you would be in mine. However, right now I don't have a place of my own to invite you to. What does a single man need with an apartment? So I am living in a room at the hospital."

"Well, not to worry. You'll come to our place," Lory said. Then he added, "I can still remember that year that I went home from school for Christmas with you. Do you remember?"

"Of course I do. How could I ever forget? We went to my friend Marco's house next door where we had the Feast of the Seven Fishes. We ate so much that we both got sick."

"I remember, my friend," Lory said. "We were rolling on the bed holding our swollen bellies." He laughed.

"And then you accompanied me and Marco to his church for midnight Mass even though you're Jewish," Lory said.

"That is because I loved you both, and I would never let religion get in the way of that love. I may not be a Catholic, but the service was quite beautiful."

"Midnight Mass is always very special." Lory smiled, then he continued. "Even though I would never want to change a single thing about my Alma, I love her just as she is: I would really like for her to see a midnight Mass one Christmas Eve."

"Let's keep the line moving," a man, who was standing behind Lory and Alma, said in a frustrated tone.

"So come by our house and see us soon. Don't be a stranger. My Alma is a good cook."

Alma smiled. "I try anyway," she said.

"Next . . ." the clerk at the desk said. He was tapping his pencil impatiently.

Lory shrugged. "I suppose it's our turn now," he said, and then he and Alma walked up to the desk to fill out and sign the registration papers.

CHAPTER 1

May 1938

Early one morning after Lory had finished his rounds at the hospital, he went to the nurses' station to record his notes. While he was writing he received a call.

"There's a Dr. Sacerdoti here to see you," the receptionist said.

"Please send him up to my office, Margie," Lory said. "I'm finished here, so I should be there in just a minute."

When Vito arrived at Lory's office, Lory stood up, and the two men embraced. "What brings you here?" Lory asked.

"I was going to come by for dinner tonight, but I wanted to check with you first to see if you and Alma had any other plans."

"You can come by anytime; there's no need to announce yourself. Just knock on our door, and both Alma and I will be thrilled to see you. I am so glad we found each other again last month. It had been far too long since the last time we were together."

"I couldn't agree more," Vito said. "What time shall I come?"

"How is seven o'clock for you? Is it too early?"

"I'm off work today. So seven would be perfect. I'll be there. Will you let Alma know I am coming?"

"Of course. She works here at this hospital with me, so I'll go and tell her as soon as you leave."

"What can I bring?"

"Yourself. You need not bring anything else. I know I can speak for my wife when I say this: we will both be happy to have you at our table, my dear friend."

After Vito left, Lory went upstairs to see Alma on the floor where she was working. When he arrived, she was in a patient's room helping the old woman to eat her breakfast. Lory smiled as he watched his wife. The compassion in her heart made her face shine. And he was awestruck by her beauty. Once she'd finished helping the patient, she tucked her into her bed and then walked out the door. When she saw Lory waiting outside, her eyes twinkled with love.

"Hello," she said. "I wasn't expecting to see you. Is everything all right?"

"Yes, my darling. Everything is fine. Vito dropped by the hospital this morning and asked me if it would be all right if he came to dinner tonight. You remember him, don't you? We invited him to dinner when we saw him at the synagogue when we went there to register."

"Of course, I remember him. He was a lovely person. And it would be wonderful for him to come to dinner tonight. What time did you tell him?"

"Seven. Is that too early?"

"Not at all. I'll make a stew. I have some fish and vegetables, and some rice. Would that be all right?"

"It would be perfect," he said. "I have to get back to my work. But, by the way . . . in case you forgot . . . I love you," he said.

"I love you too," she said, smiling.

Vito arrived on time. He brought a bottle of wine and a cake. The three of them had such a good time, they decided that Vito should drop over for dinner at least once every month.

CHAPTER 2

July 1938

One hot summer night, Lory and Alma had just finished eating dinner and were sitting on the sofa. In spite of the heat, Lory's arm was cradled around Alma's shoulder, and her head was on his chest. She was engrossed in reading the novel she had taken out from the library the day before. As he did every night, Lory was thumbing through the newspaper. She cuddled deeper into him, and he leaned down and kissed the top of her head. Then there was a loud knock at the door. Lory got up and stretched his legs. He shook his head at Alma. "Probably someone in the neighborhood is sick again," he said.

She nodded as he opened the door. A frantic woman in her forties was standing outside.

"How can I help you?" Lory asked.

"Are you Dr. Bellinelli?"

"I am. Who are you?"

"My name is Juliana Russo. I need your help. My daughter is in desperate need of a doctor."

"Please come inside," Lory said.

"I need you to come with me quickly. We must hurry," Juliana said as she walked in.

"Do you know what is wrong?" Lory asked as he was gathering his medical equipment to put his doctor's bag together.

"Please. My daughter is giving birth, and things are not going well. She has been laboring for a long time. Since yesterday morning. Now she is bleeding. There is a lot of blood. I cannot take her to a hospital. If anyone finds out that she is having a baby, our family will be shunned. You see, she is unmarried."

Lory looked over at Alma. "I'll be back," he said.

She nodded.

Then Lory grabbed his black leather bag and followed the woman outside. He ran behind her until they arrived at a run-down apartment building just outside of the Jewish Quarter. When they walked in the woman's flat, there was a large cross hanging on the gray wall. All around it the paint was chipping.

Mrs. Russo led Lory to the back of the apartment. They entered a small bedroom where Lory saw a pale young woman covered in bloody sheets. Her lips had turned blue. Lory felt his heart sink. *She looks bad,* he thought. "I'm Dr. Bellinelli," he said, taking the young woman's hand. "What is your name?"

"Tatiana." White film had formed around the edges of her mouth, and her voice was barely a whisper.

"I'm going to examine you now. All right?"

Tatiana nodded.

Sweat beaded on Lory's forehead as he worked to save Tatiana Russo's life. Hours passed; the sun began to rise. He had to turn the baby. She screamed with pain. But, finally, the child was born. The umbilical cord was wrapped around his neck, and he was dead. Lory felt so bad for the young mother. She'd suffered so much only to find that her child was gone. But, despite all the blood she lost, Tatiana was still alive.

"I'm so sorry," Lory said, taking Tatiana's hand in his own.

It was seven thirty in the morning when Lory finally informed the mother that her daughter was stable enough for him to leave. "I am sorry about the baby," he repeated as he got ready to go. "But you are young." He stopped what he was doing and walked over to take Tatiana's hand in his. He held it gently and said, "You will have more babies."

She nodded, then turned away from him to face the wall. He assumed she was crying and that she preferred to be left alone.

Lory finished gathering his things and put them back into his bag to be cleaned as soon as he got home. Then he left the room.

Juliana followed him. She stopped him when they were in the small living room.

Juliana looked at Lory and bit her lip. "I don't know what to say. Perhaps it is for the best that the child did not survive. My daughter would have been forced to leave town with him. She would have had to move away from here and go somewhere on her own. Still, I can't help but mourn for the poor helpless little one."

"I understand. You have my deepest sympathies," Lory repeated.

"I don't know what to say, except thank you, and may God bless you and your family."

Lory smiled.

Mrs. Russo was wringing her hands, but she continued speaking. "I am sorry, Doctor. I realize that I should not have come to ask for your help. You see, I don't have money to pay you. But I didn't know where else to turn. I had no choice. If you had not come here to help us tonight, my daughter would have died."

"Yes, I understand, and I am glad I could be of service." Lory sighed. "As far as payment is concerned. Pay me when you can. How is that?" He was used to this. It happened often. A person would be in need of medical help and unable to pay. Some of the other doctors he knew had begun to ask for payment in advance. But he just couldn't bring himself to do that. He believed that as a man who practiced medicine, he owed it to his patients to treat them, to help them as much as he was able, regardless of whether they had the money to pay or not.

"Bless you. Bless you, Dr. Bellinelli," Mrs. Russo said, kissing the tops of Lory's hands.

CHAPTER 3

December 1938

It was a week before Christmas when Vito dropped by Lory and Alma's apartment for dinner. He brought gifts that he'd wrapped for each of them and insisted that they wait until Christmas to open them.

"They aren't much. But they are tokens of affection for you both."

"You really didn't need to bring us presents," Alma said. "But it was very kind of you. Lory and I appreciate your kindness. And we are both so glad to see you."

"It's been so hectic at work lately that I wasn't certain that I would be able to come by until after Christmas. But it is important that we make time for fun, time to spend with those we care about, yes?" Vito said as he handed Alma a box of cookies he brought. "These cookies are very similar to the ones my mother made when Lory came to visit my home so many years ago. He enjoyed them so much that I brought them here today. Of course, my mother's were better than these. These come from a bakery; everything my mother made, she made with love. But these are the closest thing I've found." Then he put a bottle of inexpensive red wine down on the table. "I brought this wine too. I drink it often, and I really enjoy it. I hope you and Lory will like it too," he said.

Alma had not been expecting company that night, so she hadn't planned anything special for dinner. She'd come home from work and prepared a quick sauce, which Lory called a gravy, for spaghetti, using tomatoes that she'd canned, from her friend Lucinda's garden last summer. Food was becoming more difficult to acquire, and there was hardly enough for her and Lory, but Alma took a smaller portion and strategically spread it around on her plate to make it look as if her portion was larger. She loved having Vito come by for dinner, and she wanted to make sure he did not feel uncomfortable thinking there wasn't enough.

"This is such a delicious gravy." Vito smacked his lips. "Where did you learn to cook Italian food like this?" Vito asked.

"My mother-in-law taught me. This was her recipe," Alma replied with a smile.

"It's wonderful. I'm sure you added your own touches."

"A little bit. I didn't change too much. I just chopped up a little sweet pepper and a little onion and sautéed them first." Alma smiled. "I'm so glad you like it."

All through the meal, Vito told Alma stories about the comical mishaps that he and Lory had faced in their early days at the University of Bologna. The three of them laughed until their faces hurt and their stomachs ached.

After they'd finished dinner, Alma made a pot of chicory coffee, and although she didn't have any milk or sugar, they sipped the bitter liquid and ate the cookies Vito brought.

"I heard an old friend of mine came to see you, and you helped her out," Vito said. "You're a good soul, Lory."

"Who is your friend?" Lory asked.

"Tatiana Russo. She and her mother attend a church where many of my patients are members. She came to me at the hospital where I work when she found out she was pregnant. She told me in secret that she was with child and unmarried, but she couldn't come to me to help her with the birth at the Catholic hospital because people might find out she was an unwed mother. She asked me if I knew anyone who could help her out. Someone who was not connected to the Catholic hospital. I recommended that she come to see you when her time came or if she should need a doctor before."

"Poor thing," Lory said. "She had a very difficult time, and then she lost the baby anyway. But, at least, thank God, she will be all right."

"I wanted to thank you for helping her," Vito said.

"Of course. We're doctors. That's what we do. Isn't it?"

"Yes, it is." Vito smiled. "I love my job. I love knowing that I spend my days helping those who need me. That's why I decided I wanted to be a doctor. I won't say that every day is good. There are bad days. Days when we have to face death and know that it is in God's hands, not our own. But I love the work, most of the time anyway."

Lory hesitated, then he said, "This is a little off topic. But I need to discuss it with you. Have you noticed that things are not so good for the Jews here in Rome lately? I have been seeing a rise in suicide among Jewish people at the hospital."

"Yes, I know about it. It seems to me that Mussolini is taking some of his ideas from Hitler these days."

"Yes, exactly. He's banned marriage between Jews and Gentiles."

"That should not affect you two, should it? I mean you are already married," Vito asked, concerned.

"For now, it doesn't affect us. But I can only hope that things won't get worse in the future. The way things are going, who knows what laws will be put into effect. Jews in Rome are losing their rights. Did you know that they can no longer teach in public schools? I am worried."

"I've heard all of this. And quite frankly I'm worried too. I am afraid that I might lose my job at the hospital," Vito said.

"You're a doctor. They need you. Don't worry, you'll be fine," Lory reassured him. But he wasn't sure of anything.

"Please, let's not talk about Hitler or Mussolini or the state of the world, for that matter, anymore tonight. Let's just enjoy each other's company," Alma said, smiling. "It's so nice to have a guest."

"She's right," Vito said. "I want you to know that I am proud of you, Lorenzo. You married quite a girl. She's both beautiful and smart."

"I certainly did," Lory said, and he smiled at Alma.

When the evening ended, Lory and Alma both made Vito promise to return as soon as he had a little spare time. He assured them he would, and he did. He returned two weeks later. But this time, he brought all the food, which he purchased at a small local restaurant.

CHAPTER 4

Italy, 1940

Lory and Alma were sitting at their kitchen table eating slices of dry toast for breakfast one morning. Lory was skimming through the *Il Popolo d'Italia* (*The People of Italy*) newspaper. "I hate this newspaper. It's full of fascist propaganda," Lory said more to himself than to Alma. "I prefer the *Avanti*! But I can't get it safely." He shook his head. Then he stopped on a page, slammed his fist on the table. Lory put the newspaper down and looked up at Alma.

"What's wrong?" she asked.

He shook his head. Then he handed her the paper. She read it. Then she looked directly at her husband and said, "What are we going to do? It says that Mussolini declared that all Jews who were not born in Italy would have five years to leave the country.

"I know. I read it. But I don't know what we are going to do." Lory put his toast down and shook his head. "I love Italy. It is my home. But if you must leave, I will go with you. We are husband and wife. You are the woman I love. You know how government is. That lunatic may very well change his mind before our time is up. Whatever happens, we will face it together. At least we have five years to wait and see what happens. Then if we must leave here, we will decide where to go."

"I would hate to leave," Alma said. "I've come to love our lives here. I love the hospital where we work, our coworkers. Everything about Italy." She sighed.

"I know, I know," Lory said. "It's getting late; finish your food. We have to get to work."

Alma nodded, but she couldn't eat another bite.

That night Vito dropped by to visit. As always, Alma asked him to stay for dinner.

After they'd finished eating, Lory showed Vito the article he and Alma had read that morning about Alma being forced to leave Italy in five years. Vito read it quietly. Then he looked up at Alma and Lory and shook his head. "This is terrible. Just despicable. I wish I knew what to say. Do you think they will ever really enforce this?"

"I don't know. I hope not," Lory said.

"If they do, where will you go?" Vito asked Lory and Alma.

"I have a brother in America. I was born there," Alma said. "I still have my United States citizenship. But I won't go without Lory, and I don't know if I will be able to get him into the country."

"Of course you could not leave your husband. But being that you are married, and you are an American citizen, doesn't that automatically give him citizenship too?"

"I don't know. I would have to look into it," Alma said. "We just saw this article this morning. Then we both went to work. Neither of us has had an opportunity to look into it any further."

"But it's been on my mind all day," Lory said.

"Well, don't worry too much. Things have a way of working themselves out. Perhaps things will change here in Italy over the next five years. You know how this government is. Things are always changing," Vito said. He was trying to look calm, but his eyes betrayed the worry he felt for his friends because Alma wasn't an Italian citizen. And he was beginning to feel worried for himself because he was a Jew, and he knew that throughout history, it was always unsafe to be a Jew.

"That's what we are hoping for," Lory replied. "We both love our jobs here. And I know Alma would agree with me that we would both miss you terribly. We both enjoy our visits with you so much." Lory smiled.

"Vito is right. Things do have a way of working themselves out. If I were to consider all the changes in my own life over the last five years, I would be flabbergasted. Five years ago, I had no idea that I would meet my wonderful husband. I believed I would never fall in love. And look at us today." Alma smiled at Lory.

"My wife is like her bubbie, always the optimist," Lory said, then he added, "I truly hope there is a way that we can stay in Italy. I am hoping that because we are in the medical profession, and because the country always needs doctors and nurses, that perhaps they will make an exception for us."

CHAPTER 5

Manhattan, Fall 1940

I zzy Reznick went to his favorite restaurant in Chinatown. The waiter knew him as soon as he sat down.

"Yes, Mr. Izzy. You want your regular?" he asked.

"Yes," Izzy said. The regular was beef chop suey. He'd heard that chop suey wasn't really a Chinese dish, that it had been invented here in America. But he didn't care, he liked it. He loved the slight flavor of sweetness in the sauce, and he couldn't wait to drench his rice in that delicious salty soy sauce.

"I bring it for you right away. I take care of you first, before any of other customers in restaurant," the waiter said.

"Thanks." Izzy nodded. *Of course he loves me,* Izzy thought as a slight smile came over his face. *I tip him as much as the meal costs. I'll bet nobody else does that. But I know what it's like to be poor. I was poor all my life. So when I see a poor slob working his rump off trying to make a living, I don't mind giving him an extra dollar or two. Besides I'll bet it's even harder for this fella. He can hardly speak English. At least I was born here. Anyway, a couple of bucks is not enough money to make any difference to me, so why not?*

Izzy preferred to sit in the back of the restaurant where he could read his newspaper in peace, where he needn't worry about being seen by a rival gang member, who might have an unresolved issue with him.

The waiter set a pot of steaming tea and a small cup down on the table. Izzy poured himself a cup and then opened the newspaper and began to read.

He read a few boring articles, but then he stopped dead when he saw the articles that read that all men between the ages of twenty-one and forty-five are required to register for the draft. He read the article. Then he reread it. The food arrived, but Izzy had lost his appetite. His stomach was turning over, and his mind was racing. He thought about the discussions he'd heard lately about America and the war in Europe. All of his coworkers and friends agreed. They were certain that Roosevelt would keep America out of the war. They had long discussions about how so many Americans were against entering into a conflict that had nothing to do with them. Izzy listened to their conversations, but he didn't add anything. He was not so sure that America would not somehow be pulled into this European conflict. And he didn't care about what anyone said or thought. In the end, all that mattered to him was that he had worked too long and too hard to become the head Jewish mob boss. He had risked his life countless times to finally acquire enough money to live very comfortably. Now that he was living the life of his dreams, he would be damned if he was going to die in a foreign country for a cause that made little or no difference to him. He'd read that the Nazis were treating the European Jews terribly. But he wasn't European, he was an American. And although he was sorry to hear that the Jews were being persecuted, he just didn't care enough to fight for them. And now he felt sick as he read this article. With the war in Europe raging and that madman Adolf Hitler conquering countries left and right, the American government was insisting that every man between the ages of twenty-one and forty-five register just in case the country needed them. The very thought of registering put him on edge. He just didn't like the sound of it.

But it was a law, and Izzy had evaded so many other laws that he dared not ignore this one. Whether he liked it or not, he knew he must register. However, he also knew that with a medical exemption of the right kind he would be able to get out of the draft. It wouldn't be cheap, but he had enough money to grease the right palms and get himself a medical exemption. He hated to fork over so many of his hard-earned dollars. It seemed like a terrible waste of money. But when he thought about putting on a uniform and risking his life, he shook his head. *No matter what happens, I am not going to war.* Then he raised his hand and signed for the waiter, who came right away.

"I need my check," Izzy said.

"Why you no eat, Mr. Izzy? Something wrong with food? You want I get you something else?"

Izzy shook his head. "No, thanks," he said. Then he paid the check and left his usual tip. It was late when Izzy drove home. But as soon as he arrived, he called all of the government officials with whom he had made important connections over the years. Especially the ones who owed him favors. He had their home phone numbers. It didn't take long to find someone willing to write up a few important papers giving Izzy exactly what he needed in exchange for a nice pile of cash.

CHAPTER 6

Germany, 1939

In 1939 Hitler legalized what the Nazis referred to as mercy killings by physicians. Under the rule of the Third Reich, the mentally and physically handicapped were considered a burden on society. They were called useless eaters. Which meant that they took from the country but made no contributions. Hitler and his highest-ranking officers decided the best thing that could be done for these poor souls was to end their pitiful existence. Therefore, Hitler ordered that institutions be established where these useless eaters could be euthanized quietly.

The program was given the code name Aktion T4. And even though Hitler was certain that he and his men were doing a service to Germany and mankind, they still felt that it was best if T4 was kept secret from the public. The Nazis feared that the murder of the disabled and mentally ill might not be as well received by the German people as it was the by the high-ranking Nazi officers.

Facilities to carry out this murderous mission were set up in Germany and Austria. And then the process began. At first things were going smoothly. However, in spite of all of the Nazis attempts to conceal these mercy killings, the information about what was being done leaked out. And as Hitler had predicted, the murders did not sit well with the German people or the world. Hitler and his advisors decided that they preferred to keep their attempts to cleanse the world of those who were tainting German blood, a secret. So, eventually, in the fall of 1941, the program was canceled. But for Hitler, the program had been a success. Perhaps he had not been able to eliminate all of the people he felt were unfit to live, but he'd created the first gas chambers and crematoriums. This was the beginning of all that was to come. It was Hitler's first attempt to systematically and efficiently murder large groups of people. And although T4 would be dissolved, the killing had just begun.

Once the program was abandoned, the gas chambers and crematoriums that had been created were sent to the concentration camps. There they were perfected, and later they were used to exterminate human beings in even larger numbers.

CHAPTER 7

Late Summer 1941

It had been a little over a month since Luisa had discovered Goldie Birnbaum was a patient in the hospital where she worked. It had happened on the day Goldie was scheduled to be gassed. The patients, Goldie among them, were lined up outside the gas chamber waiting to be wheeled or walked inside by the hospital staff, who were hard at work trying to rid Germany of the mentally and physically disabled. When Luisa saw Goldie in that line, she felt a surge of excitement shoot through her. Before Goldie could be ushered into the gas chamber, Luisa ran to her superior and requested permission to remove Goldie from this group, at least for now. Luisa needed time with Goldie. Now that Luisa was in a place of power, this was her opportunity to make Goldie pay for how she treated her when they were young. *That Jew bitch is still beautiful*, Luisa thought to herself as she looked at Goldie, and her heart was still filled with jealousy.

Luisa took Goldie out of her room and locked her in a small room that had once been a broom closet. It was dank and dusty, and Luisa was glad when she heard Goldie coughing. Every afternoon, once

Luisa had finished her shift, she went to see Goldie. She walked in and locked the door behind her.

"Please, can I have my medications?" Goldie begged. "I need them. I haven't had them in so many days."

Luisa laughed. No matter how much Goldie begged, Luisa refused to give her any of the medications that she'd been taking. Instead, she slapped Goldie hard across the face. "The time has come for you to suffer for all of your crimes," she said.

Then Luisa took a straight razor and began to shave Goldie's thick, golden blonde hair. Luisa was nicking her head, and blood was dripping into Goldie's eyes. Goldie was crying, and she tried to get away. So Luisa punched her, and Goldie fell to the ground. Then Luisa took handcuffs out of her pocket and handcuffed Goldie to a chair. Once she was finished, Goldie was bald and bleeding. "You poor thing," Luisa said, and then she left.

The following day, Luisa returned. Goldie had fallen asleep in the chair; her head was covered in scabs. "Get up, Jew swine," Luisa said. Then she lit a cigarette and began smoking and blowing the smoke in Goldie's face. Goldie's nose and eyes ran, and she coughed profusely. "Please, I can't breathe."

"Who said I want you to breathe?" Luisa said. Then she took her lit cigarette and burned Goldie's beautiful face. Goldie let out a piercing scream and begged her to stop. But Luisa burned her again.

"Please, Luisa. I am sorry. I know I hurt you when we were young. I was wrong. I was so wrong. I will do anything. Please stop this."

"How does it feel, Goldie? Beautiful, beautiful, Goldie. When I am done with you, you will be so ugly that people will turn away rather than look at you. Then you'll know what it feels like to be me."

"Please, Luisa. Please, I am begging you for mercy. I am sorry. I am so sorry." Goldie was weeping. But the more she begged Luisa for forgiveness, the more justified Luisa felt in torturing her.

Tormenting Goldie was the highlight of Luisa's life. She couldn't wait to finish her daily tasks so that she could slip away into that small room and torture Goldie. She loved to hear Goldie beg. Each day, she gave Goldie just enough food and water to keep her alive. And she would have continued with Goldie indefinitely had she not received a message from one of the doctors, who she worked with, informing her that Hitler's euthanasia program was about to be dissolved.

Luisa rushed to find the doctor. She found him in his office writing up some important records. "How soon is the program going to be disbanded?" she asked him, hoping to keep Goldie for at least another month.

"August eighteenth," he said. "So hurry up and finish that business with the Jew you have tucked away."

"Of course," Luisa agreed. But she was disappointed. August 18 was less than a week away, and if she didn't hurry and finish Goldie off, Luisa was afraid that somehow Goldie Birnbaum would survive. *I can't let that happen. She must not live through this,* Luisa thought. *It's time to put an end to her.*

The next group of patients who were to be gassed was scheduled for that afternoon. Luisa decided it was best to get the job done as soon as possible. So when Luisa heard the sound of the patients as they were being wheeled in hospital beds and wheelchairs into the gas chambers, Luisa stopped what she was doing and went into the room where she was keeping Goldie. She unhandcuffed Goldie and then picked her up. Goldie was as light as a small child. Luisa flung her into a waiting wheelchair and then strapped her in, restricting all of her movement. Goldie was thin and weak; she had no more fight left. Her entire face was covered with scars, and her head was scabbed over with dried blood. "Where are you taking me?" Goldie asked in a small voice.

"Shut up," Luisa said, slapping Goldie across the face. Goldie winced. Then Luisa continued. "How do you still have the strength to question me? You know I am taking you to somewhere that you are going to suffer, don't you? Of course you do, Goldie. You know that I hate you. I hate you, and your suffering is my greatest pleasure."

Goldie began to cry long, low sobs.

Luisa ignored her. Instead, she wheeled Goldie to the front of the line of patients who were on their way into the gas chamber.

Luisa approached the nurse who was checking the patients in. "I want to take this one in myself," Luisa said.

"What is her name?"

"Goldie Birnbaum."

"She's not on my list."

"I know. This is a special case. Ask Dr. Muehler. He told me to make sure she was in this group."

"All right. I'll add her to the bottom of my list. You can go on and wheel her in."

"No, please." Goldie tried to appeal to the nurse who was checking the patients in. But the woman ignored her. And Luisa jerked the wheelchair hard, then wheeled Goldie into a large shower room where the walls, and the floor, were concrete.

Luisa parked Goldie's wheelchair in the front of the room right under the showerheads.

"Do you know where you are?"

Goldie shook her head.

"Look up there. You see those showerheads? You think that water comes out of them? Think again, Goldie Birnbaum. Gas comes out. You breathe the gas, and then you die a hideous death."

"No, please, Luisa. I am begging you. Please, take me out of here."

"No, Goldie. I would have kept you longer as my little toy. But, unfortunately, this program is about to come to an end, and I can't risk the possibility that you might get out of here alive."

Goldie was shaking. The reality of what was about to happen to her was terrifying. "Please, Luisa, haven't I repented for everything I did? Listen to me. I promise you, if you help me to survive, my family will give you whatever you want. Money, a house, anything you want."

Luisa started laughing. "Don't you remember that day I saw you on the street, and I told you that the time would come when all the wealth of Germany would be taken back from the Jews who stole it, and returned to the German people? Well . . . that day has arrived. Your parents don't have any money anymore. While you've been in here, they have been stripped of everything. Your father no longer owns his factory. He's nothing but a common worker there now. They are at our mercy now, just like you are. And . . . bitch, you don't deserve any mercy."

"I was just a child when I treated you badly. I was stupid, young, and thoughtless. I shouldn't have done it. I know that now."

"Oh, shut up already. You have said the same thing over and over for weeks now. I'm tired of hearing it. Say something new, or say nothing at all."

"I don't know what to say to you. All I can do is beg you to forgive me. Please, Luisa. If not for my sake, then for my mother's. She was always kind to you. I remember she gave you my clothes."

"Yes, your old clothes. The trash you no longer wanted. I hate her as much as I hate you."

"She meant well. She wanted you to have nice things."

"And you humiliated me about those clothes in front of the entire school. Do you know that I quit school because of what you did to me that day? Everyone was standing around and laughing me. I couldn't go back there." Luisa shook her head. Her teeth were bared. She was shaking. "You stupid, ugly bitch. You had no idea how much you hurt me that day. I was so proud to be wearing those clothes of yours because I wanted to be like you. Everyone called you the beautiful golden girl. And I wanted to be a beautiful girl too. But what I didn't know yet was that I was already much better than you would ever be. Our führer showed me the truth. You see, I am a pure Aryan. And you are nothing but Jewish swine."

"I didn't mean it," Goldie begged again. "I didn't know. I was all caught up in my own problems."

"Oh, yes you did. You knew, and now you will say anything to save your own life. But you meant it. You meant every word that you said on that humiliating day. And you hurt me."

"I was facing a bad situation on that day. I remember it. I had just found out that I was pregnant out of wedlock. I took it out on you. I shouldn't have. Please, Luisa. Give me a chance to live. Let me make it up to you."

Luisa leaned down close to Goldie and whispered in her ear. "I have to leave now. They are about to start the gas. Look around you. Look," Luisa said, turning Goldie's head with her hands. "We are going to murder all of these useless eaters that are sitting here in this room. In a few minutes, you will feel the pain," she said, smiling. "And remember, as you suffer, that I'll be watching through that window right over there. I'll be watching you as you die."

Goldie struggled against the restraints that held her to the wheel-chair. Then she let out a loud scream. Luisa smiled wickedly and waved goodbye. Then she walked out of the room, and the door slammed loudly behind her. Goldie felt her heart pound. Tears ran down her cheeks; her nose was running. But her hands were bound, and she couldn't wipe it. *I can't believe that doctors and nurses are about to kill everyone in this entire room. These are sick, innocent people.* But something in Luisa's words rang true. *No, no, please, I'm not ready to die,* she thought.

The hair on the back of Goldie's neck stood up, and she shivered as she heard a soft hiss that sounded like a giant snake. She looked up at the showerheads. But she saw nothing. Then a fog of smoke poured out. Her throat felt as if it had been raked over with razor blades, and her chest ached as her lungs were being squeezed until there was no air left within them. She gasped trying to draw a breath, but there was no air. She was drowning without water. She wanted to scream, but no sound came out of her mouth. The pain was so intense, and she was struggling so hard to breathe that she rocked the wheelchair until it fell on its side. Then Goldie began coughing hard, painful, deep coughs. Blood came trickling, then pouring out of her mouth. Her eyes were wide. Again, she tried to scream, but the red river of blood was so thick, it was blocking her windpipe. Then she lay still unable to move, and she took her final breath.

CHAPTER 8

Berlin, August 1941

Esther Birnbaum had just returned from a meeting with the woman's club she belonged to concerning the state of things for Jews in Germany. Since her daughter, Goldie, had been transferred out of the private mental hospital to the new facility, Esther could no longer visit her. But when the doctors had suggested the move, they'd given Esther so much hope that Goldie might be cured, Esther felt the sacrifice was worth it. But now, she had to find other ways to keep busy while Ted was at the factory. She was surprised that he'd wanted to continue working there. He no longer owned his business. The government had confiscated it. But so far, because he had friends, he was allowed to continue as an employee. It was hard on him to lose his business. That factory had been in his family for generations. And she assumed that was why he wanted to continue his work there even if he faced daily humiliation having gone from an owner to a low-level employee. She took a deep breath and sighed. Life had taken a hard turn for everyone since Hitler took power. It was late afternoon, but Esther was still unnerved due to the bombings last night. The sound had been deafening. And with the landing of each bomb, she could feel the earth beneath her tremble. She knew Ted couldn't sleep either. She'd been married to him long enough to be able to determine whether he was awake by the rhythm of his breathing. But she hadn't said a word. Instead, she just moved closer to him, and he put his arms around her. Neither of them wanted to give voice to their fears. But Esther's mind had been racing. She couldn't help but feel that each time a bomb fell, she had narrowly escaped death. *At any time one of those bombs could hit our home or hit the institution where Goldie is staying. And yet I am grateful for the British even if I must endure the bombings. Ted is very hopeful now that Hitler has attacked Russia, he might be weakened by fighting on two fronts. We can only hope.* It was getting worse in Berlin every day. She'd begun to hate walking through the streets. Because each day there was more destruction. And she couldn't bear the sad faces of women cleaning up the rubble that was scattered all over the streets from the bombed-out buildings. But far worse than the buildings were the dead bodies that lay covered by sheets. Poor innocent people who had been pulled from these broken structures that once were their homes. *They'd been sleeping safely in their own beds, and within seconds they were dead. Damn that Adolf Hitler. Because of him, no one is safe anymore.*

It was after lunchtime, but it would be several hours before Ted returned from work. So Esther went into the library in her home. She moved a bunch of books. Behind them she found her favorite literary treasures which had been banned by the Nazi Party. Then she selected a book. As she opened the novel *All Quiet on the Western Front*, by Remarque, she thought to herself that it was a terrible shame that Hitler was forbidding the German people from enjoying wonderful, thought-provoking literature like this. She'd read the book twice before, but each time she read it, she found new insights that she had not seen before. She thought about going into the kitchen to prepare a cup of tea for herself. *I'll ask Hans if he'd like one too,* she thought. Hans was the family driver. He'd been with the Birnbaums for years. And even though Gentiles were forbidden to work for Jews now, he chose to stay on with the Birnbaums. Esther yawned and put the book down, and she got up to go into the kitchen. But before she left the library there was a knock on the front door. She quickly hid the forbidden book in the drawer of her husband's desk. They no longer had a maid to answer the door, so Esther went herself.

"Who is it?" Esther said before opening the door.

"Telegram for Herr and Frau Birnbaum."

Esther opened the door and took the envelope. Then she handed the delivery boy several coins and thanked him. He nodded and left, hopping on his bicycle and riding away before she even had a chance to close the door.

Esther sighed. *It's probably a message about Goldie's progress*, she thought. Then she sat down at the desk and opened the telegram. It read—

HERR BIRNBAUM AND FRAU BIRNBAUM,

WE REGRET TO INFORM YOU THAT YOUR DAUGHTER, GOLDIE BIRNBAUM, PASSED AWAY ON AUGUST 1, 1941 OF A HEART ATTACK. THE STAFF AT SONNENSTEIN SENDS OUR CONDOLENCES. PLEASE TAKE COMFORT IN KNOWING THAT YOUR DAUGHTER'S SUFFERING AND STRUGGLES ARE OVER. SHE IS NO LONGER FORCED TO ENDURE A LIFE THAT WAS HARDLY WORTH LIVING.

SINCERELY,

DIRECTOR HERMAN PAUL NITSCHE.

ESTHER SUNK INTO THE CHAIR. The telegram fell from her hand onto the table. *Goldie is gone*, she thought. *My Goldie is gone. As confused and tortured as Goldie was, she was still my child. My precious daughter. And even after she was an adult, to me she was always my baby girl. I had such hopes for her. Such dreams.* Esther began to cry. *I believed in this program. I know I was grasping for anything that might help her, but I hoped that maybe, by some miracle, my Goldie could be cured. I wish I had known the last time I saw her that I would never see her again. I would have held her a little closer. I would have smoothed her hair like I did when she was just a child. My Goldie, gone from this earth before me. No mother should ever know such pain.*

She put her hand on her chest. *I feel so empty as if a piece of my heart is missing.*

The ticking of the grandfather clock was the only sound in the house.

Esther Birnbaum sat alone among the tall bookshelves and looked around at the familiar room. *I raised my daughter in this house. I read to her in this room when she was so small that she still believed I knew everything.* Tears burned Esther's eyes. She stood up and took down two books from the shelf of hidden books. They were forbidden copies of the children's books that Goldie had loved. Tears covered her face. *My beautiful Goldie, my precious child. This was not supposed to be your life. You were supposed to be happy and carefree. I have all the money that I could ever want, but without you I will never be happy."*

Another loud knock at the door startled her. Hans had been passing the library on his way to the kitchen. "Shall I answer it?" he asked. *Hans, dear Hans. He's such a godsend. I feel so grateful that he stayed on with us despite the law that forbids it. He takes such a chance by working for us in secret. But the truth is I don't know what I would do without him. Especially now at this terrible time. I am so glad he is here today. I need a buffer, someone who can stand between me and the world. I just can't face anyone at this moment.*

"Yes, Hans, can you please answer it?" Esther said. *I am so glad that Ted is kind to Hans and pays him well because he deserves it.*

"Of course," he said.

A few minutes passed, and Hans came into the library. "There is a Luisa Eisenreich here to see you," he said.

"I'm sorry. I can't see anyone right now. Tell her that I am not home."

But before Hans had an opportunity to tell Luisa anything, Luisa pushed past Hans and entered the library. "Hello, Frau Birnbaum. I came to see you today because I never got a chance to thank you for your generosity in giving me Goldie's old clothes. I am sure you remember me now, don't you?"

Esther looked up at the woman who stood in front of her. "Of course I remember you. And you're very welcome, dear. But I am sorry, I can't visit with you today. It's a bad time for me," Esther said. She was trying to keep calm, trying to have as much patience with Luisa as possible even though her heart was aching.

"I'll be in the kitchen if you need anything," Hans said.

"Thank you, Hans," Esther answered. She was so grateful that she and Ted had saved plenty of money, so they were able to continue to keep Hans employed with them. Although she doubted he would have left even if they had been forced to cut his salary. He was one of the most loyal men she'd ever known, and she felt honored to have him as a part of their lives.

Luisa ignored Hans. She continued speaking to Esther. "Well, I just wanted to come to see you today, so I could tell you that when I got those boxes of the clothes that Goldie didn't want anymore, clothes that Goldie threw into the trash, I felt so special. I tried them on, then I paraded around the room I shared with my mother. We lived in a single room in the back of a rich Jew's house. My mother was the maid. So I never had any nice things. But, of course, you already knew that. You came to see me at the Horwitzes' home. You brought me the clothes. I remember the pity in your eyes. Esther Birnbaum, you felt so sorry for me. So very sorry, didn't you?"

"I'm sorry. I truly am. I don't remember right now. I have a lot on my mind. Please forgive me, but I can't visit with you today. This is a bad time," Esther said, hardly listening to what Luisa was saying. She was miserable and wishing the girl would leave her alone.

Luisa ignored Esther. "But as I got older, I realized those little dresses were nothing more than Goldie's trash. And I was nothing more than trash for even accepting them. She humiliated me in front of the whole school about wearing her old clothes. Everyone laughed at me. Goldie was cruel. Yes, she was beautiful, but she was heartless too. After that I started to hate myself. But then one day, I realized that it wasn't me that I hated, it was you! You and Goldie. And everyone like you. The Jews. I always knew that the Jews were nothing but rats. But when our führer came to power, and he explained everything to me, suddenly everything in my life began to make sense. I realized the truth about you Jews. You stole everything you have from the good German people. You and Goldie and the Horwitzes, who my mother worked and slaved for, were but common thieves. Tricky, cunning, and conniving Jew thieves. Goldie only had those pretty clothes because they were stolen from the Germans. They should have been rightfully mine in the first place."

"Luisa, please, you have a warped view on things. I would love to take the time to talk to you, to help you, if I can. Because I understand that you are hurting inside. But I can't talk to you right now. As I said before, this is a very bad time for me."

"I know this is a bad time for you. I even know why, and it's about time you suffered the way I have suffered all my life. I'll tell you a little secret. I know that Goldie is dead."

Esther's eyes flew open. She stared at the woman who was smiling as she stood in front of her. "How did you know that?" Esther asked. She was shaking.

"Do you really want to know?" Luisa said. Then without waiting for Esther to answer, she continued. "All right, I will tell you. You see, Frau Birnbaum, I am a nurse. I work at the same hospital where Goldie recently died. In fact, I was with her when she died. I was her very special nurse. And what you don't know, you old Jew, is that she didn't die of a heart attack. Goldie was murdered. The previously corrupt Weimar government in Germany might have put up with people who suffered from insanity. But the Third Reich, the proud Germany of today, doesn't tolerate the mentally incompetent. We know that they are nothing but a financial burden on our country, and therefore, it's a waste to keep the useless eaters alive. Besides that, we would never want them to breed. The sooner we eliminate the useless, the better. And Goldie certainly was useless in every way."

"Enough," Esther said. She was shaking. Her hands felt as cold as ice, and her face felt hot.

"I'm not done speaking. I have much more to say," Luisa said, smirking. "So after Goldie was dead, I took a week off from work. Then I caught the train home to Berlin. I knew you would receive the telegram today, and I wanted to be here when you got the news. Do you know why? No need to answer. I'll tell you why. Because I wanted to let you know that I watched your daughter suffer, and then I watched your sweet little Goldie die. She died in a gas chamber struggling to breathe, and she suffered. Oh, how she suffered . . ." Luisa shook her head in mock pity. Then she opened her handbag and pulled out a thick hunk of golden locks encrusted with blood. She lay the hair on the desk in front of Esther. "This is for you. It's Goldie's hair. It's all that's left of your precious daughter."

"Get out of my house," Esther said, her voice a deep growl. Her eyes were fixed like a laser on Luisa's face. Her body trembling with anger.

Luisa laughed. "Are you planning to hit me? You're an old woman. You must know that you are weak. Or are you delusional, just like your pathetic dead daughter? Perhaps you do think you have the physical strength to throw me out? Well, let me tell you this—you can't fight me, old woman. I am young and strong, and you are old and ready for the grave. I once told Goldie that the time would come when all your stolen Jew money wouldn't save any of you. Well, that time is getting very close. And I must admit I am itching with anticipation."

"I said, get out. And I mean it!" Esther screamed.

Hans came running into the library. "Shall I throw her out or call the police?" he asked, trying to assess the situation.

Esther looked at Hans. She could not bring the police into this because Hans was illegally employed by her family. Besides, the police were not partial to Jews. And chances were good that Esther would cause herself more trouble by contacting them.

"No need to call anyone." Luisa stood up and straightened her skirt. "I've said what I had to say. Now, I am leaving," Luisa said, then she turned and walked out of the room and down the hall, then out the front door. But before she left, she screamed, "Trash. You made me feel like trash." Then the door slammed.

Hans went after Luisa to make sure she was gone. He looked out the front window and saw her walking away. Then he locked and bolted the door. Once he was certain that he and Esther were alone, he headed back into the library where he found Esther with her head in her hands.

As soon as Esther saw Hans, she lifted her head and tried to muster a smile. "Thank you, Hans," she said.

"Are you all right, Frau Birnbaum?" Hans asked Esther.

"Yes, I'm fine," Esther said, but she wasn't. She was shaken, horrified by Luisa's words. She sat there glued to her chair staring at the hair that lay on the desk in front of her.

"May I take this?" Hans asked as gently as possible, indicating the pile of hair.

"It's Goldie's hair." Esther's voice broke. "I would know that hair anywhere. I can still remember how I used to brush it when she was just a little girl. Look at these curls," Esther said, taking one of the golden curls between her fingers. Suddenly she was sobbing uncontrollably.

"I think it's best that I take the hair away, Frau Birnbaum. I promise that I won't throw it away. I'll just put it somewhere for now. Would that be all right with you?"

Esther nodded; she was still weeping.

Carefully, Hans gathered every strand of hair into his hands. He left the room but was only gone for a few minutes. When he returned, he did not have the hair with him. He sat down across the desk from Esther and asked, "Can I get you anything? A cup of tea, perhaps? It will help calm you."

"I don't want anything."

"Have a cup of tea. Please, Frau Birnbaum."

"All right," Esther managed to say. "That would be very nice of you Hans. Thank you."

"Of course," he said. "I'll go and get it for you right away."

A few minutes later, Hans returned. He brought a cup of tea and some cookies on a plate and set them down on the desk. Then he sat down across from Esther again. "Frau Birnbaum. I heard some of that conversation, but I am not sure exactly what happened."

"I'm sorry, Hans, I can't talk about it right now. I am too upset."

Hans quickly glanced at the telegram. Then he got up to leave.

"Thank you so much for the tea, Hans."

"If there is anything else I can do for you, Frau Birnbaum, just call for me. I won't be far away."

"I will, thank you again."

When Ted arrived home that evening, Esther was still sitting in the library holding the telegram in her hand and staring out the window. The cup of tea and plate of cookies lay untouched on the desk.

"Esther? What is it?" Ted said. He was alarmed to see her tear-stained face. She handed him the letter. He read it. Then in a whisper he said, "Oh God, no."

He got up and walked over to his wife, then he lifted Esther into his arms and held her tightly. She was trembling. "It was my fault," she said. "I could have done something more for her."

"There was nothing you or I or anyone else could've done. We've talked about this. We both tried our best for Goldie."

Then Esther said in a soft voice, "Do you remember Luisa Eisenreich?"

"No. Who is that?"

"A girl Goldie knew from school. She came by here today," Esther said, then a choked voice she told Ted what Luisa said. His face turned gray.

"That is the most terrible thing I've ever heard," he responded. "Do you think it's true?"

"I know it is. If it were not true, how could she possibly have known that Goldie was dead? She had to have been there with her when she died. Everything she said had to be true. That horrible, heartless woman had to have been the nurse who killed our daughter. Oh, Ted. My poor child. My poor little Goldie. They purposely took her life." She gasped. "They put her in that hospital, and then they murdered our daughter," Esther whimpered.

He held her in his arms for a long time, rocking her gently.

At least ten minutes passed before Esther whispered, "Ted, it's not safe here in Germany for Jews anymore."

He nodded and patted her head. But he didn't speak.

She looked up at him. Their eyes locked, and suddenly there was an understanding between them. They had to get out of Germany.

CHAPTER 9

Night had fallen, and the telegram still lay open on the desk between Esther Birnbaum and her husband, Ted. They both looked down at the desk, not at each other because they couldn't bear to see their own pain reflected in their spouse's eyes. Esther refused to touch the paper again. Yet someone must move it because it is there lying between them. A stab through the heart. A written reminder that their daughter, Goldie, is dead. Murdered by the mental hospital that had given them such promise that there might be a cure. Esther had been so hopeful that her Goldie would finally be able to live a normal life. But it was not to be. In her mind's eye she could still see the face of that horrible girl, Luisa Eisenreich. *I tried to do right by Luisa. I knew she came from a poor family, and that was why I gave her the clothing. I never wanted to hurt or humiliate her. I even bought her new dresses occasionally. And all it did was make her hate me. And more importantly, it made her hurt my daughter. Dear God, how could she do what she did? I will never understand such cruelty.*

Esther had always had a soft spot for children, especially those who were underprivileged. After all, Esther was constantly grateful for all the blessings that God had bestowed upon her family. Ted earned a good living. They owned a large factory and had many wonderful friends and neighbors. So Esther was always trying to do mitzvahs by helping those in need. But as it turned out, Luisa had been terribly jealous of Goldie who, Esther had to admit, was unkind to Luisa. Still, nothing justified what Luisa had done. Esther felt sick to her stomach when she thought about the pleasure Luisa seemed to be deriving from the misery she'd caused. Never in her entire life had Esther felt such hatred and disgust for another human being. If she had been physically stronger, she would have killed Luisa with her bare hands that afternoon. However, she was not young or strong. And she'd never hurt another person in her life. So when she began screaming, and Hans came into the room to see what was wrong, she was relieved to see him. His presence seemed to scare Luisa, and that was a blessing. Because Esther could not bear to look at her for another second. It had been hours since Luisa's visit, yet if Esther closed her eyes, she could still see that monster's face. And she was quite sure the vision would remain burned in her memory for the rest of her life.

"We have to leave Germany," Esther whispered again, more to herself than to Ted.

"I know, you're right. I didn't believe it before. But I do now. It is just so hard at our age to start over. And we will be leaving so much behind . . . the factory."

"We've already lost the factory. They've taken it from us for no reason at all."

"I am hoping that it will be returned to us eventually. But if we leave, we will never get it back. And what about our home? Every-thing we've built. Everything we've worked for?"

"And what good will all of it be to us if we are imprisoned or dead?"

"I don't believe they would go that far. Do you?"

"I didn't believe it. At least I didn't want to believe it. But now that this happened with Goldie, I know that anything can happen under Hitler."

"What a monster he is. What a plague on Germany and the world," Ted said. He put his head in his hands.

Esther knew Ted was trying to put up a brave front about Goldie for her sake. But she knew him too well, and she could see the pain and grief in his eyes.

"Yes he is. And that horrible girl, Luisa, who came today. I can't get her face out of my mind. I can't believe she would travel back to Berlin just to tell me that she'd participated in the torture and murder of my child. What kind of a person is that? What kind of people have these Nazis created?" Esther sobbed.

"Please try not to think about her. It doesn't do you any good, and it can't help Goldie anymore either," Ted said, patting his wife's wrinkled and veined hand. "We have to find a way to get into the United States."

"Maybe Sam can help. Do you think so?"

"Possibly. Can you send him a letter today?" Ted asked. He hoped that Sam wasn't holding a grudge against him for the incident that had happened when Sam visited Germany. Ted had never told his wife about the fight he and Sam had, when he had gone into Sam's room and had read Sam's private letter to Chana. Ted had discovered why Sam had refused his offer of a good job in Germany. The letter told him everything. He learned that his grandson was working as bootlegger, running illegal alcohol across the country and carrying a gun. Ted and Sam had a terrible fight. Sam was angry that his grandfather had invaded his privacy. And Ted was angry that Sam was living a dangerous life in America. From that time on the relationship between them had been cold and formal.

"I was planning on writing to him anyway. I am going to have to tell him that his mother is dead. I will have to write to Alma too. They deserve to know."

"When you write to Sam, tell him our situation. Tell him that we need for him to sponsor us to get us into America."

She nodded.

Esther went into the kitchen to write the letter . . . alone. She sat down with a pen and paper. But all she could think of was Goldie. It was true that Goldie had been a difficult child, curious, rebellious, never satisfied. But she was Esther's one and only child. Even in her womb, Goldie had given her mother a hard time. And the pregnancy had taken everything out of Esther, leaving her unable to have any more children. But in spite of all that, Esther had endured. When Goldie was born, she was the most beautiful child in the hospital nursery. All the nurses told Esther how lovely Goldie was with her bright blue eyes and silky, yellow hair. But as soon as Esther and Ted brought Goldie home, she'd had a terrible case of colic. And many nights Esther had stayed up with her rocking her while she screamed. Those were difficult times for Esther, but they only foreshadowed more difficult times to come. And the older Goldie grew, the worse she became. Then at ten years old she met Leni, a girl who led her down a dark and dangerous path which finally led to her destruction.

In her mind, Esther could see Goldie as a child running through the house, making messes, and leaving them for the maids. Demanding new clothes, new dolls, a new canopy bed. *I was to blame. I should have been stricter with her. Less indulgent. But I couldn't. I was so afraid she would grow up to hate me if I disciplined her. It turned out that she did anyway.* Then when Goldie was a teenager, she'd gotten pregnant out of wedlock, and Ted had married her off to Irving, a baker who was not the father of her unborn child. Ted had given Irving some money to start a bakery in America, and he'd agreed to marry Goldie and save her reputation. After they were married, Irving and Goldie moved to the United States where they lived for the next nineteen years and where her son, Sam, was born. They'd even had a second child, a little girl named Alma who was fathered by the baker. Once Alma was born, Ted and Esther were certain that Goldie had finally settled down. Esther missed her daughter every day. But Ted was relieved that Goldie was out of danger. However, Sam got into some kind of trouble, and the family had to leave the small town in Upstate New York. Irving lost the bakery. They moved to Manhattan. But Irving could not earn a decent living. And then Goldie returned to Berlin. It was supposed to be a visit. But it turned into a permanent move. And once Goldie was back at home, Esther could see that her daughter was worse than ever. She'd been living a restricted life with Irving for nineteen years, and now she was out of control. And each day Goldie spiraled further downward, living a life of pure debauchery until she ended up in the hospital for the insane. And now . . . she was dead. Esther felt sick to her stomach when she thought about Goldie's life.

Esther tapped the pen on the table. *I must write to Sam. First, I must tell him what happened. He must know that his mother has passed on. I won't tell him or Alma anything about Luisa. They don't need to know those horrible details. I will ask Sam if he can help Ted and I get into America. I don't like to ask for favors, but I promised Ted I would ask, so I will. Somehow, I must put all of this loss and misery out of my mind, or I will be paralyzed by the grief. I can hardly write, but I must also tell Alma. She has every right in the world to know that her mother is gone. My poor sweet Alma.*

Esther sighed, then she began to write.

CHAPTER 10

Luisa Eisenreich left Esther's home feeling satisfied that she'd finally gotten her revenge on Esther for making her feel like trash. But it didn't last long. Luisa had moved back to Berlin when the hospital closed and was now jobless except for her part-time work with the Deutscher Mädels. Bored and depressed that she no longer had the power she had so enjoyed at the hospital, she began to watch the Jewish neighborhood where the Birnbaums and the Horwitzes lived. One afternoon she was trying to think of some way to rise in the Nazi Party and get a better job, so she decided she would go to the Gestapo and turn the Horwitzes in. She hated them for what their son had done to her. And watching them be arrested had been gratifying. But still not enough. And to make matters worse, she didn't receive any kind of promotion or reward for her efforts. After that she was forced to apply for factory work which only served to make her feel as if she was sinking back into the world of poverty and obscurity that she'd grown up in. None of the jobs she worked at lasted very long. She applied at a hospital because she was a nurse, but the idea of being subservient to patients made her feel inferior.

Many afternoons, she spent sitting in the park across the street from the Birnbaums' house. She watched Hans drive the old man around in his fancy car, and she hated Hans for stooping so low. Although she knew she could have had him arrested for working for a Jew, she felt that was too small of a punishment. Instead, she would wait for the right moment.

CHAPTER 11

Berlin, Germany, September 1941

E sther and Ted had been waiting for a month to hear from Sam. They were hoping he would be able to get permission to bring them both to the United States. But, as of yet, he had not answered their letter, and the noose around the neck of the Jewish population in Germany was getting tighter each day. They had to do something now. However, they knew from friends who had tried to go to America that America was not allowing as many people to immigrate as they had in the past. And it was getting harder and harder to get in. Things were becoming even more desperate for Jews in Germany. Friends of the Birnbaums' had disappeared without any explanation. There were rumors that after Hitler took over Poland in 1939, he had set up ghettos where he sent the Jews after confiscating their property. These places were said to be overcrowded, filthy, and rat-infested housing, where entire families were forced to live with several other people in a single room or two. Even the wealthy Jews had fallen victim, and this worried Ted greatly.

"We can't wait much longer for Sam. I have heard talk that Hitler is about to forbid Jews from leaving Germany. Our friends and neighbors are disappearing all around us. The Horwitzes were arrested the other day. I saw the Gestapo go to their house and take them away in a black car. One day our friends and neighbors are here. That night we hear the sound of the Gestapo cars, and in the morning, they are gone. We never see them again. We can't wait until the Gestapo comes for us. We must do something now while we still can."

Esther spit on the ground three times. "Oy, Ted. May God help the Horwitzes" she said. Then she continued, "So what can we do? We've written to Sam; he doesn't answer. I wonder if he is even receiving our letters. I don't know where we can go."

"Well, I have a couple of ideas. We can try to get passage to China," Ted said.

"China?"

"Yes, they are accepting Jews."

"But we know nothing about China. We don't even speak the language," Esther said.

"Yes, I know. We could learn the language. We could manage. But the problem is, I don't know if we can get a visa in time before the law is passed that won't allow us out of here."

"Who told you about this law?"

"A business associate. He's a party member. His brother is pretty high up in the Nazi Party. But I've always been good to him, so he likes me."

"So you don't even know if it's true?"

"I don't. The worst thing about all of this is not knowing who to trust."

"I feel as if all of our old friends who were not Jewish have turned their backs on us," Esther said, tears in her eyes. "I don't know what we are going to do."

"Don't cry, liebsten. I have another idea," Ted said, taking a deep breath, and letting out a sigh. "I have a contact who knows Eichmann. For the right price, he says, Eichmann will make arrangements for us to get out. It might cost us everything we have, but at least we'll be alive."

"And where will we go? Where will he send us?"

"He doesn't say. All he says is we pay, and Eichmann makes the arrangements."

"Oy, Ted. Adolf Eichmann. Just the name makes me tremble. How can we trust Eichmann? He is one of Hitler's top men."

"I know that. And I realize this plan could backfire on us. It could turn out to be a trick. But what other choice do we have?"

"I am so afraid to trust any of them. Especially one who is so close to Hitler," she said.

There was a knock at the door of the study. Ted jumped as he turned around to face the sound. When he saw Hans standing in the doorway, he realized that he'd forgotten to close the door. "Hans," Ted said, startled.

"I'm sorry to have overheard you," Hans said. "But I believe I can be of help."

CHAPTER 12

Ted stole a glance at Esther. She gave him a trembling smile. He walked over and sat beside her. Then he took her hand.

"Sit down, Hans." Ted pulled out a chair for Hans and Hans sat.

The Birnbaums had always trusted Hans. He'd been working for them for fifteen years.

"What did you have in mind?" Ted asked.

"Well, let me start by explaining that Marta, my wife, has a brother who has friends that rank pretty high up in the Nazi Party. Don't worry. He has no idea that I am working here with you. But he told my wife that by next month Jews will no longer be permitted to leave Germany."

"I heard that," Ted said, nodding.

"It's like we are in prison in our own country," Esther said.

"If you look at other countries where the Nazis have taken power, like Poland, the Jews are imprisoned in ghettos. I am afraid that this may be the plan for German Jews as well," Hans said. Then he continued. "Now, I am sorry to have been eavesdropping. But, in short, what I am trying to say is that you cannot put your trust in a Nazi like Adolf Eichmann."

"So what is the alternative? We can't even get a visa to China by next month. It's too soon. It would take much longer than that to get all the paperwork approved," Ted replied.

"That's what I wanted to talk to you both about. Marta and I are very grateful to you for all you have done for us over the years. We would never have been able to afford the life we are living had it not been for your generosity. In fact, Herr Birnbaum, it was you who gave me the advance so that we could buy our home. I still owe you money for it, but you never ask. You have always allowed me to pay whatever I can whenever I can. So she and I have discussed this, and we would like to offer you a solution. We have an attic above our kitchen. It is well hidden. So no one even knows that it's there. It's small, and you would be cramped. I am sorry about this. I wish it were bigger. But it's just a storage attic. Still, I believe you both would be safe there until this madness is over."

"You want us to hide in your attic?" Esther said.

"Yes, I want to help you," Hans said, then he continued. "I heard you say that people are disappearing from their homes. I know where they are being taken. Some are going into hiding. But others are being arrested by the Gestapo and deported to the ghettos in Poland. You must get out of this house before they arrest you. You need not do anything wrong to be arrested these days. Forgive me for saying this, but all you need is to be Jewish." Hans hesitated. Then taking a deep breath he said, "Let me help you."

"We need to do what he says," Ted said to Esther. "Hans is right. It is the only way we will be safe."

"So how do we disappear from our home? How do you leave your job without being noticed? What shall we tell our friends?"

"One night, we are just gone. We don't tell anyone anything. I don't show up for work. We don't discuss this with our friends. We just go."

"Just like that?" she said, her voice barely a whisper.

"I am assuming you are planning to write to the grandchildren to say goodbye," Ted said solemnly.

"I wrote to both of them to tell them about Goldie passing. But I don't know if they ever received my letters. Neither of them has answered. I will write and tell them again about Goldie. And, some-how, I must let them know that they will not be able to reach us. But I have no idea how to tell them that. If the letters are being censored . . ."

Ted said, "When you send the letter, tell them about their mother. Then make sure to mention that it may be a while before they hear from us. Say that we won't be available to answer their letters because we are going to visit my uncle in Cuba."

"Do you think they know that you don't have an uncle in Cuba?"

"I don't know. But at least they will know that when we don't write to them it isn't because we have been arrested by the Gestapo. They might wonder what is going on. But at least they'll know that we are all right."

"And then we'll move, and we'll live in an attic?" Esther whispered more to herself than to the other two.

"Better an attic in Hans's home than a ghetto where we are crowded in with other families and no food. I've heard terrible things about those ghettos in Lodz and Warsaw."

"Hans, are you sure you want to do this? If this law actually comes to pass that Jews are not allowed to leave Germany, you and Marta would be in a lot of trouble if the Nazis find out you are hiding us," Ted said.

"Marta and I have discussed this at length. We both agree on this. If you remember back fifteen years when I had only just started working for you: I'd only been working for you for a few months when my wife became pregnant unexpectedly. Marta and I were very young, and we were so worried because we couldn't afford to have a child. I came to speak to you, sir. I had no other choice. And I was very afraid because any other employer might have fired me for asking for help. But not you, sir. When I told you of my predicament, you helped my wife and I to find a nice place to live, and you gave me a raise so I could afford to care for my family. You had faith in me, and you didn't even know me yet. I want to help you and Frau Birnbaum the way you helped me."

"You leave me speechless," Ted said, looking away because his face was filled with emotion. Then clearing his throat and trying to hide how touched he was by Hans's words, he said, "Well, I suppose we are going to have to take you up on your very generous offer, Hans."

Esther looked at her husband. "When should we go?" she asked.

"As soon as possible," Ted said. "I know it is hard to leave our home and everything we own behind."

"I am sorry, but as I said, the attic is small. There is no room for all of these things. Please forgive me. This is the best I can offer you. Please only pack things which are practical. Warm clothing, blankets, food..." Hans said. He stood tall, and as Esther looked into his kind eyes she realized, as she never had before, that he was a truly handsome man.

"How long do you need to be ready before we can go, Esther?" Ted asked gently.

Esther felt her heart begin to beat quickly as she looked around the room at all the precious things she loved. Her grandmother's vase. Her Great-Aunt Ruchel's lamp. The books she cherished. The memories that she'd brought with her when she married and the new ones she'd made as Ted's wife and Goldie's mother. They were all there, over fifty years of memories. A portrait of her parents when they were first married hung above Ted's desk. His family albums were arranged along the bookshelf. Her life . . . her entire life up until now was in this house. Esther let out a sigh, then she turned to Ted with an encouraging smile and said, "Let's leave as soon as possible."

"Are you sure?" Ted asked.

She gave him a brave smile, then she said, "Ted, these are just things. As long as we have each other, we don't need anything else."

CHAPTER 13

Berlin, October 1941

After much discussion, Hans Hubermann and his wife, Marta, decided the best time to move the Birnbaums into their home was when the Hubermanns' son would be away. One evening Hans came home from work at the Birnbaums, and Marta was preparing dinner. Erwin, their fourteen-year-old son, was in his room packing for a long camping weekend to celebrate Octoberfest with his Hitler Youth Group. Hans hated the Hitler Youth, and he'd told his son as much. But it was hard to turn the boy away from the group. After all, every one of his friends were members. There were constant activities, sports, cookouts, camping trips, even dance parties with the Deutscher Mädel's league. Hans had warned Erwin that he must be careful, never reveal the fact that Hans had continued working for the Birnbaums even after the law forbidding Gentiles to work for Jews had been instated. And he trusted that his son was smart enough to realize that if he said anything to any of his group leaders or his friends, he would be putting his father and mother's safety in jeopardy. But even so, Hans was worried about how Erwin would deal with finding out that he had decided to allow the Birnbaums to hide in their attic. This was a major offense against the Nazi Party. Harboring Jews could be punishable by death. When Hans and Marta discussed how Erwin would feel about the situation, they both decided the best thing to do was try and keep the Birnbaums' presence in the home a secret from their son.

The Hubermanns had decided they would move the Birnbaums into their home while their son was away on this camping trip. Then if the Birnbaums were quiet, perhaps Erwin need never find out they were there.

Erwin came into the kitchen carrying his duffel bag. He laid it down by the back door so he could just grab it when he was ready to leave the following day. "Hello, Vater. I didn't hear you come in."

"Camping trip this weekend, huh?" Hans said, trying to sound cheerful.

"Yes, and the girls will be coming too."

"Camping with girls, Erwin?" his mother said.

"Not exactly." Erwin smiled, and Hans thought his son was very handsome and should be quite popular with the girls. But he also knew Erwin was painfully shy around women. "Of course, the girls won't be camping with us. They will be on the other side of the campgrounds. And there will always be adult chaperones around. So you needn't worry."

"Don't do anything you will be sorry for later," his mother said in a serious tone. "If you get some girl into trouble, it could ruin your life. You will have to marry and work to support a family at a young age. It will ruin so many opportunities for you. Do you understand me?"

Hans had to smile. He had once been a fourteen-year-old boy, and if he'd had the opportunity, he would have had sex without even thinking about it. He just hoped his son would be smart and remember what he'd told him about pulling out before he ejaculated. Hans had heard how the German Youth were encouraged, even celebrated, for having children. But he didn't want Erwin to ruin his future by making some girl pregnant before he was even finished with his studies. Hans hoped his son would have the opportunity for an education, something which Hans had to forgo to help support his parents and sister. It was understandable at the time. His father had gone off to war, and there was no one else to help his mother make ends meet. Although his mother and sister both took in washing and did cooking for the wealthy neighbors, Hans was able to earn better wages working at the factories. So his future had been signed. He would always work at menial jobs. As a child, Hans had always dreamed of doing great things. But he had long since put that dream aside and was grateful to have found Herr Birnbaum, who was a kind and generous employer willing to pay him a more-than-decent wage.

"Do you think I look smart in my uniform?" Erwin said as he straightened his necktie. "I just wanted to try it on and make sure it still fit well."

"I don't much care for the Hitler Youth: you know that, Erwin," his mother said. "I think the ideology of the group is dangerous and fanatical."

"And most of all, it's cruel," Hans added. "You were raised to believe in Jesus. Would Jesus have approved of Hitler? Do you think so, Son?"

"Oh, Father. You are always worried about the Jews. You are always concerned about how the Nazis hate the Jews. But Jews are not the main purpose for our youth groups' existence."

"So, tell me, Erwin, what is the main purpose?" Hans said. His words came out more biting than he'd planned.

"To love the fatherland. To love our people, the pure Aryan people. And to work together in order to bring Germany back to a place of greatness. Until our führer took power, the rest of the world laughed at us. They watched and pitied the Germans as the Jewish bankers stole everything from our people in the Great War. Then once the war was over, our good German soldiers who'd fought for our fatherland returned home to find themselves unemployed and destitute. Our führer is in the process of changing that. You'll see! Germany is growing more prosperous and respected around the world every day."

Hans took a deep breath. His son was so young and idealistic. But Hans wasn't. Hans could see that Hitler was conquering all neighboring countries, swallowing them up like a shark swallows tiny fish in the sea. And, ultimately, Hans was sure Hitler would lead Germany into a war in hopes of dominating the world. The führer, as he called himself, was a frightening and hateful man who would take his country down a path that would end in its ultimate destruction. *But how does a father convince a son of what he knows to be true. Especially when his son is certain that he is much smarter than his father. Was I not once a young man, and did I not think I knew better than my parents? In my eyes when I was a young boy, I thought my father was just an old man who was out of touch with everything going on around us. Now I can see his wisdom, and now my son thinks of me the way I once thought of my father.* Hans shook his head.

"I love you. Please be careful. And . . . Erwin . . . be smart," Hans said.

The next morning Marta and Hans had breakfast with their son. Hans could see how excited Erwin was to be leaving for this short vacation. *They pull these young people into their clutches with sports and holidays. This youth group is fun. Erwin and his friends love it. And in between the dances and the cookouts, they teach them to follow the Nazi doctrine without question. I would like to forbid Erwin from attending these things, but if I do, he will only love them more and hate me and everything I stand for.*

"I have to go; I don't want to be late," Erwin said as he raced out the door.

Hans watched his handsome young son, on the brink of manhood, wearing that terrible uniform. He held his breath as the door slammed behind Erwin. *Don't believe everything they tell you, Son,* Hans thought.

CHAPTER 14

As soon as Luisa left the Birnbaums' home, she did some research on Hans and his family. She discovered Hans and Marta had a son named Erwin and that he was a part of the Hitler Youth. Erwin was coming of age; he was a handsome but shy teenager. She had read everything in his file. His troop leaders wrote that he was shy and awkward, but he was devoted to the party and had potential for future growth. She knew Erwin was leaving for the Hitler Youth Octoberfest camping trip today. And she was pleased because she would be attending this trip as well, with her troop of Deutscher Mädels. *I am not dumb. Hans is a real Jew lover. He's going to stick by those Birnbaums to the end. Goldie's father knows they are rounding up the filthy vermin, and he is probably going to pay Hans to hide him and his wife. And isn't it just like a rich Jew to try and pay someone to put their own life at risk for him. Jew pigs. Hans would be just stupid enough to do it too. That's probably why he didn't join the party. He hasn't got the sense to know that the future of Germany lies with our führer. Now, I don't think Erwin would stand by and allow his father to hide these Jews. It would ruin his chances for a promising future. So if I had to bet, I would think Hans would use this time, while Erwin was away, to move the Birnbaums into his house. I have to know if I am right. I can't let*

them slip by me. I'll just wait here in Berlin for a day and watch the house. Then I'll leave for the trip.

CHAPTER 15

Hans and his wife spent the next four hours cleaning the attic as best they could. It was a small, cramped space, and they were unable to stand upright. Being forced to crouch down while they cleaned made it even more difficult. But they dusted and scrubbed the floor and the walls until the dirt and cobwebs were all gone. Then Hans laid a mattress on the floor. The Hubermanns didn't own any extra bedsheets, but Hans knew he could tell the Birnbaums to bring their own. They had plenty. However, he told them they must not pack a suitcase. A couple carrying a suitcase, even if it was only from the car to the door of his house, could easily draw suspicion from neighbors. Therefore, the sheets must be rolled up carefully and stuffed under Ted's jacket. Hans had an old desk that he'd never used which he had already stored in the attic. He sat down in the chair, but he had to crouch so his head didn't touch the ceiling. *I feel so bad that this is the best I can do for the Birnbaums. This damn attic is so uncomfortable, but at least there are no windows. We won't have to worry about anyone peering in and seeing something they might report,* Hans thought. And even though the neighbors might not want to turn Hans and his wife in to the Gestapo, Hans knew that anyone who reported the hiding of Jews to the authorities would receive a reward. And he wasn't stupid.

Although most of the neighbors were friendly with the Hubermanns, they were poor and starving. Extra food rations, or a few extra reichs-marks, would go a long way during these trying times. And that meant there was a good chance that if someone saw the Birnbaums, they would turn them in. Yesterday, which was the last time he'd been at the Birnbaums' home, he'd taken a bag of candles and a few books with him hidden under his jacket. Now he lay the candles and books on the mattress. The days would be long, and the nights probably even longer, for poor Ted and Esther. His heart ached for the kind people who were no longer young, so it seemed probable that they would be living the last years of their lives here in this cramped closet-like room. Hans wished he could offer them a better place to spend their old age. But this was all he had.

CHAPTER 16

Rome, Italy 1941

L ucinda Fortini carried the heavy basket filled with vegetables that she'd just harvested from the orti di guerra, the war orchard. This was a small plot of land in the park that was allotted to any of the citizens in Rome who wanted to garden. Lucinda was on her way to her friend Alma's apartment to drop off some of the bounty of her recent harvest. Since Alma was so busy with her work at the hospital, she was unable to tend her garden properly. And since Lucinda had four children to care for, she was at home all day. The two had become friends when Lucinda's husband, Anthony, was in the hospital. He was a large, muscular man who worked in construction and developed a hernia from lifting.

While Lucinda waited for her husband, she and Alma talked about gardening. And when Alma heard that Lucinda loved tending to plants, they'd agreed that she could farm Alma and Lory's plot as well as her own. With two plots of land, Lucinda had plenty of harvest, which she shared with Alma and Lory. And often there was so much that she was able to sell some of it.

A cool autumn wind rushed through the trees as she turned down the street to Alma's apartment.

"Lucinda!" Alma was waving as she called from down the street. She was still wearing her white nurses' uniform.

"Alma, I was just on my way to your apartment," Lucinda said in broken English. "I have vegetables for you. Look at this! Zucchini, potatoes, tomatoes, and bell peppers. Some cucumbers too!"

"Oh good! I am so glad. Come, I'll make you a cup of carcade." Alma waited for Lucinda to catch up with her.

When Lucinda reached Alma, she put down the basket and the women hugged.

"Are you sure you have time for a cup of carcade? When will Lory be home?"

"Not for another hour or so. Come in. I'll put up a stew for dinner, and we can have a nice chat."

"I'd love that."

"I can't believe all the vegetables you produced out of that small plot. This is wonderful." Alma smiled. Then she stopped and opened her mailbox and collected the mail, then she helped.

"Here, let me take that. I'll carry it up the stairs. It's the least I can do," Alma said, taking the basket from Lucinda.

"The least you can do? If it weren't for you allowing me to farm your plot as well as my own, we wouldn't have so much produce. It took both plots for us to have such a good harvest."

When they got to the second floor, Alma unlocked the door, and the two of them entered the modest apartment. Alma laid the mail on top of Lory's desk, then she put the basket down on the kitchen counter. Alma put a pot of water on the stove to boil, and soon the fragrance of African hibiscus filled the air.

"I love this carcade," Alma said, drinking in the scent.

"I like it so much better than the chicory that passes for coffee these days," Lucinda said. Then she added, "Here, let me help you cut some of these vegetables. You can use them in your stew tonight."

"I can't thank you enough for doing all this gardening for us."

"Don't mention it. It helps my family too. And besides, I love it," she said, handing Alma some ripe tomatoes.

Alma began chopping vegetables. Then Lucinda began chopping a bright green zucchini. Alma added them both into a pot with water with some seasonings. Then she poured a cup of the hot carcade for herself and one for Lucinda, and they sat down at the table.

"How is your job?" Lucinda asked.

"It's hard work," Alma said. "Every day is a challenge."

"I am sure it is. You save lives. It must feel good to make a difference in the world. Sometimes I wish I could have had some kind of career of my own. But growing up here in Italy, we girls were members of the figli della Lupa, and there we learned that our jobs in life were to be wives and mothers. They taught us every aspect of that job. Until I met you, I never knew a woman who was married and had a career. Before you, I was foolish enough to believe that women who had careers were always just old maids."

"I wanted a career from the time I was just a small child. In fact, I wanted to be a doctor."

"I think you would have made a wonderful doctor. You are so compassionate," Lucinda said.

"I would have loved to be a doctor. And you are right, I am compassionate. I care so much about each of my patients. By the way, where are your boys?"

"My mother-in-law is watching them," Lucinda said. "She is a big help, but she also drives me crazy. She is very demanding of me."

"I understand. Mine was that way too. She recently passed away. God rest her soul. Lory was devastated."

"Italian men and their mothers. I sometimes think that if Anthony could have married his mother, he would have. He thinks the sun rises and sets on her," Lucinda scoffed. The she sighed. "But I suppose Anthony is a good husband. Don't get me wrong. I appreciate all he does for me and the boys. But can I tell you a secret?"

"Of course. I would never share anything you told me in confidence," Alma said.

"I resent it that whenever his mother and I disagree, Anthony takes her side. Was it like that with Lory and his mother?"

"Actually, no. I tried to avoid any disagreements with my mother-in-law for my husband's sake. I did whatever she asked of me, for the most part anyway. But on the rare occasions when she and I argued, he always took my side."

"That's unusual," Lucinda said. "You are a lucky girl. Your husband must love you a lot."

"I believe he does. And I love him too," Alma said. She saw the sadness in Lucinda's face, and then she added, "I am sure Anthony loves you very much. It's just that he doesn't know how to stand up to his mother."

"You think he does? I often wonder."

"I know it. I saw it in his eyes when he looked at you when the two of you were at the hospital."

"I love coming by to visit you, Alma, because you always make me feel better about everything."

Alma smiled.

After they finished their drinks, Lucinda stood up. "I had better be on my way. My mother-in-law will wonder where I am."

"I'll see you again soon?" Alma asked.

"Next week, more vegetables." Lucinda smiled.

"I look forward to it."

While the stew was simmering, Alma set a pot of water on the stove to boil to make noodles. Once the noodles were cooking, she sat down and began to sort through the mail. When she saw the envelope addressed to her with her grandmother's beautiful curling handwriting, she smiled. Then she tore the envelope open.

CHAPTER 17

Alma heard Lory's key turn in the lock. She wanted to fall into his arms when he walked in, but he was carrying a box of chocolates and a small paper package.

He planted a kiss on her lips, then went into the kitchen and put the things he'd brought home with him down on the table. "I have some wonderful surprises for you," he said, smiling. "Remember when I went to that young girl's apartment last month to deliver her baby? The girl who Vito told to come and see me? And if you remember, I worked on her for ten grueling hours while she was in labor. Then the poor thing couldn't afford to pay me?"

"Of course I remember. I was so worried about you that night. After you were up all night delivering the baby, you had to go into work at the hospital on no sleep at all. I wanted you to call in, but you refused. I still remember you telling me that this is what a doctor is supposed to do. I was worried anyway."

"Yes, I knew you were worried, and I felt bad about it. But they needed me at the hospital the next day, so I didn't think much about it. And I never expected to be paid. The poor thing was lucky to be alive. So I just figured it was . . . how do you say it in Yiddish? A mitzvah."

She had to laugh in spite of how sad she felt after reading her bubbie's letter. Her Lory, her beloved husband, had such a sweet way about him. "Yes, we call it a mitzvah."

"Well, today, the father of the baby came to see me at the hospital. He has decided that he loves the girl who he'd gotten pregnant. So he plans to marry her. And as payment for my work, he brought me these"—he indicated the packages—"black-market chocolates from Switzerland. And a chicken that we can put right into the stew you are making tonight."

"A chicken! Oh, how I have longed for meat or chicken," she said.

"Well, my dear. Tonight we shall feast. To accompany our brown sawdust bread, we will have chicken!"

"You make the bread sound so unappetizing."

"Well, it is made from sawdust. And if I had my way, we would never eat brown bread again."

"Oh Lory," she said, ready to weep. Her tone of voice startled him.

"What is it? What's wrong?" He ran over to her. "Not the bread?" he asked, unsure of what had upset her.

She shook her head. "No, it's not that," she said. Then she handed him the letter she'd received from her bubbie.

He read quietly. Then he took her in his arms and held her. His tender caress made her feel as if she could let her guard down. And she began to weep.

"I never loved my mother. So why do I feel so bad now that she's gone?" she said.

"Because she was your mother."

"I can't believe my mother is dead. I will never see her again. Never."

"Shhh . . . it's all right." He took her into his arms and whispered into her hair.

"I shouldn't care so much but I do. She was a terrible mother."

"But she was the only mother you ever knew. It's understandable," he said.

Lory held her in his arms for several minutes. Then she said, "Did you notice that my bubbie's letter sounded strange too? Why is she going to Cuba? When I asked her to come here to Italy and bring my zede with her, she said she couldn't because the doctor told them that

Ted was not to travel. Now, all of a sudden, they are going to Cuba? That makes no sense to me at all. Besides that, I didn't even know that my grandparents had family in Cuba. No one ever said a word about Cuba. My mother never mentioned it. And I think she would have. She was always talking about her parents and their connections. It's very strange to me."

"It is. I agree with you," he said. "So write to her and ask her why they are traveling so far with Ted's condition and all. I am sure she'll explain everything to you."

"Yes, that's a good idea. I'll write to her tomorrow. I can't tonight. I am so overwhelmed. I have so many confusing emotions. But if my bubbie and zede are on the way to Cuba, they won't receive my letter until they return."

"Everything will be all right. They'll write when they can," he said. "Let me cut up the chicken and put it in the stew while you take a nice hot bath."

"Are you sure you don't mind?" she asked. "You worked all day; you must be tired."

"You worked today too. Besides, I'd do anything for you, my love," he said.

After dinner, Alma lay on the sofa in her husband's arms trying to read a book. But she was unable to concentrate. Her heart was aching. He sat quietly beside her and held her.

"I can give you a little something to help you sleep if you would like," Lory said.

"I would. I don't normally like to take medications, but I am feeling so on edge tonight."

"I know, dear," he said.

Once Alma had fallen asleep, Lory went into the living room to read the paper. It had been a year since Italy had joined forces with Germany and entered into a war that Lory felt certain was a terrible mistake. He had never liked Mussolini, and now that Italy had joined forces with Hitler, he was certain things were going to get worse in Rome. He knew how Hitler felt about the Jewish people, and he was afraid it could become unsafe for Alma in Italy. If it did, he would do anything to protect her even if it meant risking his entire career and his life. She had become the very essence of his life, his reason for living, and he often wondered how he'd ever gotten along before he met her. Hitler's hatred for the Jews was why the letter from Alma's grandparents worried him. He didn't tell Alma what he was thinking because she was too distraught. But he had heard that Hitler was arresting all Jews and sending them to Poland and imprisoning them there. He wondered if that was why the Birnbaums had set off on a voyage to Cuba. So many thoughts clouded his mind. He was exhausted but he couldn't sleep. And he had an important surgery to perform in the morning.

CHAPTER 18

Berlin, Germany 1941

When the T4 euthanasia program was canceled in the late summer of 1941, Luisa Eisenreich had been terribly disappointed. The program was supposed to be top secret. However, the secret leaked, and there was such a public outcry that Hitler decided it was best to cancel the entire effort. Luisa had gone to her superiors to make a plea. She told them they should reconsider. She explained these were mercy killings. As a nurse who had been directly involved with the euthanization of the patients, she'd seen firsthand that this was the best thing for these poor people, who were incapable of contributing anything to society. "After all," she explained, "who would want to spend their life as a useless eater bringing nothing to the country and all the while draining its resources?" But in the end, the program was terminated. Luisa did not tell her superiors the real reason she'd enjoyed working for the hospital in the T4 program. It was the power. The power to decide who would live another day and who would die. All of her life she'd felt small and powerless. But now as she had stood at the little peephole and watched as these worthless beings were destroyed, she felt in control and superior. Sometimes, just for her own amusement, she would pull one of them out just before the doors were about to slam and the gas was to end their lives. "You have been chosen to live another day," she taunted them. Other times she just watched them die. However, the most satisfying day had been when she had been a part of the killing of Goldie Birnbaum. That was because Goldie was everything she'd always wished she could be. A rich, spoiled girl who had everything. To make matters worse, Goldie's mother had thrown Luisa a bone by giving her Goldie's old clothes. Goldie's trash. Meanwhile, Goldie had a fur coat for winter and cashmere sweaters with fine wool skirts. Luisa hated Goldie, but not only Goldie, she hated Goldie's mother too. She hated Esther Birnbaum because she knew Esther pitied her. And that pity made her feel worthless. Once in a while, Esther would bring Luisa a brand-new dress from the Birnbaum Ready To Wear clothing factory along with Goldie's hand-me-downs. At the time, Luisa had been elated. But later, when she grew up and remembered her childhood, she despised herself for being so needy and pathetic. And so many times she'd wept in her bed as she remembered her childhood. This always left her feeling like dirt and wishing she could punish Goldie and Esther for reminding her of her own feelings of worthlessness. Then, like a miracle, unexpectedly, her wish had been granted. And she'd made the most of it. She'd tortured Goldie every chance she got all the way until the end. And then she'd felt a terrible letdown when it was over. So she'd asked for time off from work. That was when she decided to take the train home in time to meet the letter that was sent to the Birnbaums. The letter that was nothing but a gentle lie. It said that Goldie had died of a heart attack. But Luisa couldn't wait to see the look on Esther's face when she told her the truth. "Goldie was murdered. And I was there when it happened. I helped to kill your daughter."

At first Luisa was satisfied to be done with the Birnbaums. Then after the program ended, and she returned home to Berlin, Luisa began to think about Goldie's parents more often. She'd enjoyed the satisfaction she'd derived from Esther's pain. And so she began to keep an eye on them. She made it a point to know everything they were doing.

And because she did, she was aware they were breaking the law by keeping Hans on as their driver when it was absolutely forbidden. But she wasn't quite ready to turn them in yet. She enjoyed the power she felt knowing they were oblivious to the fact she was watching them and waiting for the right moment to strike.

CHAPTER 19

Manhattan, New York City, February 1942

M orty Laevsky, the Jewish mob boss, who had also been Sam Schatzman's boss, was dead. He died unexpectedly in his office. And the last person to see him alive was Izzy Reznick, one of his employees.

The shiva for Morty Laevsky took place at Morty's home. The people who had been present at the burial were now trickling in. Fannie, one of Laevsky's oldest friends, was helping to set up the shiva. And although Laevsky had a large home, she was certain it was going to be crowded. Laevsky knew lots of people. But she was searching for one person in particular. Her best friend Chana. Chana and her husband, Sam, had suffered a terrible loss when their young daughter died. The strain it put on their marriage had broken them up. But Fannie knew they were still in love, and that the breakup was destroying them both. About a half hour ago, Sam had confided in Fannie that he had lost all hope and was planning to go to the recruiting office and join the army. Fannie was frantic. She felt that she must find Chana before Sam did something rash.

When Chana walked in with Izzy at her side, Fannie saw her immediately. *Thank God she's here. I hope she can get to Sam in time.* Fannie rushed over to Chana, and forcing herself to stay calm, she said, "Izzy, I need a little help. Can you put these knishes on a platter for me, and then put them on the table?"

"Sure," Izzy said, but he was looking at her skeptically.

"I just a need a minute alone with my good friend," Fannie said.

Izzy nodded, but Fannie could see he was not pleased that she was going to be speaking with Chana alone. She assumed that he probably knew she had something to tell Chana about Sam. It was no secret that Izzy had always been in love with Chana, and the last thing he would want was for Chana and Sam to get back together.

Then Fannie gave Izzy a quick smile and grabbed Chana's arm. She pulled her into the bathroom where they could talk without anyone else hearing them. Then she locked the door.

"Chana," Fannie said, out of breath, "listen to me. You might only have a few minutes left to change everything that's about to happen. Sam was here, but he left a very short time ago. He was terribly distraught. He told me he was on his way to the recruiting office to join the army. I tried to talk him out of it, but he is determined. He thinks he has nothing left to live for. If you still love him, you'd better get over to that recruiting office in a hurry."

Chana stared at her friend for a second. Then her eyes flew open wide with understanding. "The army? If he joins, he'll be going off to fight."

"Exactly," Fannie said. "That's what I am telling you. Please hurry, Chana."

Chana was still holding the box of cookies that she'd brought to the shiva house. She looked at Fannie. The box fell from her hands. The cookies spilled all over the bathroom floor. But Chana never looked back. She ran out of the bathroom and then out of the house.

As she dashed down the street, her high heels were slipping on the ice. But she dared not stop, not for a second. Her heart was racing. *Sam, please, Sam, I'm coming. Don't do this. I love you.*

CHAPTER 20

"Have a seat," the army recruiter said.

Sam sat across from the older, heavyset army recruiter who spoke with a heavy Southern drawl and looked him straight in the eye. "How old are you, son?"

"Thirty-two. Is that too old?"

"No, not at all. I just wanted to know your age for my paperwork over here, is all."

"And I don't know if it matters, but I speak fluent German," Sam said.

"Sure does matter. We can use a boy who can communicate with them Krauts. Do you have an accent when you speak German?"

"When I was in Germany, I was told I sounded like a native."

"How do you know how to speak German so well?"

"I'm Jewish. My father spoke fluent Yiddish. Yiddish is very similar to German. When my family and I went to Germany to see my grandparents, I caught on to German pretty quick."

"That sure could be helpful," the recruiter said, tapping the pen on the desk. Then he laid the paper and a pen in front of Sam. "Once you sign this paper you're in for good. Are you ready to fight for your country? Are you willing to die for America?" the recruiter said with enthusiasm.

But Sam didn't feel enthused. He felt sick and desperate. Sam picked up the pen. It felt cold in his hand. Then he thought, *I have nothing left to live for.*

Sam Schatzman's hand trembled as he signed the paper.

"Welcome to the Armed Forces of the United States of America, son."

Sam nodded. Then he put his hat and coat back on and headed for the door. As he walked outside, he saw Chana running toward him. She slipped on a patch of ice and fell. He ran to her.

"Chana, are you all right?"

She was trembling. "Sam, you didn't join, did you?"

"Yes," he said.

"Oh, dear God." She felt her knees buckle, and she couldn't stand up.

He lifted her up and set her on her feet. But he didn't let go: he held her in his arms. "You're so cold."

"I know," she said as she felt the tears forming in her eyes. "Sam, I wish I could have stopped you before you signed. I came because I wanted to tell you that I still love you. I know we have hurt each other, but I believe you still love me too. We both miss Ida; we always will. But if we are together, we can have another child. I want to make things right between us."

Sam hugged her tighter. Tears fell down his cheeks and froze on his eyelashes. "I do love you. I've never stopped loving you. Will you wait for me to come back?"

"Oh, Sam, I'll wait for you forever if I have to. Just promise me you'll return. Promise me you'll be careful." Her entire body was trembling.

"I swear to you, Chana. No matter what happens, I'll find a way to come back to you."

She looked up into his eyes. "I can't lose you again. I just can't."

"You won't. I promise you. You won't," he said as he pressed his lips to hers. She sighed. "I love you."

CHAPTER 21

The following month was filled with days of cuddling, romantic dinners, making love for hours. Sam and Chana were even more blissful than they'd been when they first married. They'd found each other again. And sometimes Sam would look across the room and catch a glimpse of Chana, and he would feel butterflies in his stomach, like a young teenager in love. They took walks at dusk and stopped at quiet restaurants where they held hands over a candlelight dinner for two. Fannie dropped by once, but she didn't stay long. Sam was sure she could sense that he and Chana wanted to spend every minute that they had left in each other's arms.

It was a bittersweet month filled with beauty, ecstasy, and pain. They loved more deeply than they'd ever thought possible, but at the same time there was always that haunting voice in the background whispering, "This is only temporary. You have three more weeks, two more weeks, one more week." Their lovemaking was filled with sweet desperation. They held each other through the nights. And told each other how much they cared. They watched the sunrise with cups of steaming hot coffee. But the weeks passed, and then the days, and then the hours, and finally the minutes.

"Do you want to come to the bus station with me?" Sam asked as he packed his duffel bag.

"Yes, of course," Chana said. But she was already crying.

"Maybe it would be better for you if we said goodbye here."

"No, I want to come."

They were both silent as Sam drove to the station, but their hands were locked together in a tight grip. Once they arrived, Sam parked the car. Sam and Chana waited for the bus to board.

"All aboard for Ft. Benning, Georgia," the conductor said. "We leave in five."

"I love you, Sam. I really love you," Chana said as she pulled him into a bear hug. His jacket was wet with her tears when she finally released him.

"I love you too. I love you more than you will ever know."

"Last call, everyone aboard."

Sam kissed Chana, and she let out a cry. "Sam. Please, Sam. For God's sake, be careful."

CHAPTER 22

Ft. Benning, Georgia, April 1942

The bus ride from New York to Georgia seemed endless. The constant rhythmic motion of the bus made Sam sleepy. When they made a stop for a bathroom break, Sam got out and stretched his legs. *I wish I had never done this. If only I'd known sooner how Chana felt,* he thought as he stood outside a service station in the moist heat of summer. A man with a cart was selling strawberries nearby. He walked over and bought one. When he bit into one, the sweet juice ran down his chin. *I wish I were on my way home to Chana.*

"All aboard," the driver called out.

Sam finished his strawberries and got back on the bus. Then he slid into his seat. His buttocks and legs protested against returning to the bus by causing him tingling pain. He would have liked to walk the rest of the way to Georgia rather than sit on that bus, but, of course, that was impossible, so he took out a pad of paper and began to write.

Dearest Chana,
I am on my way to Georgia for basic training. Every time I close my
eyes, I see your face. I long to hear your voice and to hold you in my

arms. I think about our honeymoon and how good old Laevsky came through for us. He was a good friend. I miss him too. It was so nice of him to send us to Niagara Falls. That will always be a special place for me. It seems that water has always had some sort of strange signifi-cance in my life. Our marriage began on that honeymoon in the Falls. And then a part of my life ended when we lost our Ida to the ocean in Coney Island. I both love and fear water. That's strange, isn't it? If I could take back one day of my life, it would be that day that I told Ida to wait for me while I went to get her ice cream. I should have taken her hand. But the sun was so hot, and the sky was so blue, somehow, I didn't think anything bad could happen. How could a child be alive and laughing one minute, then swept beneath the waves the next? I will never forgive myself for what happened that day. It still haunts me constantly. But if I could hold you in my arms, I know that I would feel stronger. I wish I could come home and look into your eyes. It would mean the world to me to see the forgiveness in your face once again. You can't imagine how it healed my heart when you found me in front of the recruiting office. I had waited so long to see forgiveness in your eyes, and then finally there it was. But now that I know you have forgiven me, I have to wait to hold you again. Oh, my darling, you are my life. And when I return to you, I will never do anything to hurt you again.

Love, Sam

As the bus continued the way to its destination, Sam drifted off to sleep. In his sleep he remembered that he'd been so distracted by his own misery that he'd forgotten to send in any of the paperwork for his grandparents, and the thought awakened him. *Damn it. I forgot again. I am such an idiot. My grandparents wrote and asked me if I would send the papers in to sponsor them to come to America, but I kept forgetting. I never even answered their letters. I meant to, but I've just been too busy with my own problems. They said they were going to Cuba to see an uncle. I didn't even know we had relatives in Cuba. I was so drunk during that time in my life. I'd just lost my daughter and Chana left me. Then they sent that letter asking me to help them and telling me that my mother had died. How was I supposed to cope with all of it? I couldn't. So I didn't. I should probably send them a letter explaining. But I can't. I'm too ashamed. But since they went to Cuba, I am not going to worry. It sure looks like they have found another way out of Germany. My grandfather is so stubborn that he has probably taken control of the whole thing and bought his way out. After I get out of the army, I'll write and tell them that I sent papers in, but I never received any word from the US government before I left for basic training, and that's why I didn't write.* For a moment he thought about his mother. *It's hard for me to believe my mother is dead. She wasn't the greatest mother in the world. And I am still angry about what she did to Dad. But it hurts to know she's gone. Death has stolen so many people from me, my dad, Laevsky, my precious Ida, and now my mother too. I wish more than anything that I could go home to Chana and start a family. Start over. I know that Chana and a child would fill this terrible emptiness inside of me.*

CHAPTER 23

U pon his arrival at Ft. Benning, Sam was taken into a room where his hair was shaved. Then his personal belongings were taken away to be returned to him after his tour of duty was over. Next, all the new recruits were sent into a large assembly hall. Once everyone was seated, a drill sergeant came into the assembly hall and handed out serial numbers. After the drill sergeant had given everyone a number, he quieted the men down and began to speak.

"You are soldiers now, and each one of you is an important part of a unit. From this day forward you must no longer see yourself as an individual. You must realize that the lives of all the men in your outfit will depend on each one of you putting the group first and yourselves second. No matter what you are feeling, no matter if a superior offends you, no matter what . . . you must treat your superiors with respect, and you must follow their orders without question. Is that clear?

"Sir. Yes, sir," the men said in unison.

"I can't hear you."

"Sir! Yes sir!" they repeated loudly.

"I still can't hear you!"

"Sir!! Yes sir!!" they hollered.

"Better. Now go and find your bunk."

Once everyone had chosen a bunk, the drill sergeant appeared again to take roll call. He stood in front of the men.

"Jenkins"

"Here"

"Wright."

"Here"

"Black"

"Here."

"Schatzman"

"Here," Sam said.

"Ashurst"

"Here."

The officer continued down the line. But Sam wasn't listening. He was watching the man who was called Ashurst whose bunk was across the aisle from his.

"Kike," Tyler Ashurst mouthed the words.

Sam turned away. The last thing he needed was trouble on his first day in the army. He was certain that if he started off badly with the drill sergeant, the animosity would continue and grow during his time at this base.

"Listen up, men. I expect each of you to be up and dressed and to have your bed made at the crack of dawn. Be prepared to exercise. Now, get some sleep because you're going to work hard tomorrow. For most of you, it'll be harder than you have ever worked in your life. Get acquainted with each other. Lights out in twenty."

Then the sergeant walked out leaving the men alone. Sam began putting his things away and putting the sheets on his bed when Tyler Ashurst said, "I know you, Schatzman. Aren't you the bastard who kidnapped that little girl in Medina?"

Sam was stunned. He had hardly expected to hear someone mention that terrible incident in Medina. He dropped his duffel bag and turned to see a heavyset blond man, with a ruddy complexion, glaring at him.

"What's a matter? Don't you recognize me, Schatzman? I was there when you got the shit knocked out of you for kidnapping a kid and then raping John Anderson's girl. You dirty Jew. He's a Jew. Schatzman is a Jew," Tyler called out so that everyone in the barracks could hear him.

"You son of a bitch. I never did either of those things."

"Yeah? Keep lying. It's just like a filthy kike to lie about everything."

Sam didn't want trouble on his first day in boot camp. But he lost control and went over to Tyler Ashurst and punched him in the face. Tyler's lip began to bleed. He was far bigger than Sam. When he returned the punch, Sam went flying across the floor. But he got up and hit Tyler again. Sam's nose was bleeding, but he didn't stop fighting until the drill sergeant came into the barracks.

"Stop it, you two clowns. Now, because of you, the rest of the troop is going to face the same punishment. I want all of you men out on the field in five minutes. You hear me?" he said, then he pointed to Tyler Ashurst and Sam. "You two, come with me."

Ashurst glared at Sam as they both followed the drill sergeant.

It was raining outside but that didn't stop the punishment. When the rest of the men came out, the sergeant said, "Get on the ground and give me a hundred push-ups. And you can thank these two boys right here for the privilege."

Everyone glared at Sam and Tyler.

"And as for you both. I want two hundred push-ups in the dirt, in the rain. Get down," the sergeant yelled. "Drop, now!"

The rain was so heavy that Sam couldn't see in front of him. He knew his nose was still bleeding because blood mingled with the rain-water as it ran down his face.

Once they'd finished, the men were sent back to their barracks.

"You filthy kike," one of the other men said as Sam dried his face and body with a towel. He wanted to go back and hit Tyler again. But he knew the others would face more punishment, and he was already starting off badly. Once he'd changed his clothes, he sat down on the edge of the bed and wrote to Chana.

Dear Chana,

I'm here. I wish I wasn't, but I am. One of the men here recognized me from Medina. And he brought up everything that happened there. But he didn't tell the truth. Instead, he told a whole bunch of lies. And now all the men in my troop hate me for being a Jew. When does this perse-cution of Jews stop? I have been forced to deal with it my entire life. You wouldn't think it would follow me here to the army, where I am putting my life on the line for America, now, would you? Chana, I am an American, born and raised. But I don't feel welcome here. I wish I could talk to you. You would know what to say and what to do. You always knew how to handle things. Dear God, how I miss you.

Love, Sam.

The following evening Sam returned to his barracks exhausted. He sat down on his bed and took out his pad of paper to write another quick note to Chana when Tyler came into the barracks covered in sweat.

"I don't much appreciate having to sleep in the same room as a Jew," he said loud enough for everyone to hear him. "Do they have a special place where they put dogs? Because that's where you should be sleeping, Schatzman. Why don't you ask about it?"

Sam ignored him.

"I'm talking to you, Schatzman," Ashurst said.

"What's it to you?" Sam answered.

"I don't much care for Jews," Tyler Ashurst said in his deep Southern drawl. "Jews don't make good soldiers. They ain't used to hard work. They're soft, like little girls. And I sure wouldn't want to put my life in the hands of one."

"That's your problem, not mine."

"Oh yeah? Well, what if I make it your problem?" Tyler growled. Sam could see he was itching for a fight.

"I don't want any trouble. I just want to get through this basic training without any more problems," Sam said. Even though Tyler Ashurst was a large man, Sam thought he could probably kill him if he chose to. He'd learned ways to fight from the other mobsters he'd worked with in the Jewish underworld. And although he wasn't proud of it, he'd already killed a man, John Anderson. John was a man who he believed wholeheartedly deserved to die. A man who had caused him so much grief. But killing that man had not satisfied his lust for revenge. All it did was make him feel sick. And he'd always wondered if God had punished him by taking his daughter because he committed murder and broke God's commandments. Now he was more careful of his actions. He had come to fear God's wrath. He would not let his anger or emotions control him because he didn't want to do anything to make God punish him again. All he had left in the world was Chana, his bashert. He'd lost her once, and he didn't want to lose her again.

"He doesn't want any trouble," Ashurst mocked Sam in a girly voice. Then he added, "Jews are cowards. Always have been, always will be."

"Shut up, Ashurst," another soldier said. "I don't want to listen to you. You caused us all kinds of trouble yesterday. I didn't enjoy doing push-ups in the rain, and I don't want to do them again. I just wanna get some sleep."

"I'm gonna keep an eye on you, Jew," Tyler Ashurst said.

Sam tried to ignore him.

"I heard that John Anderson was killed in New York City. Didn't you move to the city when you left Medina?" he asked. "And you sure had a reason to want revenge, didn't you?'

The last thing Sam wanted to bring to light was the fact that he'd murdered John. There was no doubt in his mind that John deserved it. He had not only led a band of his KKK friends to attack and beat Sam up, but he'd led that same group to find Sam's sister, Alma, when she was alone, and rape her. *This bastard suspects that I was John's killer. I must stay calm and be cool. I can't let on. If I am found out, I'll be arrested.*

Sam shook his head and did not look directly at Tyler. He hoped no one could see that his hands were shaking when he placed the pad of paper back into his duffel bag. He had mailed the two letters to Chana already, and he wanted to write another one. But he was so tired that he could hardly stay awake. He put the paper away and got into bed and went to sleep. Although he was very tired, he slept fitfully that night. He didn't trust Ashurst to not attack him while he slept. And he was also filled with questions that woke him twice during the night. *I regret murdering John. It was not my place to take a life. It is up to God. I wonder if God forgives a man for killing another man during combat.* When the bugle sounded in the wee hours of the morning, Sam was jarred awake. Following the direction of the others in his platoon, he made his bed and rushed outside to line up for roll call.

The first week that Sam spent at Camp Benning was difficult for him. He wasn't used to waking up early nor was he used to following a schedule. When he and Chana broke up, he'd quit his job, and he'd been spending his days drinking and sleeping in the room he'd rented at a cheap hotel. He drank excessively because the alcohol dulled his senses and helped him to cope with the death of his daughter and the loss of his wife. But now that he'd joined the army, he was required to get up before dawn and begin his program of extreme physical training which lasted an hour and a half every day. He was required to run a hundred-yard dash in fourteen seconds, jump three feet nine inches, as well as throwing a baseball 125 feet. From working with the Mafia, Sam was already skilled at shooting a gun and a rifle. He impressed his superiors with how easily he was able to take aim and hit his target. His body, which had always been muscular, began to train quickly. And by the third week, he was feeling better than he'd felt in years. There were drills which required him to march for long periods as well as time in the pool when he was swimming laps. At first the swimming left him winded, but he soon was able to keep up. Chana was on his mind all the time. Sam missed her terribly. He wrote to her every chance he got. But even though he was happy about the situation with Chana, he still had constant thoughts of his eight-year-old daughter, especially when he was swimming. And he still constantly chastised himself for leaving her alone on the beach that fateful day. Sometimes at night he would dream he was back at Coney Island with Ida. In his dream he was able to change everything. Instead of saying, "Ida, wait here for me and don't move," he said, "Ida, come with me. Give me your hand." His heart yearned for that second chance. *If only I had taken her with me,* he could hear his himself say as he felt his heart weeping. *If only I could go back in time and change that one precious moment.* But when he awoke, alone and in a cold sweat, Ida was still gone, and no matter what he did, he could never bring her back.

CHAPTER 24

Each day, Tyler Ashurst found unique ways to annoy Sam. On a bright, sunny morning, all the men piled into the mess hall to have breakfast. Tyler, who was seated across from Sam, gave Sam a sly smile. Sam shook his head and looked away. Then he began to eat. But when Sam looked down at his bowl of cereal, there was a big, black, dead fly floating in it. It was early in the morning, and the sight turned Sam's stomach. He couldn't eat another bite. Laying his spoon down, Sam pushed away from the table. Tyler let out a loud laugh.

"You did this?" Sam asked. "You put a fly in my cereal?"

Tyler didn't answer. He was laughing too hard.

Sam shook his head and looked away. He would have liked to punch Tyler in the mouth, but he restrained himself. *This didn't really hurt me. He's acting childish. It's not worth getting the whole platoon into trouble over*, Sam thought.

That afternoon there was a supervised boxing match. When Tyler won against one of the other men, the drill sergeant asked, "Who wants to go up against Tyler next?"

Here's my chance. I can get in a few punches at this jerk without having any problems with the sergeant. Sam raised his hand. The drill sergeant looked at Sam curiously because Tyler was a large fellow. Much taller and heavier than Sam. But the sergeant knew there was some bad blood between Schatzman and Ashurst, and he would rather they duke it out in the ring than in the barracks again. So the sergeant didn't question Sam. Instead, he told Sam, "Come on up here, Schatzman."

Sam got into the ring and the fight began. At first, Tyler knocked Sam down with a punch to the jaw. But then Sam countered, and Sam could see by the expression on Tyler's face that he was surprised to feel how hard Sam's punch was.

"You're pretty strong for a Kike," Tyler whispered into Sam's ear. "I heard the fellas raped your sister too. I wasn't there. But I sure would have liked to have been."

Sam punched Tyler so hard that he fell. The sergeant who was acting as the referee began to count, but Tyler got up. His face was a bloody mess.

The two men fought for three rounds. Sam gave Tyler a good fight before Tyler knocked Sam out.

CHAPTER 25

A few days later, Tyler began to pal around with Hank, who was another KKK member who hated Jews. He was a good ol' boy from Mississippi. Hank and Tyler made it their business to ensure that the rest of the platoon knew that Sam was Jewish. They started anti-Jewish rumors. The result was that no one wanted to sit beside Sam in the mess hall. And when the men worked in small units to learn the importance of building teams, Sam was not chosen by any of the team leaders. The appointed commander in charge had to place Sam on a team. Sam had experienced this sort of thing before, but that didn't make it any easier. He was the only Jew in his platoon, and he felt like an outcast. The only bright light in Sam's life was when he received a letter from Chana. It was two weeks into basic training, and he was terribly alone when the letter arrived. He took it outside and sat under a tree where he devoured every word.

Dear Sam,

I received all of your letters at once! I cried when I read the sweet things you said. I miss you more than I can ever express, and I promise you that we will make things right as soon as you get home. We will start our lives over again, like newlyweds. Maybe we can even go back to Niagara Falls for a second honeymoon. And just so you know, I have a surprise for you. I missed my period. I think I am pregnant. I have a doctor's appointment next week. I hope I am. If it's a boy I would like to name him Irving for your father. Keep your fingers crossed.

Fannie drops by to visit me every so often. It's good to see her, but she wants me to come and work at the bakery with her. I know she doesn't need me. After all, I am no baker. I am sure she wants me to come so that I don't waste away here all alone. I might take her up on it. I haven't decided yet.

Izzy has taken over for Laevsky. I know you and he have had your differences, but he's really not such a bad fella.

And I send you all of my love.

Love, Chana

Sam read the letter over again. He couldn't help but be worried about Izzy trying to move in on Chana. Sam knew Izzy had always loved her. But he was stuck here, and it would be a while before he would return home. So he had to pray and put his trust in Chana that she would remain faithful to him.

One afternoon Tyler and Hank were talking during an exercise. The drill sergeant caught them and punished the entire unit by forcing them to do a hundred sit-ups. As they were doing the exercise it started to rain heavily. It was pouring so hard that Sam couldn't see in front of him. One of the men complained, and the drill sergeant added another hundred sit-ups. If he could have done so, Sam would have punched them all in their faces and told them to just shut their mouths and finish the task at hand. But there was another complaint and another hundred sit-ups added. By the time Sam finished he was soaked to the bone and his body ached.

That night, several of the men attacked Hank and Tyler and pounded them with their fists. They beat them up until they both had black eyes. Sam watched as the men in his barracks descended like angry warriors hungry for blood upon the two who'd caused them trouble, and at that moment Sam realized that he'd been lucky that the fight between himself and Tyler had taken place that first night when everyone was still unsure of themselves. But now that the men had been there for a while and were comfortable in the army and with each other, he realized that no matter what happened, he must never cause his troop to be punished again.

It was strange that the day after the beating, all was forgotten. Tyler and Hank forgave the others, and the others welcomed them back into the clique. But even though Sam had never done anything to warrant the hatred that was directed his way, he was still being treated as an outcast. *All because I'm a Jew.*

Over the next several weeks, Tyler met several new men with similar convictions to his about Jews. And together they found ways to make Sam's life at boot camp even harder. Sam was losing his patience. He had too much on his mind to tolerate much more of these childish antics. One afternoon, Tyler had jammed Sam's gun during target practice. Sam was furious. He didn't care that Tyler had won the boxing match against him. He was ready to fight him again, and this time he would fight dirty, the way he'd learned to fight from the other mobsters. In the ring no kicking was allowed, no hitting below the belt. *Too many rules,* Sam thought. *I can knock him out if I don't have to worry about all those damn rules.*

"Hey, Jew, how does it feel to have had half of your dick cut off when you were too young to protest?" Tyler teased.

Sam knew Tyler was referring to circumcision. It was well known that male Jewish babies were circumcised. Sam had woken up with a headache that day, and he was in no mood to put up with Tyler. He was about to punch Tyler in the mouth when one of the senior officers came over to where Sam and Tyler were standing and pulled Sam aside. "It says here on your paperwork that you speak fluent German. Is that right?"

"Yes, sir," Sam answered.

"Come with me."

Sam followed the officer into the building. Then they went down the hall to an office where two other men waited.

Sam saluted when he entered.

"Private Sam Schatzman?" the man behind the desk said.

"Yes, sir."

"When you've finished your basic, you'll be sent to Fort Ritchie for special training. We need men who can speak the enemy's language fluently."

CHAPTER 26

Ft. Ritchie, Maryland August 2, 1942

Sam was glad to be done with his basic training. Although he'd come to enjoy the calisthenics and the drills, he was tired of Tyler and his friends. But it was disconcerting to think he might have to face more men like Tyler in his new training camp. *I've signed up to serve my country, and this is the treatment I get from my own men*, he thought as he boarded the bus that would take him from Maryland to Ft. Richie.

When Sam arrived, he was shown to the barracks and assigned a bunk. He looked around at the other men in his room, but he didn't greet them in any way. Instead, he began to put his things in the locker. When he'd finished, he took his sheets and made up his bunk.

A freckle-faced, red-haired man, who looked more like a teen than an adult, walked over to him and extended his hand. "Mike Applebaum," he said.

"Applebaum?" Sam said. "Are you Jewish?"

"Yeah, I sure am. And so what?" Mike glared at him ready to fight.

"So am I! Schatzman. Sam Schatzman."

"Another member of the tribe." Applebaum laughed. "Hey, it's nice to meet you, Schatzman."

"My friends call me Shatzy."

"Let me introduce you to the rest of the tribe. This handsome fella over here is Evan Lieb, another Jew." Mike smiled.

Sam nodded and smiled.

Evan Lieb was sitting on his bed, but he smiled and saluted without standing up.

"And this is Joe Shapiro. Short for Jonah. This is Shatzy, Joe. He's new."

Sam smiled. "Nice to meet you, Joe."

"Same by me."

"You can feel right at home here. We're all Jewish," Applebaum said.

Applebaum noticed Sam looking at a copy of a *Captain America* comic laying on Applebaum's cot. "You ever see this?" he asked Sam, handing him the comic book. On the front was a picture of Captain America punching Hitler in the face.

"No, I've never seen it. Is it recent?"

"Nope, you know what's so amazing about it? It's from March of forty-one. We hadn't even entered the war yet, and good ol' Captain America already knew Hitler was a shtunk, a good-for-nothing, nasty stinker. Like my bubbie would say, Hitler should only have a messa masheena, a horrible and tragic death."

"How do they treat you boys here being that you're Jewish?" Sam asked.

"Pretty good. We all speak German fluently, and we speak it without accents. The army appreciates that."

"Finally," Sam said.

"Jonah is a German Jewish immigrant."

"My parents were Jewish immigrants from Germany," Sam said.

"Welcome. So you are now officially one of the Ritchie boys!" Jonah said.

"The Ritchie boys, huh?" Sam said.

"Yep." Applebaum smiled. "And you know what? Every Friday night we have a service and a Shabbat dinner."

"Are all of you religious?" Sam asked.

"Some, not all. But there's a cantor here with us. His voice is haunting, and you'll be surprised at how touched you are when you hear the service. Whether you're religious or not."

The following morning Sam was sent to a classroom where there were only a handful of male students. Then a tall, slender man with golden-brown hair walked into the room and stood up in front of the class. He paused for a moment and looked around, then he introduced himself.

"I'm Sgt. Clayton Lee," he said. "You boys are here because you've been selected for special training. And I am going to teach you the art of interrogation. In this classroom you are going learn how to get information without using torture. Now, I am not going to tell you that we never use torture. But let's just say that once you learn these techniques, torture should be your last resort."

Sergeant Lee walked around the room. "Now I know that all of you speak German fluently. That's why you have been chosen for this very important mission. You will be trained extensively here. Then once you have finished, you go back to serve in the regular armed forces where you will be a part of a squad. However, if or when your squad takes a prisoner that's when your special training comes into play. You will have the responsibility of working on that prisoner to make sure that you out any information he might have which could be of importance to our country. Am I making myself clear?"

"Yes, sir," the men answered in unison.

"All right, then. Let's begin. There is a pad of paper and a pen in front of you. I suggest you take notes and study them every night. Now, there are three basic types of interrogation techniques we are going to study and master in this room. They are as follows." The sergeant went on to explain.

Although Sam had never liked school, and he'd never been one to study, he took extensive notes. There was no doubt in his mind that he had been chosen for something crucial, and he didn't want to fail his squad if they ever needed him.

The first week, Sam learned techniques to use when he was trying to bribe a prisoner, using things like cigarettes or chocolate. And then he was taught how to strategically build a friendship with his enemy by finding things they had in common and thereby instilling trust in the prisoner.

Each afternoon, the men were put into groups and told to practice the techniques they'd learned that morning.

Then one afternoon, at the beginning of the second week, the sergeant came in and placed a gun on the table in front of him. He pointed to the gun and said, "When you have a stubborn prisoner, and you can't get him to talk, walk into the room and put a gun on the table between you. Then stare at him and don't say a word. Just keep staring at him. Don't avert your eyes for a second. Keep this up for an hour if you have to. Some men are unnerved by this technique, and they start to spill everything. But, of course, always make sure that the prisoner's hands are tied securely before you try this, or he'll grab that gun and blow your head off as sure as I'm standing here."

The men laughed.

The sergeant cracked a smile. But Sam knew he was serious and that he'd given them good advice. The last thing he wanted was to be shot by his own weapon.

The following day, the sergeant came in and said, "All right, men, here's another important technique that may work in certain circumstances. This may sound strange, but always give the prisoner the impression that the Americans are all knowing, and that withholding information would not be beneficial to their side. Warn them that you already know everything, but they must divulge all of their secrets if they want to gain your trust. Assure them that if they do reveal some important information, you will make their lives easier. And then promise you'll give them more food. But if they refuse to talk, it isn't going to help their cause at all; it will make life much worse for them. They will suffer needlessly. They will receive less food. In fact, you mention that you might withhold their rations for a day or two."

In his final week of training, Sam was sent to another class where he was taught how to recognize the subtle signs that would be displayed by Nazis who had grown disheartened with Hitler and the war. He learned how to talk to them and how to use their loss of enthusiasm for the Third Reich. He studied exactly what to say in order to befriend these disgruntled soldiers and gain their trust. The training was intense and grueling. But Sam got along well with all the Ritche boys, and he found that even though he was working hard, he liked this training camp.

Each night since Sam had arrived at Ft. Ritche, he retired to his bunk exhausted. He found that studying and learning psychology was far more difficult than the physical training he'd received at boot camp. He hadn't written to Chana as often as he would have liked. It wasn't that he didn't want to. He thought of her constantly, but as soon as his head hit the pillow, he fell asleep. But tonight, he didn't lay right down. Instead, he sat up on his bed and wrote. He wanted to let Chana know how much he loved and missed her.

My dearest Chana,

You are the light that keeps me going. I love you with all my heart and I think of you constantly. I am angry with myself for letting all that time pass when we were apart. I just didn't know what to say to you. I was stupid and prideful. I was hurt and I felt guilt too. I still do. A day doesn't go by that I don't wish I could change that terrible day with Ida. But I must face the fact that I can't. You are my one true joy in life. And God willing, we will have more children. I will be different this time. I won't try to make you into someone you are not. I know selling your business wasn't easy for you. So if you want to open another business, I will be there to help you. And each and every day, I will be grateful for you just the way you are. The more I think about what we had together and what I did, the more I know that I was wrong. And now that I am away from you, all I want is to come back home and to hold you in my arms. Be well and be safe, my darling. I am going to bed now, but I know I will see you in my dreams. And, by the way, I've been transferred to a wonderful platoon of all Jewish soldiers, really nice fellas. If I have to be away from you, I couldn't have chosen a better group to be a part of.

All my love to you,

Sam

Then two weeks later, he received this.

Dear Sam,

Guess what!!! I am pregnant!!! The doctor says I am due in December. I am so excited, and I know you will be too when you receive this letter. Sam, now that we are going to have a baby, you must return home to us. You must be very careful because your child and I are waiting for you. I can't wait until we can make every day like those days we shared in March before you left.

In your last letter you mentioned feeling bad about having made mistakes. But you should know that you are not the only one who was at fault in our marriage. I, too, made many stupid mistakes. And you can bet that when you return home, I am going to spend the rest of our lives making it up to you. I love you, Sam. I was foolish to put that business before my family. It's just that when I was young, I was so poor. And I never wanted to be poor like that again. I didn't want Ida to have to do the things I did to survive. I wanted her to have a better life. And even though you were earning money, I was afraid that because your sources weren't legal that they would someday dry up. But I now realize that being poor and having those you love around you is far better than being rich and being alone.

Love, Chana

CHAPTER 27

Berlin, Germany, Summer 1942

Erwin Hubermann was packing to leave for the Hitler Youth summer camp when his father, Hans, came into the room.

"Do you have everything you need?" Hans asked. Hans and his wife had taken great care to keep their son from learning that they were hiding the Birnbaums in the attic of their home.

"Yes, Father."

"Good," Hans said. Then he added, "Do you really enjoy these summer outings with the Hitler Youth?"

"Very much."

"What is it that you enjoy?"

"We play sports and make campfires. The girls make camp on the other side of the lake, and we get together with them and have cook-outs and sing. It's loads of fun."

Hans nodded. *How am I to compete? I want so much for my boy to see all the wrongs that the Nazis are doing, but their leaders are so clever. They keep the youth happy. So between sing-alongs and cookouts, the young people learn their ideology. And because they are having so much fun, they follow it blindly. I can never tell my son about Ted and Esther. He wouldn't understand.*

"I wish you would join the party, Father. I think it would do you good. You would make a lot of friends. And you might even get a better job too."

"You know me, Son. I am not much of a joiner. I don't care for groups. I just enjoy the company of my own family." Hans smiled.

"But the party offers so much. Wouldn't it be something if you were able to find a better position."

"I am happy driving for Herr Schultz."

"He is a party member, isn't he?"

"Yes, he is."

"And you drive him to and from party meetings."

"Yes, I do. But I also drive him to work and everywhere else he is required to be."

"You have so much more to offer, Father. I don't know why you are satisfied being a chauffeur. But I must admit I am glad that at the very least you are no longer working for those Jews. That was embarrassing. And I was constantly worried because I knew that you were breaking the law. They've been taken away, haven't they? I know that the Birnbaum factory is now under pure Aryan ownership."

"Yes, they were taken away." Hans sighed, wishing he could talk openly to his son. He loved Erwin, but he was relieved that the boy would be gone for the next three weeks. *At least I won't have to worry about him hearing any noises coming from the attic. My biggest fear is that he'll hear something and go and investigate the sound by himself. What would I tell him if he found the Birnbaums in our attic? How would I make him understand why I felt I must help them? He believes so strongly in this whole terrible lie about the racial superiority of the German people.*

CHAPTER 28

As soon as night fell, Hans went up to the attic carrying a single candle. He was on his way to bring food for Ted and Esther. It was only a half loaf of bread, a small bowl of boiled potatoes, and pitcher of water. But it was all the extra food Hans was able to acquire.

"How are you both?" Hans tried to sound cheery when he walked in crouching, so his head didn't hit the ceiling.

"How should we be?" Ted said, taking the food. "Not good, Hans."

"I am sorry, Herr Birnbaum. I know it's hard living up here in the attic. But for now, it's the best we can do," Hans said. "But I have some good news. My son, Erwin, just left. He will be away at a summer camp for a few weeks. So you won't have to be as worried about being quiet. As you know, he doesn't know you are here. I think it's best we keep it from him. With all the Hitler nonsense he learns in school, I don't know how he would respond."

"I agree," Esther said.

"It's nice that we don't have to worry about making a little noise. But to tell you the truth, we don't make much noise anyway," Ted replied. "Most of the time, Esther and I play cards or read when the sun shines in this room and gives us some light. Then as soon as it gets dark, we wait for you to come and bring us a little food. This"—Ted threw his arms up in the air—"is what my life has been reduced to. Who would ever have thought that this is where I would be spending my old age?"

"I don't know what to tell you, Herr Birnbaum. All I can say is that I wish I could offer you more. And I know I've said that a hundred times. But I don't know what else to say," Hans said as he was wringing his hands.

"We're all right," Esther assured him. "We are safe, and we have food to eat. In these troubled times, we are very fortunate to have you, Hans. And believe me, both Ted and I appreciate everything you do for us."

"Yes, my Esther is right. She's always looking on the bright side," Ted said with just a hint of sarcasm in his voice. "Hans, I gave you all my money, and all you can bring me is a little bread and potatoes?"

"I'm sorry, Herr Birnbaum. I am doing my best," Hans said.

"Are you having trouble buying food on the black market?" Esther asked.

"Yes, a little. I can't buy too much at once because I don't want anyone to wonder where I am getting the extra money or why I am buying so much."

"I think that's very wise," Esther replied. "You're doing a good job, Hans."

"Meanwhile we are starving," Ted said.

"We are not starving. We may not have a lot to eat, but at least we have some food." Esther glared at her husband. "Besides, you could afford to lose a little weight."

"I will do my best to get more food," Hans said.

"Hans, forgive my husband. He is having a hard time adjusting to all of this. But, believe me, in his heart, he is very grateful for what you are doing for us."

"You have both been very kind to my wife, Marta, and I over the years, and we are happy to be able to help you," Hans said.

"It was always our pleasure to help you both." Esther smiled.

"I am going to go back downstairs now. I will see you at around the same time tomorrow night. And I'll do what I can to get more food."

Ted got up and patted Hans's shoulder "I'm sorry, Hans. I don't mean to be so irritable. It's just very difficult for me. But I really do appreciate everything you have done."

"It's all right, sir. I understand."

CHAPTER 29

After Hans left, Esther sat down on the cot beside her husband. "He is a good friend to us," she said.

"I know he is. But I am sure he must be tempted to turn us in. After all, there is a reward for turning Jews in to the Gestapo, and he and Marta could use the extra food they would get." Ted shook his head.

"Yes, but I trust him. He's been with us for a long time. He would never turn us in."

"He's the only employee we ever had who we could rely on."

"I have to agree," Esther said.

Then Ted lay down on the cot and patted the pillow beside him. Esther laid her head down. He cradled her in his arms. "Do you ever feel like just giving up?" he asked.

"Giving up?"

"Like ending our lives. Doing it together, so we would never be forced to say goodbye to each other?"

"Ted, life is God's greatest gift. We can't just throw it away. We have to keep fighting."

"For what? What is it that we are fighting for? We don't own the factory anymore. If we do survive this, we won't have any money. Who knows what has happened to our home? For all we know it could have been destroyed by a bomb. Our daughter is dead. Tell me what we are going to do if we survive?" Then he sighed. "Just look at this place. We always lived in such a beautiful home and now are stuck in an attic with a small cot. I can't even stand up in this place. I'm too tall. I keep hitting my head."

"I know. I know," she cooed at him softly. Then she whispered, "Close your eyes, Tedaleh."

"You haven't called me that since we were first married."

She squeezed his arm gently. "Come on, please, just close your eyes."

"For what?"

"Because I asked you to."

It was dark in the room, and Esther would never have known if he had really done as she'd asked.

"All right, they're closed."

"Now I want you to remember back to our trip to Paris that year before Goldie was born."

"That was so long ago. I don't know if I can remember."

"Sure you can. Remember that beautiful summer day that we went to that small restaurant and asked them to pack a lunch for us. Then we walked hand in hand all the way down to the river and had a picnic under that flowering tree."

"I remember it. White flowers."

"Yes, my love. White flowers. They were beautiful."

"Not as beautiful as you," he said, taking her hand in his and raising it to his mouth to kiss it.

"We ate, and then we took a long walk holding hands. Do you remember what we did next?"

"How could I forget." He laughed. "It had grown dark, and we went off into that secluded little area and made love."

"Yes, exactly."

"Are you blushing?" he asked.

She laughed. "I am."

"My sweet Esther. My best friend, my bashert, and my wife."

She reached over and caressed his arm. "As soon as this is over and the Nazis are gone, we are going to make a trip to Italy to see our Alma and her husband, Lory. We will bask in the sunshine and eat until we can't eat another thing. And I promise I won't complain about your weight the entire trip."

He sighed. Then he said in a pained voice, "I was such a powerful man, Esther. I am lost without my wealth and status. I've worked my entire life to be an important man. And now I am dependent on other people to bring me a crust of bread. To house me in an attic. Do you have any idea what this feels like for me? I feel like I have been reduced to less than an ant."

"You are still and always will be an important man to me. I love you, Ted. You don't need to have a big factory or a big house for me to be happy. I can smile as long as we still have each other. Just think about it. We are truly so blessed to be alive and to have Hans to help us."

"How do you do it?" he asked.

"Do what?"

"How do you always find a way to make-believe that things will get better. How do you always find a way to look on the bright side, even when there is no bright side? You've done it since the day we met."

"Because I believe that things will get better. I always believe that things will get better. Besides, what good does it do you to be miserable. We have a lot to be thankful for." She smiled in the darkness and took his hand in hers.

He kissed her forehead. "You want to eat the food Hans brought, or should we save it until morning?"

"Let's get some rest. We'll have a nice breakfast."

"A nice breakfast? You can't possibly have forgotten what a good breakfast is like. We had so many nice meals in the past. Do you ever think about them?" he asked, but he didn't wait for her answer, he just continued speaking. "I know we were never religious, but do you remember the high holidays when we were invited to our friends' homes for dinners? Or how about that wonderful dinner party you gave to celebrate our thirty-year anniversary. There was so much delicious food. When I think about all of the food we gave away to charities, I get so angry."

"We had a lot then. So I gave what we could to those in need."

"But when you think of it now, don't you wish you had it?"

"I am glad we were able to help others at the time."

"You amaze me. Are you sure you want to go to sleep? Aren't you famished? Are you sure you don't want get up and eat now?"

"I'll be all right," she said as she curled up in the crook of his arm. Then she whispered, "Ted, it's been years since we made love."

"Yes it has," he said.

"What about tonight?"

He leaned over and kissed her gently. "Yes, that's a good idea," he said. Then they made love. After they'd finished, he said, "I feel like a young man again."

"Ted, you are the man I love. To me you are ageless," Esther whispered, then she curled up in the crook of his arm, and they both fell asleep.

In the middle of the night they were awakened by the thunderous roar of low-flying planes followed by the crash of a bomb. The tiny attic room trembled. *That one was close,* Esther thought. Outside, screams of fear followed by more heartbreaking cries filled the streets. Ted pulled Esther to him and held her tightly. She buried her head in his chest. Neither of them said a word.

CHAPTER 30

December 1942

Dear Sam,

You have a son. He came into the world on December 4 at three in the afternoon. He has your dark hair and dark eyes. In fact, he looks like a miniature version of you, my darling. His expressions make me laugh. He squints his eyes when I sing to him, the same way you do. He is a true joy, and I can't wait to introduce you two. You are the two most important people in my life. His name is Irving, and I know your father, wherever his is, he is watching, and he is so proud that your son will carry his name.

I love you with all my heart. Be safe. Please, Sam, please, be safe. Your son and I are waiting for you to come home.

With love, your wife, Chana

CHAPTER 31

Germany, July 1943

Erwin Hubermann loved going away to the summer camp that was provided by the Hitler Youth organization. He loved the physical exercise and the comradery of his friends. They all shared the same ideals; they loved their country, and they believed that their führer was a god.

Last year he'd been interested in the girls, but he'd been too shy to actively pursue any of them. But this year, at fifteen, he was obsessed with girls. It seemed that girls were the only thing the boys in his group talked about these days. And there was one in particular that he really liked. Her name was Dagmar, and she was a member of the Deutscher Mädel's league. Dagmar was a tall and slender, graceful girl with long blonde braids. They'd never spoken. But he caught her looking at him at the cookout that they'd attended the first night they arrived at the camp, and he decided he had to find a way to talk to her. Then the following day, when he saw her in her exercise outfit, and when he could see a faint glimpse of her nipples through the thin cotton of her T-shirt, he thought he might go mad with desire.

One evening after the group finished swimming, Erwin was

helping to gather wood for the campfire they were preparing for that night. As he picked up a bunch of branches, his friend Gundolf walked over to him. Gundolf took some of the branches and began to help Erwin carry them to the campfire area. "Want to have some fun?" Gundolf whispered as they walked.

"What do you have in mind?" Erwin asked. He'd known Gundolf since they were ten years old. And he knew Gundolf was always pulling pranks and getting into trouble. Although Erwin and Gundolf had been friends for years, last year the camp leaders had advised Erwin to stay away from him. They told Erwin that Gundolf would get him into trouble. Erwin didn't doubt the truth of their words, but he couldn't help himself; he liked Gundolf. It was probably because Gundolf was always doing something interesting even if it was something that would be frowned upon by the leaders. Or he was up to antics that were amusing even if they involved playing a prank on someone, and pranks were clearly against the rules. But one thing everyone agreed upon, Gundolf could make you laugh. One year he'd been sent home early for putting green dye in Fraulein Eisenreich's shampoo. Fraulein Eisenreich was one of the head counselors at the league of the Deutscher Mädels camp. And everyone knew she was very mean, especially to the boys. So when she came out of her cabin one morning with a green stain covering her mousy-brown hair, everyone laughed until the leaders threatened to send them all home. Then to make things even funnier, the following morning Fraulein Eisenreich came out of her cabin with her hair as black as shoe polish. Her round plum face was red as could be, and everyone could see she was furious. And since she couldn't get the dye out of her hair she would be stuck with that dull black color until it grew out. Gundolf was sent home. His parents were notified of his bad behavior, and the following year, Gundolf had been forbidden to return to summer camp. But as time passed, his prank was forgiven. He'd since proven himself a good sportsman and an avid future leader for the Reich, so he was now back at camp with all the others. And he had been back for the last two years. He hadn't lost his sense of humor, but he also had not played any pranks that were serious enough to get him sent home. Erwin glanced over at Gundolf. He saw that twinkle in Gundolf's eyes, the twinkle that would come when he was about to engage in some serious mischief.

"Why don't we sneak away from camp tonight when everyone goes to sleep and spy on the girls? We can watch them if they go into the washroom; there is a small window we can look through. Maybe we will see one of them change clothes or shower. We might get to see some bare breasts."

"I don't know. We could get into a lot of trouble for that," Erwin said.

"Only if we get caught. Wouldn't you like to watch Dagmar get undressed? Who knows, she might go into the bathroom while we are watching."

Erwin blushed. "Of course, I'd love to see her naked. But if we get caught, they'll tell our parents."

The boys both dropped their loads of branches onto the top of the stack.

"We won't get caught. Trust me," Gundolf reassured him as he picked up two twigs and threw them on the pile. "What do you say?"

"I say it's dangerous. But why not. I'll go," Erwin said. He couldn't help himself. He knew this could cause him a lot of trouble, but when he thought of seeing Dagmar naked, he felt slightly out of control.

"Good. I knew you would. So as soon as the group leaders give the call for lights out, and we know for sure that they're in their rooms for the night, we'll climb out the window and head over to the girls' camp."

"Then what?"

"Then we hide in the shadows. We stand where we can see the bathroom window and we watch and wait."

Erwin felt a stirring in his groin when he thought about the possibility of seeing Dagmar's small naked breasts. He remembered the way her gym shirt had shown a slight definition of her breasts' shape. "What about the other fellows in our room? What if they decide to tell on us?"

"I'll bribe them. I'll promise them that they can come with us tomorrow if they keep their mouths shut."

"All right. We'll go tonight," Erwin agreed.

Erwin was a bundle of nervous excitement throughout the entire cookout. He sang along with the others when they sang their songs of devotion to the fatherland, but his mind was on Dagmar's perky breasts. And he could hardly wait for the evening to be over so he and Gundolf could be on their way. It seemed like forever, but finally the group leaders told the boys that the time had come to extinguish the fire. Erwin's knees and feet were tingling as he helped to clean up the campgrounds. Then once the leaders declared that the fire was out, they sent everyone to the cabins. Gundolf winked at Erwin as they walked side by side.

Everyone in Erwin's cabin was busy getting ready for bed. They had ten minutes before the leaders came to check to make sure the boys were all in their bunks. After the room checks, they called for lights out. Once Erwin heard the door to their cabin close, he knew the group leaders had left for the night. He had heard from boys who swore that they had spied on the male leaders and saw the male leaders meet with the female leaders after the campers went to bed. These boys swore they saw their counselors drinking together and having sex. Erwin thought it could very well be true because once the leaders left for their own cabin each night, they didn't return until morning. *They never bother coming back during the night to check up on us because they're busy with the women*, Erwin thought.

Once all was quiet, Gundolf and Erwin began climbing out of the window. Erik, one of the other boys in their room said, "Where are you two going?"

"Never mind," Gundolf hissed at him under his breath.

"I want to go too."

"You don't even know where we're going," Erwin said. "How do you know you want to go?"

"I don't care where you're going. If Gundolf is going, I know it's going to be fun. And I want to go too."

"Fine. Come on," Gundolf said.

The other boy, Kurt, who was sharing their room, had always been a top athlete who never got into trouble. Everyone said he was headed for work with Hitler's elite SS. Even now, Kurt was quiet. Erwin didn't know if he was asleep. But if he had to make a wager on it, he would have bet that Kurt didn't want to get involved. He didn't think Kurt would report them. From what he knew of this boy, he assumed if they were caught, Kurt would just claim that he'd slept during their escape through the window.

Once they were outside, the three boys began to run toward the girls' camp. It was dark, and there were a lot of trees between the two camps. Erwin shivered slightly as he remembered frightening fairy tales his mother had read to him. Stories of children who'd been lost in the woods, taken by wild animals or by witches. But he would never dare to mention his fears to Gundolf. He knew Gundolf would laugh at him and tell everyone else that Erwin was weak and that he still believed in childhood fairy tales. The last thing a boy in the Hitler Youth wanted was to be called weak.

They arrived at the girls' camp. It was dark in their cabins.

"Do you know which one Dagmar is staying in?" Gundolf asked. "We could take a look inside and see if we can see her sleeping if you'd like."

"I know which cabin is hers. I've been watching her. But I think it would be too dark to see anything through her window," Erwin said.

"What are we doing?" Erik said.

"Spying on the girls."

"But they're sleeping," Erik said.

"He's right," Gundolf said. "What a genius you are, Erik." Gundolf let out a soft but sarcastic laugh. "That's why we are going to go to the latrine. There we can keep watch at the window. Perhaps one of the girls will come in there, and we can get a look at her."

"You promised we'd get to see Dagmar," Erwin sneered.

"We'll try, but any girl we get to see using the latrine is better than none. If we're lucky, we might just get a look at her private parts." Gundolf giggled.

"All right," Erwin said. He was curious. He was an only child. He didn't have a sister. And so he'd never even had a glimpse of a girl's private parts. Erwin was curious and excited.

The boys stood in the darkness for over an hour until one of the girls came into the latrine. Gundolf elbowed Erwin so hard that Erwin winced. The girl looked around. She wasn't sure if she'd heard something or if it was just a sound coming from the woods. The boys crouched down so they could not be seen. But when she squatted to urinate, they poked their heads up. The girl saw them, and she let out a loud, piercing scream. The three boys began to run away but not before Fraulein Eisenreich grabbed Erwin by the back of his shirt.

"Stop, all of you, right now," she called out, but the other two boys kept running.

"What were you doing here looking through this window?" she asked Erwin angrily. "And who were those other two boys?"

Erwin didn't know what to say. He was shaking. Fraulein Eisenreich pulled him by his shirt into the office building. "Sit down," she said to him as she indicated a chair across from a desk. Then she sat down behind the desk. He did as he was told. Erwin was trembling. He knew he was in trouble, and he was trying to decide whether to snitch on his friends and give her the names of the other two boys. He thought she might let him off easy if he gave her their names.

"You know what you were doing was wrong, don't you?" Fraulein Eisenreich said.

He nodded, looking down at his shoes. "Yes, ma'am."

"Then why would you do it?" She shook her head. She looked angry. But inside she was smiling as a plan began churning in her head. "What is your name?" she asked.

"Erwin Hubermann."

"I thought so. Isn't your father Hans Hubermann?"

"Yes," Erwin said. Then he nervously added, "Please, I beg you not to call my father."

This is perfect, Luisa Eisenreich thought. *I've been waiting for an opportunity like this.*

CHAPTER 32

Rome, Italy June 1943

It was a warm night. Lory and Alma were detained at work, so it was late when they arrived back at home. Vito was outside their apartment building waiting for them. They had a dinner date that night, but an emergency surgery had kept them both at the hospital. And now it was too late for Alma to prepare anything for dinner.

"Would the two of you like to take some food down to the river for a picnic? It's only seven o'clock. We can make it back before curfew. And it might be nice. What do you fellows think?" Alma asked.

"I like the idea," Vito said.

"Me too," Lory agreed.

"Give me a few minutes. I have some fish that I smoked and a full loaf of bread. I'll pack it all up, and we can be on our way."

Alma packed the food for Lory, Vito, and herself, and the three of them walked down to the river for a picnic. They sat on an old, worn blanket. And as they ate, it began to grow dark outside. For a while they were all quiet as they watched the light from the stars reflect like diamonds on the water.

Then Vito said, "I know you have heard that the Nazis demanded a huge ransom be paid to them in gold, or they plan to arrest all of the Jews in Italy."

"I have been so busy at work I haven't heard anything about it," Lory said. "Sometimes, I feel so out of touch with everything. The only newspapers available are the fascist papers, and they never give a clear or true account of what is going on."

"I heard a little about it from one of my patients. She didn't know much," Alma said. "But she told me that many of the people in Rome have given what they could of their own gold in order to help their Jewish neighbors."

"Yes, I've heard that too," Vito said, "and you know what else? The Vatican has also made a large donation. They knew that the Nazis had imprisoned all the Jews in the ghetto in Rome and that the Jews didn't have any money."

"How much were the Nazis asking for?" Alma asked.

"Fifty kilograms of gold," Vito said.

Alma gasped. "That's a lot of gold."

"Did the Vatican pay the entire amount that the Nazis demanded?" Lory asked.

"The friars at the hospital said that between the wealthy Jewish population in Venice, the Italian people, and the Vatican, the Nazis have been paid in full," Vito said. "So now that they have their money, we should not have anything to worry about. But I just don't trust them. And I still can't help but worry."

"Italy is so different from Germany," Alma said. "I feel that the Italian people care about the Jews here. Even Goebbels, their minister of propaganda, hates that the Italians treat the Jews as well as they do. I've read articles he wrote about how he thinks the Italians are too kind to the Jews."

"Yes, I agree with you, Alma. However, the people of Italy are powerless against the Nazis," Vito said.

Lory nodded. Then he said, "It seems that everyone is powerless against the Nazis."

"Not everyone." Vito winked.

CHAPTER 33

September 1943

Lory was with a patient when Vito arrived at the hospital one afternoon. He saw Vito standing at the door and nodded to him. "I'll be right with you," Lory said.

"Don't hurry. I have plenty of time," Vito answered.

A few minutes later, Lory walked out of the patient's room. He found Vito sitting in the waiting area.

"What brings you here?" Lory asked as he walked over and hugged his friend.

"I came because I wanted to see you." Vito smiled.

"Will you come for dinner this week?" Lory asked.

"Yes, and I will bring my rice rations as well as some additional rice I purchased on the black market."

"Good," Lory said. "We can make a nice soup. We have some tomatoes and zucchini in the apartment. And Alma has some wheat that she was given as a gift, so we'll make a fresh bread too."

"Sounds good."

"Bring your dirty laundry with you," Lory said. "Alma traded some sugar for soap last week, so we are going to wash our clothes.

We'll wash your clothes at the same time; that way we can save on soap. It's so damn hard to get."

"You are so good to me," Vito said. "Will that be all right with Alma?"

"Of course. She adores you. You are my oldest friend," Lory said.

Vito brought a bottle of wine and plenty of rice that he'd gotten on the black market. Alma chopped some vegetables and put the rice, vegetables, and some dark liquid into the water.

"What is that?" Vito asked.

"It's salt. You won't believe it. But one of my patients worked for the railroad from Milan to Switzerland during the winter last year. They used salt on the tracks so the trains wouldn't slip. He brought some home with him. I took good care of him, so he gave this jar."

"Why is it brown, and why is it liquid?" Lory asked. "And what's that stuff in it?"

"My patient told me that the brown color is from the iron in the rails, and although he had to put the salt into a cloth and then pour water over it to strain it, it was impossible to get all of the debris out of it. But it's the best we can do in these hard times. After all, our salt rations are so small, five tablespoons, if we are lucky, and they are gone within a couple of days. And this salt mixture does make the soup taste so much better."

Once Alma set the pot on the stove, they all sat down in the living room and waited for the soup to boil. As they sat together sipping wine, the conversation turned to the state of the country.

"I am very worried about Germany taking us over. I don't know who's worse, Mussolini or Hitler. I started to worry in July when Mussolini was removed from power and placed on house arrest. But I read in the paper that last week Hitler sent paratroopers into Italy and they rescued him," Lory said.

"I read that too. He is in charge of some territory in Northern Italy," Vito answered.

"But what will happen to us if Mussolini is not in charge?" Alma asked.

"That's what I am worried about. Hitler is in control of Italy. And that is not good. I think he may very well be worse than Mussolini," Vito said.

"Let's not talk about this now. It's upsetting. In fact, it's giving me heartburn." Lory smiled. "Let's enjoy our dinner, yes?"

Vito nodded. But they were all worried.

CHAPTER 34

Rome, Italy October 16, 1943

There was a commotion in the Jewish Quarter of Rome. Loud guttural voices seemed to make the earth shake. "Achtung!!! Mach Schnell!!!" Big trucks began lining up along the side of the street with armed guards in front of each one. Nazis stood in the streets in full uniform. They were holding crowds of people at gunpoint. Not criminals. But innocent women and children along with men, and elderly people who were being rounded up like cattle. Babies screamed, crying and clutched on to their mothers. A woman held her daughter in her arms and fell to her knees begging as a guard pulled the child from her. The crowd were told they must put their hands in the air, a gesture of surrender.

CHAPTER 35

Tibor Island, Rome October 16, 1943

D r. Lory Bellinelli had just finished performing a knee surgery. He was tired and hungry as he headed back to the nurses' station. If there were no emergencies to be taken care of, he was planning to record his notes and then go back to his room to eat the lunch Alma had packed for him. When he arrived at the nurses' station, it was quiet, so he placed all the white folders down on the counter and began to write.

As Lory was finishing his notes, one of the nurses who he and Alma had become friendly with came running to the nurses' station. She was out of breath as she shook Lory's arm. "Dr. Bellinelli, the Nazis, they are in the ghetto. They are rounding up all the Jews and taking them away. You must find Alma quickly and hide somewhere," she said.

"Rounding up the Jews," he said, stunned in disbelief. "Why? How do you know this?"

"I don't know why. But the doctors are trying to hide all Jewish patients. The say they are afraid that the Germans will come into the hospital and take the Jewish patients away. Please, you must hurry.

There is no time to think," the nurse said. She remembered how Alma had brought her a hand-knitted baby blanket when her son had been born a year ago. And how Lory had always been helpful when she had medical questions. She had nothing against the Jews. And with all she'd heard, she was afraid for Alma.

Lory looked at the young nurse. Her face was flushed. *I don't know if this is all true, but if it is, and she is right, I must get to Alma quickly,* he thought, then he got up and ran to the stairwell. Lory climbed the stairs two at a time up to the fourth floor.

"Can I help you, Doctor?" the nurse at the desk asked.

"Where can I find Alma Bellinelli?" he asked, out of breath from the stair climb.

"Oh, I think she should be with the patient in room 406."

Without thanking the nurse, Lory ran frantically into the patient's room. He saw Alma looking like an angel as she was gently washing the face of an old man who lay in the bed. *Keep calm,* he thought. *Don't alarm the patient.*

"Alma. I must speak with you," Lory said. He could hear his own voice shaking.

"Yes, Doctor, I will be finished here in just a few minutes."

"I'm sorry, but I must see you right now," he said, then he turned his face to the patient and said, "Please excuse us."

Alma studied her husband for a moment, and she saw the fear in his eyes. "Excuse me. I'll be right back," she said to the patient and then walked outside the room with Lory.

"What is it?"

He didn't answer. He grabbed her hand and pulled her into the stairwell. Then he pulled her with him as he ran down all four flights of stairs. He continued to pull her until they had gotten all the way to the basement. She was out of breath. But she held fast to his hand as he led her behind some large pieces of equipment. Once they were hidden from view, Lory whispered, "They are rounding up all the Jews in the Quarter."

"Who is?" Alma was puzzled. "I have to get back to my patient, Lory. He's waiting for me."

"The Nazis are rounding up all the Jews."

"Why?" she asked.

"I don't know. But I know they are up to no good. So we must hide here until they're gone. Then we must come up with a plan. We can't go back out there. Not now."

"My patient," she said.

"It doesn't matter. You can't go."

She nodded. Suddenly she was starting to understand. Then she asked, "All the Jews?"

"Yes, women, children, old people."

"I wonder why. I can't imagine where they are taking them."

"I don't know. But I pray for them."

"What about our patients? Do you think they'll come in here and take our patients?"

"I don't know. But we can't worry about them now. You and I must stay here and hide until this over."

CHAPTER 36

L ory and Alma waited in the hospital basement until late that
night. When they emerged from the basement, they found the
hospital dark and in ruins. There was no one around. The patients, the
doctors, the nurses were all gone. The hospital was closed.

Lory and Alma stared at the mess for a few seconds. Then Lory
looked at Alma. "We'd better get out of here fast."

She nodded in agreement.

He looked outside to be sure the streets were clear of Nazis.

"I don't see any of them," he said. "We can only hope they're
gone."

Then taking her hand, Lory and Alma ventured outside. Careful
not to be seen by anyone, Lory and Alma went directly to the
Fatebenefratelli Roman Catholic Hospital.

When they got inside, a pretty young woman at the reception desk
greeted them. "I'm sorry. But visiting hours are over," she said in a
kind voice. But Lory observed that she looked frazzled.

"I am here to see a friend. Can you please direct me? His name is
Dr. Vittorio Sacerdoti."

"Of course. He should be on the second floor."

"Thank you," Lory said.

When they arrived at the nurses' station on the second floor, Vito was filling out some paperwork. "Lory, Alma," he said, "I'm glad you are here. I was going to come and find you both as soon as possible." Vito put down his work and then said, "Follow me. We need to talk."

They followed Vito into a private room at the end of the hall. "I sleep here," he said. "I'm sorry. It's a bit of a mess."

Lory nodded. "It's all right."

"But more importantly, we must discuss what happened today in the Jewish ghetto. I have been worried sick about you two. Because I am Jewish, I didn't dare leave this hospital until things settled down in the streets."

"We hid in the basement of the Israelite hospital where we work. They've closed it down."

"I know. Some of the patients escaped. They are here."

"This is terrible. As you know, Alma is registered as a Jew. They will be looking for her."

"I know. I am glad you came here. I have a solution for you."

"You do? I was hoping you would have some ideas. I must admit I am all out."

"Wait here. There is someone I want you to meet."

Vito returned ten minutes later. "Dr. Borromeo, my boss, will be here in a few minutes. He's a good man. He will help you."

It was less than two minutes before Dr. Borromeo, a tall, slender, distinguished-looking man, walked into the room. He quietly closed the door behind him. Then he turned and extended his hand to Lory. In a soft, refined voice he said, "I'm Dr. Borromeo. You must be Dr. Bellinelli and Alma."

"Yes," Lory said.

"It's a pleasure to meet you. Vito speaks very highly of you both. Now, I am not sure how to begin." Dr. Borromeo took a deep breath. "He told me that Alma is Jewish and that the two of you were going to need help. Vito and I, along with another doctor, have put a plan into effect to help the Jewish citizens of Italy. The third doctor will be here in a few minutes to meet you. Just to be certain that Vito has the right information. You are Jewish, aren't you, Mrs. Bellinelli?"

"Yes," Alma said.

Dr. Borromeo nodded. There was a knock at the door. Alma felt her heart jump. Dr. Borromeo saw her face and smiled reassuringly. Then he opened the door and said, "It's all right. This is Dr. Adriano Ossicini. He's the man I was just telling you about."

Adriano was a slender man with black-rimmed glasses. He smiled and nodded at Alma and Lory.

"All right. So we are all here now," Dr. Borromeo said. "I will tell you my plan." Dr. Borromeo glanced around the room. Then he took a deep breath. "I have some inside information. I can't tell you how I acquired this information. However, I will share what I know. The Jewish people that were rounded up and taken away by the Nazis today, have been transported out of Italy to a place called Auschwitz in Poland. When they arrive there, the Nazis plan to exterminate them."

"Exterminate?" Lory said, shocked.

"Yes. Murder," Dr. Borromeo clarified. "The Nazis plan to murder all of them. The three of us doctors who are involved in this Syndrome K hoax are strong antifascists. And together we have put a plan into motion that we hope will rescue many of the Jewish people here in Italy."

Lory looked at the doctor in shock. "I can't believe that they would just murder so many people."

"Yes, it's appalling, and so horrific that it's unbelievable. But I promise you that I received this information from a very reliable source," Dr. Borromeo said. Then he sighed and continued speaking. "First of all, as part of my plan, I would like you, Dr. Bellinelli, to begin working here at Fatebenefratelli. I would venture to say that your compensation will probably not be as good as it was at the hospital where you are working now, because we are owned and run by friars. But when lives are at stake, material things are secondary."

"Please . . . tell me more about your plan. I am very worried about my wife," Lori said.

"Rightfully so." Dr. Borromeo nodded his head. Then he said, "Perhaps it would be better to show you." The doctor stood up. "Won't you both follow me?"

Lory and Alma followed the three doctors up the stairs to the third floor. They walked down a long hallway and then stopped in front of a room. On the door there was a frightening-looking sign written in large red letters that read "QUARANTINE! DO NOT ENTER!!!!! SYNDROME K PATIENTS INSIDE!!!! THIS DISEASE IS FATAL!!!! HIGHLY CONTAGIOUS!!!!!"

"Syndrome K?" Lory asked. "I've never heard of that syndrome."

Dr. Borromeo winked at him.

Alma quickly looked inside the window above the door of the quarantined room. She saw beds filled with people. Most were adults, but some were children.

"You've never heard of it because it doesn't exist," Dr. Borromeo whispered. "We created it."

"I don't understand," Lory said.

"You will. Let's go back to Vito's room where we can talk privately, and I'll explain further."

CHAPTER 37

When the three of them got back to Vito's room, everyone sat down. Vito and Dr. Ossicini were there waiting for them. After Dr. Borromeo locked the door, he turned around and said, "Nazis are terrified of disease. Especially any disease that is painful and disfiguring. They are horrified by coughing. So we three doctors created this imaginary disease. The ward that you just saw is filled with perfectly healthy Jewish people. Dr. Sacerdoti, or Vito as you call him, rescued these poor souls from the October sixteenth roundup. They brought them here, then the three of us doctors created this quarantine where we put them. If the Nazis come looking for them, and we expect that they will, we plan to terrify them. We are going to warn the SS that the disease is highly contagious and most often fatal, and if they risk going into that room, chances are good that they will contract it. The patients know what we are up to, and they have been instructed to cough like mad if they see a German uniform."

"Fascinating," Alma gasped.

"I agree. It's absolutely brilliant. But why call it Syndrome K?" Lory asked.

Dr. Borromeo laughed. "Dr. Ossicini came up with the idea to name our fictitious syndrome after SS Chief Kesselring and SS Chief Kappler.

I'm sure you are familiar with the works of two good-for-nothing, murderous Nazis. We all decided that there was no one better to name a horrific disease after. Don't you agree?"

Lory laughed. "I am amazed at how magnificent this all is."

"It's true they are monstrous men, and they do deserve to have a disease named after them," Vito said.

"The three of us all share a hatred of Mussolini and of Hitler and, to be quite frank, of anything fascist. The friars here at the hospital back us up on this; they don't care for fascism either. They are aware that we have installed a radio in the basement in order to keep in contact with the partisans," Dr. Ossicini added.

"This is a Roman Catholic hospital. How does the Vatican feel about all of this, or do they even know?" Lory asked.

"Absolutely, they know. They feel that our Italian Jewish population are as much a part of Italy as everyone else who lives here. They are completely against the persecution of the Jews."

"I must admit, this plan, in its simplicity, is superb," Lory said.

"Yes, if it works, it will be a wonderful godsent miracle. We can only hope," Dr. Ossicini said.

"And . . . I hate to bring this up. But what happens if it doesn't work? If the Nazis don't fall for it, then what?" Lory asked.

"Then we are all in trouble," Dr. Borromeo said. "But we all agree that saving lives is worth the risk. So we are willing to put our own lives in danger to help those in need."

"Alma, how do you feel about all of this?"

"I think we must do it," Alma said.

"What about our apartment? I suppose I would have to go and clean it out tonight. All of our things are there."

"You must not. You must leave everything behind. Alma will be moved into the Syndrome K room tonight, and you will be moved into one of the doctor's rooms," Dr. Ossicini said.

"I don't know. Everything we own is in that apartment."

"Leave it all behind, Lorenzo. Alma's life is worth more than all of it. You two must never return to your place in Rome. They could be waiting there to arrest you. Safety is the most important thing. Just move in here tonight."

"I suppose it's all right with me. My wife is the most important thing in the world to me," Lory said. "Is it all right with you, Alma?"

"Yes," she said.

"Now, this is very important, so listen to me. If, for some reason, you are asked anything about Syndrome K by anyone, even another staff member, you must never tell them the truth. You just tell them that your wife came down with a terrible case of Syndrome K, which is a horrific and often fatal disease. And that is why you came here in the middle of the night because you knew she needed to be quarantined in the Syndrome K ward. You will also tell them that you have changed jobs because you wanted to be close to your wife in case she needed you for anything. Believe me, no one, not even any of the staff here at the hospital, will want to go into that room to see if your story is true. They will be too afraid of catching this deadly virus," Vito said.

"We have no clothes," Lory said, "only the clothes we are wearing."

"I'll see to it that you are given a doctor's coat and trousers. Alma will be given a hospital gown," Vito said.

Lory looked at Vito with concern in his eyes.

"Don't worry, my friend. Everything will be all right," Vito said.

"I don't mean to be rude, Vito. But how is it that you are not in that Syndrome K room? Aren't you afraid that the SS will take you? You are registered as a Jew."

"Yes, you are correct. Dr. Vito Sacerdoti is registered as a Jew. But Dr. Vittorio Salviucci is not."

"Who is Dr. Vittorio Salviucci?"

"Why, it's me, of course." Vito winked. "My dear Uncle Elio purchased papers for me. So I am now officially working here as a Roman Catholic doctor."

"Can your uncle get papers made for Alma?"

"I don't know. I plan to ask him. But until he responds, the best thing to do is have her admitted to the hospital with Syndrome K."

Lory nodded.

CHAPTER 38

The second day that Alma was in the Syndrome K quarantine room, a child was brought in. She was a small girl with a mess of knotted, dark hair tumbling across her tiny shoulders and wide, dark eyes. She sat in her bed sucking her thumb and staring around the room looking terrified. Alma walked over to her.

"Hello, I'm Alma," she said, sitting on the edge of the bed.

The child stared at her but didn't speak.

"What's your name?"

The child stared at Alma but still didn't answer. Alma studied her and decided she was probably about six years old. She wondered if the child was deaf or unable to speak.

"Can you speak, sweetie?"

The little girl stared into Alma's eyes.

"It's all right. You don't have to speak. How about if I brush these knots out of your pretty hair. Would you like that?"

The child didn't respond. Alma got up and went back to her own bed. She took a brush out of her handbag and walked back over to the little girl who was watching her. Then Alma gently began to brush through the little girl's hair.

Finally, after a few minutes passed, "My name is Isabella," the child whispered.

"What a pretty name," Alma said, not wanting to sound shocked that the child had spoken. "How old are you?"

"Seven."

"Seven. That's a very good age to be. I remember being seven," Alma said as she finished the girl's hair. Then she put the brush down. "Look at how lovely your hair is." Alma smiled.

"I am scared," Isabella whispered.

Where is her family? Alma thought. *Why is she here all alone? I'd like to ask her, but I don't want her to stop talking again. I am afraid that if ask a question that she doesn't want to answer, she might very well close up again.*

"You'll be all right. Why are you so frightened?" Alma said, stroking the girl's back.

"They hurt my mother. I think she is dead."

"Who hurt your mother?"

"There were these scary soldiers coming. They were yelling in German, and they had very mean faces. My mother and I saw them marching into the Jewish ghetto where we lived. My mother was scared. I'd never seen her so scared, and it made me feel scared too. Then she told me that I must hide under the floor. I begged her not to leave me, but the space under the floor was too small for her to fit. I tried to climb out. But she hollered at me and told me to stay there. My mother never hollered at me like that. I was shaking. Then she started crying. So I started crying too. But she stopped herself and told me that I was forbidden to cry and that no matter what I heard I must be absolutely silent. She said that I must not move from this spot under the floor until I didn't hear any more noise. Then she closed the door, and that tiny little room was so dark I couldn't even see my hand in front of me. I was all alone. I wanted to scream and call for my mother, but I was afraid. I heard them come in. They were yelling at her in German. She was begging. But then there was a terrible sound. I don't know what it was. It sounded like a bomb. But I don't know. I sat there shaking and hoping my mother would come back but she never did. I waited a long time. I was so scared, and I had to go pee so badly that I wet my pants. I am still all wet. I haven't peed in my pants for years."

"It's all right. I'll get you a hospital gown, and I'll send my husband to the store to buy you some underwear."

"Your husband is here?"

"He's a doctor here at the hospital. Do you want to tell me the rest of your story or would you rather not?"

"I'll tell you. There was a lot of yelling. Then when it got real quiet, I peeked out, and my mother was laying on the ground with blood all around her. I threw up. I didn't know what to do. I ran over to her and tried to get her to talk to me. But she didn't answer. I think she is dead. Finally, I had to leave the house. I needed to find help. So I left and went to all my friends' houses, but no one was there. I went to everyone's house that I knew. All our neighbors. My parents' friends too. Everyone I could think of. The whole ghetto was deserted. I was all alone. Then it started to get dark outside. And I was hungry and so scared. I wanted my mother so badly. I wished she was not dead. I still wish she was not dead. I sat down on the curb of the street and started to cry. Then this man came over to me and told me that he could help me. He was wearing a white doctor's coat. I was afraid to go with him. My mother had always told me not to go with strangers. But I was even more terrified to stay there all alone. So I got up and followed him. He brought me here. I know this is a hospital because I visited my grandmother when she was in the hospital before she died last year. But I don't know why I am in a hospital. I'm not sick."

"I know. But it's very important that you pretend that you are sick. Do you know how to play pretend?"

"Sure. I used to play with my girlfriends. We all pretended we were princesses from the Hans Christian Anderson fairy-tales book."

"That's very good. You must be very good at this pretending. Whenever you see a soldier come near this room, or you hear someone speaking in German, you must start coughing as hard as you can and pretend that you are very sick. Can you do that?"

Isabella nodded.

"Show me," Alma said.

Isabella started coughing. She coughed until her face turned red. Then she gasped for breath.

"That was very good. Someday you might just become a famous actress."

"You really think so?" Isabella asked.

"I do." Alma smiled. "Now, don't forget. When do you act sick?"

"Whenever I see someone wearing a uniform or speaking in that terrible language."

"Absolutely right!" Alma smiled at her. "But it's very important that no one ever knows that you are pretending. Everyone must believe you are really sick. All right?"

"Yes, all right."

CHAPTER 39

Lory came into the Syndrome K ward. When he saw Alma sitting with Isabella, he walked over to them both and introduced himself.

"I'm Alma's husband, Lory."

"Nice to meet you," Isabella said, "and you're a doctor here too, right?"

"Yes, I am!" Lory smiled.

"Is it possible that you can bring me some things for Isabella?" Alma asked.

"Of course."

"She needs some undergarments, and some books that might be of interest to a young girl of seven."

"Of course," Lory said, "and I don't suppose either of you will be needing dresses. But in case you were wondering, you both look stunning in those hospital gowns."

Alma and Isabella laughed.

"Well, you do," Lory said, then he smiled and added, "Later today, I will go out and purchase the things you have requested."

Then Lory turned to Isabella and asked gently, "Would it be all right if I had a word with my wife alone, sweetheart?"

Isabella nodded.

"I'll be right back," Alma said.

Lory and Alma walked to the door of the room where they could speak privately. Then he leaned close to her and whispered, "I missed you last night. We haven't slept apart since the day we were wed. I kept reaching over to the other side of the bed to hold you in my arms, but you weren't there."

"Oh, Lory. I miss you too. So did you stay here at the hospital?"

"Yes, I've been given a room right down the hall. I have agreed to be available to patients all night in case there is an emergency."

"I wonder how long this will last?"

"I don't know. All I know is that your safety is the most important thing in the world to me."

"I love you," she said, and tears dripped down her cheeks. "I want to go home and sleep in your arms."

"I know. I want that too. But we can't. Not yet."

CHAPTER 40

Lory returned with a big pad of paper and crayons for drawing and coloring. He brought underclothes for Isabella and several storybooks.

Alma was helping to pass out the food that had been left at the door for the patients. The staff would not enter the Syndrome K ward. They left all the food at the door. It wasn't much, just a hunk of bread and some tea. But everyone was hungry.

Alma quickly finished passing out the food and then sat down beside Lory.

"Still my little nurse," Lory said, taking her hand.

"I miss my job."

"I know. But believe me, you are needed right here. That little girl looks up to you. She has no one else."

"Her mother was killed by the Nazis."

"Her father too?"

"I don't know. She didn't mention him, and I am afraid to ask. She is very fragile. When I first met her, she wouldn't speak."

"Really?"

"Yes, she was traumatized, I am sure."

"Poor thing. The Nazis are such horrible people."

"Lory . . ."

"Yes, love."

"I am worried about my bubbie. I have written to her several times and she doesn't answer. I don't know what happened to her. I don't know if she ever returned from Cuba. And I am afraid that if she did, the Nazis might have done something to her."

"I want to comfort you. I want to tell you that she is all right. But the truth is, Alma, I don't know. I don't understand these kinds of people. I don't understand this kind of cruelty. So I don't know what they have done. But I will pray."

"I am praying every day," Alma said.

He put his arm around her, and she leaned into him. "We must do the best we can to stay strong. It is the only way we will survive this."

"I agree with you. I am so afraid that they will come here to the hospital and take all of us away. I am so afraid that they will see right through this Syndrome K lie."

"If there is one thing I've learned about the Nazis from the other doctors here, it's that they are terrified of getting sick. Their fear will keep them from seeing the truth."

In spite of the situation, Alma let out a short laugh. Then Lory laughed too. "We must keep them frightened."

"Yes, we must," she said.

"I'll see if I can get my hands on some red lipstick so you can draw marks on everyone's face. That, along with the coughing, should keep them far away."

That evening Vito walked into the Syndrome K quarantine room with a young girl by his side. She looked terrified. As soon as Vito saw Alma, his face broke into a smile, and he went over to her.

"How are you doing?" he asked.

"I'm fine. I have my little friend, Isabella, to keep me company. Lory drops by when he can. It's not so bad."

"I have bad news. I am so sorry, but the source that my uncle used to buy my papers has been arrested. He says he will try to find someone else, but for now, you are best off to stay here in this Syndrome K room. With God's help, you will be safe."

"Thank you for trying."

"I will keep trying. You know that."

"Of course I do." She smiled.

"I have someone I'd like you to meet," he said, gently easing the little girl out from behind him. "This is Luciana. She's my cousin."

"Hello, Luciana," Alma said. "How old are you?"

"Ten," Luciana said.

"Well, that's just wonderful! "Alma gave the little girl a big smile. Then she continued, "I have great news for you. There is another little girl here in this room with us, who is just a few years younger than you. Her name is Isabella. Would you like to meet her?"

Luciana nodded. "Yes, I would like that very much," she said.

After Alma introduced the girls, she walked back over to Vito. "She's adorable," she said.

"She's a good girl. It's a terrible thing that these young children are forced to hide from the monsters in the SS," he answered. Then he added, "I introduced my little cousin to Lory before we came in here."

"So you saw him. Then you must have told him about the man who was forging the papers?"

"Yes, I told him. He was very upset. He was really hoping my uncle would be able to have papers falsified for you. I feel so bad having to disappoint you two."

"I know. I was hoping he could help us too. I would like to get out of this room and work as nurse here in the hospital. I miss nursing. But I must face facts. That is just not possible right now. So all we can do is just keep our faith in God and stay strong," Alma said. "And believe me, Lory and I are very grateful to you for everything. We both know you did the best you could, and we couldn't ask for a better friend."

Vito nodded. "God bless you, Alma," he said, then he left.

CHAPTER 41

The outskirts of Berlin, Germany 1943

Luisa studied Erwin. Up until this last incident, he had never gotten into trouble. Even so, had it been any of the other boys, she would have reprimanded him and called his parents. Depending on her mood, she might even have sent him home, disgracing his family. And she might do just that to the two others when she got their names from Erwin. But she had a more interesting idea as to what she planned to do with Erwin.

"So," she said, sitting behind the small desk, "who were the other boys who were with you on your perverse little adventure?"

"I'm sorry, no matter what you do to me, I cannot tell you," he said.

"A man of honor, huh?" She laughed. "I like that. You have character, don't you? You like our ways of doing things? You enjoy the Hitler Youth?"

"Yes, of course."

"Do you believe all that you have been taught?"

"I don't know what you mean."

"You don't know what I mean?" She acted appalled that he had not understood, but in fact she had hoped he'd ask for an explanation.

"Being a senior member of the Hitler Youth, you should know our doctrine and our ideals very well, shouldn't you?"

"Of course."

"How do you feel about the fatherland and the führer?"

"I love them both. Germany is my homeland, and the führer is our savior. I would give my life for them if it was necessary."

"And how do you feel about the Jews?"

"I don't like them or trust them. They are the reason that Germany lost the First World War. They have done nothing but try to destroy our beloved country. That is because Jews are a lower species. The truth is that they are not even human. But they are dangerously tricky because they appear to be human."

"You have a very good grasp of our truths." She smiled. "Now let's discuss why you were hiding in the darkness outside of the latrine."

His face turned crimson with embarrassment. "I'm sorry," he said.

"No you're not." She laughed "You're a boy. And you're just coming into manhood. You wanted to see if you could get a glimpse of a naked girl. All of you boys are nothing but little perverts," she said.

He turned away unable to face her.

"I was only joking," she said. "To be truthful, it's only natural for a boy your age to want to see what the other sex has to offer."

He was stunned by how at ease she was. He'd expected her to be angry. But instead she made him feel that somehow what he'd done was all right.

"You've never had a woman that way, now, have you?"

Erwin looked down at his shoes. He shook his head. "No," he said in a whisper.

"Would you like to?"

His face felt so hot that he thought his skin might burn off. He couldn't speak.

"Why don't you answer me?" Luisa asked, then she gave him a sweet smile and continued. "I am not making fun of you, Erwin. Your feelings are only natural."

Luisa stood up and locked the door of the office. Then she began to unbutton her blouse. At first Erwin was repulsed by her large, pendulous, naked breasts. She was older than him by many years. She was at least forty, that was for sure, and not pretty at all. Luisa reached over and caressed his inner thigh. He would never have chosen her to be his first lover, but she was a woman, and his young body was alive with hormones. His manhood stirred at the touch of a woman. So when she turned off the lights and put his hand on her breasts, he felt his penis growing hard. She gave him instructions, and he followed them, but when he'd finished, he felt disgusted with himself.

"It's late. I should go back to my cabin," he said.

"Of course you should. And, Erwin . . . let's let this little encounter we shared this evening be our little secret. Do you agree?"

"Yes, I won't tell anyone. I promise," he said, and he hurriedly got dressed. Then he ran all the way back to his room.

"What happened?" Gundolf whispered to him in the dark. "Was that Frauline Eisenreich?" he asked.

"Yes."

"Does she know about me and Erik being there with you tonight?"

"No, and she's not going to call my parents either. She just said that I had better watch myself and not get into any more mischief."

"Wheew," Gundolf said "Maybe we should stay on the straight and narrow for a while."

"I think it's best," Erik said.

CHAPTER 42

E rwin couldn't concentrate on the sports activities at camp the following day. All he could think about was the night before. He had so many mixed feelings. He found Luisa Eisenreich to be repulsive. But when he thought about the way his body had responded to her, he felt heat run through him. *I've had sex*, he thought. *I wondered for so long if it would ever happen to me. I am not the most handsome boy or the most athletic, and I've always doubted that any girl would let me do that to her. Now, granted, Fraulein Eisenreich would never have been my choice, but she had the right equipment, and she was a good teacher.*

That night the boys and girls had a cookout and sing-along planned. The boys gathered wood after they had finished their swimming exercises. Then they got ready for the evening. The girls marched over to the boys' camp when it grew dark. They could be heard singing the songs of the Reich as they approached. The night before with Luisa had given Erwin more confidence than he'd ever had. After the group finished eating and the singing began, he got up and walked over to the girls' side of the campfire and sat down beside Dagmar. She turned and looked at him. Then she smiled, and he felt his entire world light up. They sat together through the sing-along, but when the leaders began to bring out the marshmallows, she moved and went over to sit down beside Arthur, a very handsome boy, who was one of the most popular boys in the Youth group. Erwin felt rejected. He watched Arthur slip his arm around Dagmar's shoulders, and he couldn't eat the sweet, gooey treats. *She doesn't like me. Why would she? She's the prettiest girl in the Deutscher Mädels. She could have any one of these fellows that she wanted. Why would she ever choose me? I was deluding myself.* Erwin stood up. He tried to slip away from the group without being noticed. But once he had walked far enough away from the others and was hidden by a cluster of trees, Luisa came up behind him.

"What's a matter, loverboy? Did Dagmar reject you?"

He shrugged.

"Don't worry about her. She's just a child. Why don't you wait until the cookout is over, and then meet me at my office where we were last night?"

He couldn't look into her eyes. He found her hideous, yet he knew he was going to go to the cabin and meet her as soon as he could. The idea of having sex again, even if it was with her, was driving him wild. "All right. But I have to wait until my counselors call for lights out. Then I'll slip out the window."

"If your friends ask where you're going, don't breathe a word of this. Just tell them to mind their own business."

He nodded. "I will."

That night after they had sex, Luisa said, "You see how much better this is with a mature woman?"

"Yes, Fraulein Eisenreich," he said.

"You might as well call me Luisa. After all, we have been intimate," she said.

"Luisa," he repeated.

These meetings with Luisa continued for the next two weeks. During that time Erik stopped asking where he was going, but Gundolf hounded him. He refused to tell Gundolf anything, but Erwin was certain Gundolf had followed him and knew what Erwin was up to.

Camp was almost over, and Erwin was confused. He wasn't sure why he was having such strange feelings for Luisa. He was very sad to see their affair ending. It had become an important part of his life.

Having these secret sexual rendezvous gave him a feeling of superiority to the other boys in his age group. *I have done things that they have only daydreamed about. I don't want to let Luisa go. I don't know how this happened, but I think about her all the time, and I think I may have fallen in love with her.*

On the last day of camp, the bus to take the boys home to Berlin arrived early. Erwin gathered his bags and looked around the campsite for Luisa. He knew he had a half hour before the bus was scheduled to leave, so he quickly ran to the girls' camp and searched for her. She was nowhere to be found. Time was passing, and Erwin was feeling as if a deep cavern had been carved into the pit of his stomach. *She's gone. It's over,* he thought, and hurt and disappointment came rushing through him like a river. *I don't care about her,* he told himself as he boarded the bus. *She's old and ugly anyway.* But he was unsettled the entire ride home. Erwin was glad that at least the boy who was sitting next to him on the bus had fallen asleep. He didn't want to have to deal with talking to anyone.

Erwin arrived at home in a foul mood. In the past when he'd returned from a Hitler Youth outing, he'd been filled with exciting and funny stories that he couldn't wait to share with his parents. But today he was too depressed to talk to them. And when his mother asked him how everything was on his trip, he just said, "Fine." Then went up to his room and locked the door. Erwin usually unpacked as soon as he returned home. But he didn't. He put his bag in the corner of his room. Then he lay on his bed and began thinking. *It will be a year before I see Luisa again. What if I never meet another female who likes me enough to have sex with me. I'm not the kind of fellow that girls fall all over themselves for. I wish I was. But I don't think I have the right looks. I think my nose is too big, and I am too tall and scarecrow-like looking. Besides that, when I get around girls, I am so shy. I never know what to say.* Erwin, like every other adolescent, was sure he had too many faults for anyone to ever fall in love with him.

The following Monday school began. Erwin studied fiercely trying to erase thoughts of Luisa, and what they had shared, from his mind. But the harder he tried to forget her, the more he wished he could go back to those warm nights they had lain naked on the floor in the back of that office. But because he was focused on his schoolwork, his grades improved. And he could see that his parents were pleased he was doing better in school. As he had done every week since he was ten, he attended his Hitler Youth meetings. Erwin knew his parents didn't care for the Hitler Youth, but because all of his friends attended, they allowed him to attend the meetings. The other boys in his group had questioned him about his father in the past. Because they knew his father had been working for the Birnbaums, the rich Jews who owned the big factory. And they also knew that Hans had never joined the party. Erwin was certain their parents discussed it with them. But Erwin tried to sound casual when he made excuses for his parents. He told the other boys that his father hated Herr Birnbaum and only worked for him because he paid his father well. Then recently Erwin was relieved when Herr Birnbaum and his family were suddenly gone. He was certain the Gestapo had taken them during the night one night. After that, Erwin was relieved when his father finally joined the Nazi Party. Erwin knew his father had joined because the Birnbaums had disappeared. He would never have done so if that old rich Jew were still around bribing him with a good-paying job. Since the Birnbaums' disappearance, his father had gotten another job which didn't pay as well. But Erwin was hoping now that his father was showing an interest in the Nazi Party, Erwin would be like the other boys, and he would not stand out so much or have to explain his parents' odd behavior. And perhaps, if his father were clever and made the right connections, he might be offered a better position and more money.

Two weeks after school had begun, Erwin was gathering his books together to leave school for the day. There was a Hitler Youth meeting that night that he planned to attend. So he knew he would have to rush home and finish his homework quickly. He walked outside and began to make his way toward home when he heard a female voice behind him.

"Erwin, wait up."

He stopped and whipped around. "Luisa?" he said, his heart was pounding.

"I've missed you," she said, smiling.

He was glad to see her. Even in the bright sunshine, he could no longer see how he had once found her to be unattractive. All he could think about was the things she'd allowed him to do to her and how much he wanted to do them again. As he looked at her, his body grew hot all over.

"I've missed you too," he said, and he had missed her. Then he mustered up all the courage he could find and added, "I looked for you all day on the last day of camp. I searched everywhere before I left, but you had already gone. Why didn't you find me and say goodbye?"

"I was in a hurry. I had to get back to my job in Berlin." She smiled. "So you searched for me, huh?"

"Yes," he said, looking away.

"That's very sweet. I didn't think you cared."

"I do," he said, looking down at the sidewalk. He felt awkward.

"Aren't you wondering what I am doing here?" she asked.

"Actually, I was," he said, not knowing what to say next.

"Well . . . don't you have a Hitler Youth meeting tonight?"

"Yes."

"Would you be willing to miss it and meet me in my hotel room?"

He felt his face turning red. "Yes, of course."

She let out a laugh. "Good," she said, and she handed him a piece of paper with the name and address of the hotel and her room number. "What time does your meeting start?"

"Seven."

"Can I expect you to be at the hotel by seven thirty?"

"Yes. I'll be there," he replied swallowing hard.

CHAPTER 43

Luisa went back to her hotel room where she lay down on the bed. She closed her eyes and surrendered to the excitement she felt. She was drunk with the power of knowing that Hans was hiding the Birnbaums. It made her excited to watch them from afar knowing their very lives were in her hands and at any time she could turn them in. She stroked her breast when she thought about it. But then she stopped when she remembered the truth. Things had begun to look dismal for Germany, and it appeared that the Nazis could very well lose the war. So although she relished the control she felt, she knew the time had come to escalate things. She must decide what the best way would be to put an end to Esther Birnbaum. She wasn't quite sure how she was going to go about it. Luisa wanted to do whatever she could to make things as horrific for Esther as possible. *I want Esther to feel like trash, the way she and that daughter of hers made me feel. And as far as Hans is concerned? He disgusts me. He deserves to be punished for taking the side of these Jews and offering them his protection.* So when she had caught Hans's son, Erwin, peeking into the girl's latrine, she'd been thrilled. Young, naïve, and easily manipulated, Erwin Hubermann was the prefect catalyst to set her newly devised plan into motion.

CHAPTER 44

I t was a cheap hotel. The room was sparsely furnished, and Erwin noticed that the bedspread had several unidentifiable stains. *Why am I so sexually driven?* he asked himself. *I know she is too old for me and that I shouldn't be doing this. My parents would never approve. Yet here I am in this hotel room, shaking like a leaf, glad to have her back in my life. I must be in love with her. But at the same time, I wouldn't want my friends to see me here with her. They would make fun of me. The truth is I am ashamed of her. I am so confused because at the same time I am drawn to her, and I can't take my mind off of these things we do in bed together. My mother would be so appalled by my behavior. She would think Luisa was a pig. Yet I can't stop myself.*

Luisa didn't waste time making small talk. As soon as the door to her hotel room closed, she began to undress Erwin. Then she turned off the light and removed her own clothes. She climbed on top of him and attacked him like a hungry lioness, and he responded with equal passion. After they were finished, she rolled off of him. Then Luisa lay down beside Erwin and leaned over. She began to run her fingers along his hairless chest.

"Would you like for me to come and visit you once in a while? We could meet at this hotel. What do you think about that?"

"Yes," he answered, "I would like that very much."

"Of course you would. And I would too," she said. "Now, I have an important question to ask you. But you must promise to answer me with complete honesty. Can you do that?"

"Yes," he said, "I hope so."

"Do you trust me?" Luisa asked.

"Of course."

"Are you certain?"

"Yes, of course I trust you," he said.

"Then there is something you must know. And there is also something you must do. That is, of course, if you want me to keep coming back to see you."

He turned toward her. In the darkness all he could see was the shadow of her face.

"What is it?"

"It's about your parents."

"My parents?"

"Yes, your parents need help. And you can and must help them."

"I don't understand."

"You will," she said. Then under the covers she caressed his manhood.

CHAPTER 45

Esther and Ted Birnbaum had just finished playing a game of cards when the sun began to set. It was too late to start another game because soon the light would be gone, and they would remain in the darkness until morning.

"I'm very tired," Ted said.

"Hans will be here soon with our food. After he leaves, we can get some sleep."

"I don't know why I am so exhausted all the time. It seems that all we do is sleep."

"It's all right. It helps the time pass," Esther said, then she added, "Here, I saved you some of my bread from this morning."

"I'm not hungry," Ted replied.

"Do you feel all right?"

"Not really. I feel sick to my stomach. My head aches, and my jaw hurts. I guess it's just old age."

"How many times must I tell you that you're not old. You are in your prime, Ted Birnbaum. And soon this will all be over, and then you and I will have the time of our lives traveling to Italy."

"We have no money. How will we travel?"

"Don't worry about that now. We'll figure it out when the time comes." Esther smiled at him.

"I'm too tired to stay awake. I'm going to take a little nap. Wake me when Hans arrives," Ted said. "I love you."

"I love to hear you say that. And, of course, you know that I love you too," Esther said, then she picked up the book she'd been reading and added, "I'm going to take advantage of these last minutes of daylight."

CHAPTER 46

It had just turned dark outside when Hans came through the secret entrance to the attic.

"Good evening, Frau Birnbaum," he said. "My son is not home; he is at a meeting from that youth group of his. How I wish he would quit. But, of course, I dare not push that agenda. It would only bring suspicion on us. I don't know if I told you and Ted, but Marta and I have recently joined the Nazi Party. We did this to avert any distrust our neighbors have toward us. We don't want anyone watching us too closely. Anyway, Marta is downstairs, but otherwise, we are alone in the house. So you needn't be worried about whispering."

"How are you, Hans?" Esther said.

"I'm all right. I brought food and water."

"You are so kind to us."

"Ted is asleep?"

"Yes, he decided to take a quick nap. But I am sure he'd love to see you. He asked that I wake him when you arrive." She smiled. Then Esther turned to Ted and shook his arm gently. "Ted, Hans is here," she whispered, not wanting to jar him awake. But he didn't move. His arm was cold to the touch.

"Ted," she said in a frightened voice. "Ted . . ."

He still did not respond. Esther and Hans looked at each other.

"Ted." Hans shook Ted a little harder. Then he took Ted's pulse. "Esther . . ." he said in a strained voice, "he has no pulse."

She couldn't believe what she was hearing. This had to be a nightmare. Her whole life began to feel like a nightmare. She wanted to scream and cry, but she knew it would do no good. "It can't be," she said, and she shook Ted hard. But he was unresponsive. "Ted . . ." she said loudly. "Ted, I know you can hear me."

But he didn't move. And she had to face the fact that Ted was gone. He'd left her to bear this alone. Esther's shoulders slumped. She felt as if all the life had seeped out of her.

"Esther, I am sorry," Hans said.

She nodded. "At least he won't suffer anymore. This was very hard on him," she said. "At least he is free of all the fear and humiliation now." She had tried not to cry, but now the tears were uncontrollable as they spilled down her face.

Hans took Esther's hand. "I am so sorry. He was a good person."

"Yes, in his heart he was. He could be coarse and difficult. But under that hard shell, he had a heart of gold. I will miss him so much." *I don't know how I am going to go on living in this attic without Ted. I can't imagine being here alone every day, missing him. Thinking about the past and our lives together.*

Hans took a deep breath. Then he said, "I don't know how to say this. It seems like such a crude thing to address right now. But, unfortunately, we don't have the luxury of calling someone to help us. I must take his body out of here myself. I am so sorry, but I must. I will come late tonight when it's very dark outside and the streets are empty, and also after my son has gone to bed. Then I will do what must be done."

Esther wanted to ask what Hans planned to do with Ted's body, but she couldn't bear to hear the answer. So she just nodded.

CHAPTER 47

Erwin's heart was racing. He couldn't believe what Luisa was saying.

"Your parents are hiding Jews right in your home."

"You are mistaken," he said, pushing her hand away from his penis and moving away from her on the bed.

"I am not mistaken. I know this for a fact. Your father worked for the Birnbaums. He is hiding them in your attic."

"How do you know this?" he said.

"I know," she said firmly as she reached for him again.

"You're insane," he answered her. Then he jumped out of the bed and away from that evil hand of hers that made him lose control and lose sight of what was right and what was wrong.

"Come here and sit beside me," she said, sitting up in the bed.

"No."

"Listen. I am not going to turn your parents in to the authorities. If I had wanted to do that, I would have done it already. I don't want them to suffer, and the only way to prevent that is for you to help them. It's only a matter of time before someone in your neighborhood finds out, and they won't be as kind as I am. You know that there is a reward for turning people in who are hiding Jews. Your neighbors know it too.

Don't you think that at least one of them will decide that they care more about the extra food and money than they do about your family? Think about it, Erwin. Only you can prevent your parents from being arrested."

"So what should I do?"

"There is only one way that you can save your parents. Tomorrow, instead of going to school, you must go to the authorities, and you tell them that you know your parents are hiding Jews in the attic of your home. Explain that you love your parents and that you are member of the Hitler Youth. So you are fully aware that what they are doing is very wrong. Let the authorities know that you want the Jews arrested, and you would like the authorities to help your parents to be reeducated. Tell them that you want them to help your parents to understand why they cannot trust Jews. Explain that your mother and father are good Germans and that you don't want them to be arrested. Tell the authorities that is why you, their son, has come to ask for help. *If you don't go to the police station tomorrow and your parents are caught, the authorities will think you were a part of this. Then you will be arrested too."

"And what will they do if I go to them? Won't they arrest my parents and send them away?"

"No, of course not. They won't do that because their son has come to ask for help. Instead, they will go to your home and take the Jews away. Then they will send your parents for classes."

"Classes?"

"Yes, reeducation classes that will remind them of how tricky the Jews can be. They've been tricked by the Jews. The Nazi authorities understand this. They've seen it before. And because you are the son of two good German people, and you are an upstanding member of the Hitler Youth, and you have come to ask for help, the authorities will take a personal interest in your parents. And they will help them."

"Perhaps I should go upstairs into the attic tonight to be sure that there are really Jews there."

"I wouldn't do that. Jews are dangerous, Erwin. They are sneaky, and they wouldn't think twice about killing you and both of your parents. This is a matter that is best handled by the authorities. It will be safer for all of you that way. You trust my judgment, don't you?"

"Yes, but are you sure that my mother and father won't be arrested?"

"I'm quite positive." She took his hand in hers and squeezed it. Then she touched his cheek. "You and I have a special bond between us, don't we? These things we do in the dark are our secret, correct?"

"Yes," he whimpered.

"And I have kept our secret. I've even covered for you when I caught you looking into the latrine that night. You realize that I never turned you in for that. You can trust me, Erwin." She moved her hand back between his thighs.

"I do trust you, Luisa," he said.

"And if you are really worried that the police will arrest your parents, then I will make a promise to you. I will promise that if, for some reason, things don't go the way we planned, I will intervene. I won't let them take your parents away. I will make sure that your mother and father are sent for reeducation classes and nothing more. You see, I have a strong position with the Deutscher Mädels. And because of this, the police will surely listen to me."

"You promise you will stand behind me?" he asked.

"Of course I do," she said. "You are my lover, no?"

"Yes," he said, blushing in the dark at the sound of the word lover.

"So you'll go to the police station in the morning?"

"Yes. I will if you really think it's the best thing to do."

"I know it is."

CHAPTER 48

E rwin returned home later than usual. But neither of his parents said a word about his being late. So he ran upstairs and cleaned himself up. Then he got into bed. *If Luisa is right, and my parents really are hiding the Birnbaums in our home, then it is a good idea for me to go to the police. If someone else finds out and turns us in, there will be hell to pay. We will all look like traitors. This way, I will come across as a devoted member of the Nazi Party. And they will be willing to listen to me and help my parents. Luisa is very wise. And I think she really cares for me. So I'll go first thing in the morning as I promised her.*

CHAPTER 49

E sther lay beside her dead husband holding his hand. She talked to him in a soft voice as if she were certain he could still hear her. "Ted, I wish you hadn't gone away without saying goodbye. I need you so much now, and I am so afraid of being alone here in this attic without you. You've always been my rock, and I've always leaned on you. In a few hours, Hans will come and take you away. And I will never see you again. I wish I could turn on a light so that I could look at you and memorize your face, every feature, every line so I could I bring it back in my mind. Our lives weren't supposed to be like this. We were supposed to grow old together. Two little old people walking hand in hand. That was the way I imagined it. Of course, that was before Hitler came to power. Now, nothing is what I thought it would be. Our Goldie has left us and gone to heaven. You are probably already there with her. Take care of her, Ted. She has always needed extra special attention. I know it's selfish, but I wish I could have gone first. Now, I'll have to make that trip to Italy to see Alma, all alone." Then she burst into tears. "Oh, Ted, if it weren't for Alma, I would ask Hans to get me some kind of narcotic that would put me to sleep forever. But I won't do that to her. If I survive this, I will go to her, and I will tell her that she was the reason I made it through."

Hans entered the attic. As always, he was crouched over. Both he and Ted had been too tall to stand up fully in the attic. Esther was just tall enough.

"I am sorry to have to do this," Hans said; his voice was cracking. "Please don't watch me. I feel like this is a terribly disrespectful way to treat a man such as Herr Birnbaum. But I cannot carry him through this room because I cannot stand up fully. So I must drag him. Again, please forgive me, Frau Birnbaum."

"I know you are doing the best you can, Hans. And may God bless you," Esther said. Then she turned away as Hans dragged Ted's body out of the room. After Hans closed the door, Esther heard noise coming from outside the attic, and she assumed Hans had hoisted Ted onto his back. She listened as the heels of Hans's shoes clicked softly on the floor. And she knew he was walking downstairs. Then there was silence.

Goodbye, my love. Until I can be with you again, I will carry your memory forever in my heart, Esther whispered into the empty darkness.

CHAPTER 50

Erwin slept without moving at all that night. After the night of overzealous lovemaking, he'd been worn out. And it wasn't until the following morning, when his mother came into his room to wake him for school, that he remembered the task that awaited him. Erwin had a way of putting things out of his mind until the very last minute. He could erase thoughts that made him uncomfortable until he was absolutely forced to face them. Now as he was getting dressed, knowing what he must do in less than an hour, he felt a little sick to his stomach. Today would be the first time he'd been in a police station in his entire life, and the very idea of it made him frightened and nervous. His parents had warned him to stay out of trouble. They'd told him that if he ended up on the wrong side of the law, the police could be cruel and unjust. But he refused to believe them even if his stomach was uneasy from fear. He assured himself that Luisa was right when she told him the police were not his enemies; they were there to help him and his family. After all, she understood his way of thinking. And she knew the world of the New Germany far better than his parents did. They were stuck in a pre-Hitler mindset.

Erwin climbed downstairs and sat down at the breakfast table. His mother had made him two slices of dry toast which he was nibbling on. He watched her as she sipped her ersatz coffee. *How could my mother be involved in something like this? Luisa must have been mistaken.* But when he glanced at his father, his tall, proud father with the strong, determined chin, he knew his father was capable of hiding Jews. He'd always known how fond his father was of Ted Birnbaum. In fact, Erwin remembered once when he'd first joined the Hitler Youth, he'd asked his father why he worked for that dirty Jew, and his father had gotten angry. Hans had almost slapped his son, but he stopped himself and took Erwin by the shoulders holding him a little too tightly and said, "I don't ever want to hear you referring to Herr Birnbaum in that manner again. Do you understand me?" Erwin nodded. But he'd never forgotten how disgraced his father made him feel that day. And the truth was that he didn't understand his father at all. He couldn't figure out why Hans was so devoted to a rich Jew. His parents had constantly told him that the Birnbaums had been kind and generous to his family. They always sent gifts for his birthday and things for Marta and Hans at Christmas and sometimes just for no reason at all. However, although Erwin liked the gifts, in his mind the Birnbaums were still Jews. He'd learned in his youth group that the Jews were liars and thieves, and that everything the Birnbaums had given to his family rightfully belonged to the German people anyway. He'd tried to explain that to his father; he tried to tell his father that Ted Birnbaum was manipulating him, but Hans had just stared at Erwin and shook his head. "You know better, don't you, Son?" he'd said. "You know that's just nonsense."

"Do you want some coffee?" Erwin's mother asked, bringing him back to the present moment. "You can dunk your toast in the coffee, and it won't be as dry."

"Yes, thank you, Mutti," he said.

Once Erwin had finished his toast, he said goodbye to his parents and went outside. For a moment he wished he could just break his promise to Luisa and ignore her warning. He longed to be ignorant of the situation and turn in the other direction and head off to school. Then the next time he saw her he would just tell her that he had lost his nerve. She wouldn't like it. He knew that. The Hitler Youth demanded that its members be strong. They were repulsed by weakness or sensitivity. And she would probably remind him that in order for the world to recognize the new order of German superiority, the German people must prove to be a powerful race of Aryan men and women. He would nod, and then she would again insist that he go to the police to help his parents. *Maybe I should do this before it is too late and the Gestapo finds out on their own, and then my parents and I will be in big trouble, or worse, those Jews could turn on us, and then my parents and I could be murdered in our beds while we sleep. I hate to go to the police station. But I must do this. I must.*

It was a fall day, and the fragrance of burning leaves filled the crisp autumn air. Erwin loved that fragrance. He sucked in a deep breath and assured himself, *What I am about to do is the best thing I can do for my parents. Especially for my father. He really needs these classes that Luisa spoke of. They will give him a better understanding of what is expected of a German man and how he must behave in the new Germany. They will also explain why he must not trust the Jews, not even Herr Birnbaum. Still, I can't imagine that Luisa is right. I haven't heard a sound. Wouldn't I have heard something if the Birnbaums were in the attic in my home? Perhaps the police will go to the house and find that nothing is there. But at least if they do, then Luisa will be satisfied, and she will not bother me about this anymore.*

Erwin took a detour. He walked by the school and stood across the street where no one would notice him. He watched his friends and fellow classmates enter the large brick building. Then he continued walking until he reached the police station.

When he arrived at the police station, he took a deep breath before he entered. A man in uniform sat at a desk near the door. Erwin was trembling as he approached him.

"Yes, what can I do for you?" the police officer, a middle-aged man with a thick, fleshy face asked in a firm voice.

"I need to speak to someone. My parents need help. They need to take the special classes that you offer to help people who need to readjust their way of thinking. You see, my parents have lost their way." He could hear himself rambling. His palms were wet with sweat, and his face felt flushed. But now that he was here, he must continue. "My parents are hiding Jews in our attic."

The police officer looked up. His eyes were fixed on Erwin. "What's your name?"

"Erwin Hubermann."

"Wait here, Herr Hubermann. We can help you."

Erwin waited for several minutes before two younger officers came out from the back of the station.

"Hello, Erwin, I am Oberleutnant Bauer, and this is Hauptmann Herrman. We are with the Gestapo. The officer told us a little about your situation, and we would like to help you. Can you please tell us a little more?"

Erwin nodded. Then he said, "I need you to help my parents. I've been told that if I came to you, you could send them to classes. Classes that would help them better understand the new rules and to also understand that they must follow these rules if Germany is ever to rise to her rightful status in the world?"

"Of course we can help," Oberleutnant Bauer said. "Come with us. You can direct us to your home, and then we will do what we can to help your parents. All right?"

Erwin nodded. Oberleutnant Bauer smiled.

They walked to the black automobile. Hauptmann Hermann opened the back door and Erwin got in.

"So where are they keeping these Jews?" Oberleutnant Bauer asked in a friendly, gentle tone.

"In the attic, I believe. But I am not sure it's true. I heard it from someone who says she knows that it is true. But I haven't seen any evidence of it at all. So when we get to my house, there might not be anything there at all."

"Well, better safe than sorry, right? So we'll all go and check it out together." Officer Bauer turned to look at Erwin in the back seat. Then he smiled.

"How many Jews are there supposed to be in your attic, according to this source?"

"If my source is correct, there should be two: a husband and wife."

"Do you know who they are?"

"Yes. Ted and Esther Birnbaum."

"Oh! What a find! The Birnbaums, the ones who owned that big factory. Those rich Jews who stole so much from the German people?"

"Yes, those are the ones. They owned the Ready To Wear factory. My father worked for them. He was their driver. If they are actually in our attic, that is how they conned my father into taking them in."

"I see," said the oberleutnant.

CHAPTER 51

Berlin, October 1943

As soon as Erwin had left for school that day, Hans locked the door. Hans was going to head up the stairs and through the trapdoor into the attic. Normally he would not go up there until after dark in case someone was watching through the window. But he couldn't leave Esther Birnbaum to face the loss of her beloved husband alone. He knew she would need to be comforted, and so he was going to do what he could. When Hans told Marta that Ted had passed away, Marta wept. He told her that he was going to take the last of their bottle of schnapps and share it with Esther. "That is, if it is all right with you."

"Of course it is. Poor woman. She is stuck in that tiny attic alone. My heart goes out to her," Marta said.

"We will help her all we can," Hans said, patting Marta's shoulder. "There isn't much we can do, but from now on we must try to spend a little more time with her during the day while Erwin is at school."

"But what if the neighbors see us going up to the attic? What if they are looking through our window? You know how desperate everyone is these days. They would do anything for a reward. And turning us in would get them one extra food, some extra money."

"I know, Marta. Believe me, I know," Hans said, then he added, "So before we go up, we'll pull the drapes."

"That will create suspicion. Don't you think so?" Marta asked. "If our neighbors walk by and see our drapes closed, they'll wonder what we are up to."

"I know, but what else can we do? All we can do is hope for the best."

"I know, we can't just leave Esther up there to face this loss all alone. She has always been so good to us. Even when she didn't have to. Do you remember when Erwin was born, and he was sleeping in an old broken dresser drawer that you found in the trash because we couldn't afford to buy a crib?"

"Of course I remember, and I remember how as soon as Frau Birnbaum heard about our infant sleeping in an old drawer, she insisted that I drive her to that fine children's furniture store. Then she bought us a crib for Erwin and sheets for the crib too."

"Then the Birnbaums told me that I should take the car so I could bring that crib home," Hans said. "They have always been so good to us."

"Yes, they have."

"I wish I had more schnapps to give Frau Birnbaum. But that's all we have left," Marta said.

"I know her, and she'll be grateful for anything you send to her. That's the way she is. But poor Esther is suffering. So I am going upstairs now to spend a little time with her."

Marta nodded.

CHAPTER 52

E sther Birnbaum was awake when Hans entered the attic. Her face was puffy, and her eyes were red from crying.

"I wanted to come upstairs and see how you were doing," Hans said.

She shrugged. "Thank you." Then she added, "It must have been difficult for you last night. I know you had to carry Ted and find a place for him to rest."

"Yes," he said solemnly.

"I don't want to know what you did with his body. I don't believe my Ted's spirit is in that body anymore. I-I know he is with God," she stammered.

"I believe that too," Hans said. He'd left Ted's body in the grave-yard behind the church. He had not known what else to do. When the Birnbaums went into hiding, Ted gave Hans his car. So Hans used that car. He had put Ted's body into the back seat as gently as possible. Then he drove around not knowing what to do until he saw the grave-yard. He couldn't take the time to bury him. He had to get away as quickly as possible. Hans had been sweating in spite of the cool wind that was blowing through the trees. His hands were trembling so badly that he could hardly hold the steering wheel. He had been terrified that he would be caught with a dead man in the back of the automobile. A dead Jewish man. And if the police asked questions, he had no explanation that they would accept. So he pulled the car around the back of the graveyard. Then he surveyed the area. Once he was sure no one was watching, he carried Ted's body and laid him on the ground. He quickly said a prayer. It wasn't a Jewish prayer, but he believed that God had heard him. Then he'd gotten back into the car and sped home.

"Dear, dear Hans, I am so sorry. I know Ted and I have caused you a lot of extra work and trouble. I want you to know that I am truly grateful for everything you've done for us. And Ted was too. He told me more than once how much he appreciated your loyalty."

"I wish I could do more," Hans said. "I brought up some schnapps. Would you like a drink?"

"Yes, I could use one. Thank you," Esther said.

Just then they heard the roar of the Gestapo horns as the black car came speeding down the street. Esther looked at Hans. And they both knew.

CHAPTER 53

The two Gestapo agents climbed out of the car. They slammed the door. Erwin got out of the back seat and followed them.

"How do you get into your attic?" the oberleutnant asked.

"There is a hidden door in the ceiling right behind the pantry in the kitchen. There are a few stairs that will help you reach the door," Erwin said. "I'll show you where it is."

The Gestapo agent knocked on the front door of the house. Marta cracked it open. "What do you want?" she said. Then she saw her son. Her eyes flew open wide with shock. "Erwin?" she said. "Why are you here with the police? You should be in school. Are you in trouble?" Her voice was high pitched and quivering. Her hands were shaking, and when Erwin looked at her, he knew she was terrified.

The two Gestapo agents pushed past Marta and entered the house.

"What is going on here? Erwin, what do they want? What have you done?" Marta asked her son.

He looked at his mother. "I am only doing what is best for you and Father," Erwin said, but he was shaking, and his voice was cracking. "You two need help. And these men are going to help you."

"Erwin." Marta's hands flew up to her mouth. Her mouth was frozen open. She looked like she was screaming, but she was silent.

"Show us the entrance to the attic."

"I-I . . ." Erwin stammered.

"Now, son. Show us."

Erwin's fingers were trembling as he pointed to the trapdoor.

"Where are those stairs you mentioned?"

Erwin pulled out a ladder that had been hidden by a door behind the pantry. The two officers climbed the ladder, and then the hauptmann opened the door, and both Gestapo agents entered the attic.

Hans was sitting on the bed beside Esther. She was shaking her head and looking down. "I am so sorry, Hans," she said.

"Shut up, Jew." The officer was crouched down. He was too tall to stand up in the attic. "Where is the other Jew? The boy said there were two."

"There is no one else here. My husband died before we left our home," Esther said.

"Didn't I say to keep your mouth shut?"

"Where is the man?" the officer asked Hans.

"He passed away before Frau Birnbaum came here. She is alone."

The two agents looked around the small room. One of them got on the floor and looked under the cot. Then one of them nudged Esther with his gun. "Let's go."

Hans stood looking on helplessly.

"You too, traitor. You didn't think you were going to get away with this, now, did you?" the oberleutnant said to Hans.

On the way out, the hauptmann pointed his gun at Marta. "Come on. You're under arrest," he said.

Then Frau Birnbaum, Marta, and Hans were led outside. Erwin followed; his skin had turned as white as death. "Why are you taking my parents?" he said "Why are you arresting them? You promised that they would only have to attend classes."

As the officers led the three prisoners to their car, Luisa stepped out from behind the house where she'd been waiting for this moment.

"Good afternoon, Frau Birnbaum," she said. "I am quite sure you remember me."

"Luisa, they are taking my parents away. Help me. Tell them that you said my parents would not be arrested. Tell them that my parents should not be taken away. The police are supposed to help them, not arrest them," Erwin was screaming in a high-pitched voice.

"You stupid boy," Luisa said. "I tricked you. And you fell for it. You turned your own parents in. They will suffer greatly for what you have done. And they deserve it. But I don't give a damn about you or your family. I arranged all of this for you, Esther Birnbaum. I did this as payback for all the humiliation and misery you caused me."

"You are a terrible, evil person, Luisa. God help you," Esther said.

The Gestapo agent hit Esther in the mouth with the butt of his gun. Her lip started bleeding. The blood ran down her chin and onto the front of her dress.

"Get in the automobile," the hauptmann said as he pushed Esther, then Marta and finally Hans into the back of the car.

Erwin screamed, "No, this is not what was supposed to happen. Please, no. Don't take my parents away. Help them. Reeducate them. But don't arrest them."

The Gestapo officers ignored Erwin. They got into the car. Erwin stood watching and wringing his hands as the car sped away.

Erwin saw his father looking at him through the car window, and the disappointment he saw in his father's eyes broke him down. As the black police car turned the corner, Erwin fell to his knees on the sidewalk and began to weep.

Luisa never turned around to look at Erwin. She just walked away.

CHAPTER 54

Esther glanced over at Hans and Marta as they rode in the back of the black police car. Her heart sank. She was terrified of what these men were going to do to them. But even more she was overcome with guilt over the fate of Hans and his wife. This couple, in the prime of their lives, with a young son to care for, were now going to be punished for trying to save her and her husband. The sound of the Gestapo's blaring horn that was meant to terrify anyone who heard it made her head feel as it were reverberating. Hans was putting on a brave front, but she could see that Marta was trembling. *If only I could comfort her,* Esther thought. *They are afraid of what is going to happen. They don't know if they will ever see their son again. And I am certain that it hurts and devastates them to know that it was their own son who turned them in. Even though Erwin has done a terrible thing, I can't help but worry about him. I believe he is confused and was manipulated by that horrible Luisa.* Esther reached over Hans and patted Marta's hand. But Marta seemed angry. She withdrew her hand and looked away from Esther. *I can't blame her for hating me right now. If it had not been for Ted and I, she would be at home concerning herself with their family dinner instead of here with me on the way to some terrible place where the Gestapo punished those who broke their laws.*

Hans saw what happened between Esther and Marta. He glanced over at Esther and then patted Esther's hand and whispered, "It's not your fault."

Her lips trembled as Esther tried to muster a smile, but tears fell down her cheeks.

Then the two officers stopped the car in front of the Jewish cemetery on Rosen Street. A crowd of at least a thousand people were lined up outside the cemetery. They were surrounded by guards who held them there at gunpoint. The officers got out and opened the car door. "Get in line, you filthy pigs." Esther got out first, then Hans and Marta. "I hate Jews. But I hate Jew lovers even worse. And you are the worst kind of Jew lover. You have betrayed your country to save a couple of Jew rats. But don't worry, Hubermann, you are going to pay a hell of a price," he said, then he hit Hans with the butt of his gun. Hans's nose started bleeding. Marta and Esther both gasped. But Hans stood there stoic. He didn't reach up and wipe the blood away. He let it run down the front of his shirt. And he didn't beg for mercy. He took his wife's arm and then Esther's and led them into the line. The two officers stood watching. Esther was certain she saw a faint glimpse of respect on their faces. Then they got back into their black car and drove away.

About a half hour later, several open-air trucks began to arrive, and the prisoners were loaded onto them. Marta refused to look at or sit beside Esther. She sat on the other side of her husband instead. No one spoke as the truck carried them through the countryside and across the border into Poland.

Ted, as much as I wish you were beside me, and I do because you have always been my strong and levelheaded husband, like a solid tree I could always lean on, I am glad you are not here. I don't know where they are taking me. Perhaps they plan to kill me. I am not afraid to die. Although I hope it is quick and painless. I'm an old woman, and I know how brittle my bones are. But if they plan to end my life, at least I will be on my way back into your arms before we know it. And we will laugh at how God brought us together for a second time. I am putting my trust in God, fully and completely, and I am desperately looking for God's work all around me. For instance, right now, I am in the back of an open-air truck, and as I've said, I don't know where I am headed. But being that the Nazis are in control, I am certain it will not be a spa in the country. I know that upon hearing that comment, wherever you are, you are smiling. You always enjoyed my dry sense of humor. And right now, I am trying to think of the good things. So I am reminding myself that at least I am here outside getting fresh air. We had been in that attic for so long that the air on my skin feels like a bit of heaven. Instead of looking at the guards with their guns pointed at us, I am trying to keep my mind centered on the wind in my hair. As we drive along, I look at the countryside. Germany is a beautiful place, and I am glad to have been born here even if this is how it will end. I see the beautiful fall colors of the leaves on the ground, and I treasure every breath I take. It's just so hard for me to understand how the German people, a brilliant, civilized lot, could allow these monsters to take control of our country. Ahh, Ted. How I wish I could talk to you. I do miss you so.

When the truck arrived at a railway station, the prisoners were ushered off. Esther was having a hard time jumping down from the bed of the truck. Hans tried to help her, but a guard forced him away. Then that same guard pushed Esther with the butt of his rifle. She tried to jump, but she fell hard onto the pavement and skinned her knee.

"Get up!" the guard yelled at her. Esther tried, but the pain was excruciating. "Did you not hear me, old Jew? I said, 'Get up!'"

Esther tried again. Tears of pain came to her eyes. But she forced herself to stand. Then the guard pushed her into a line. Esther was separated from Hans and Marta. She saw Hans holding his wife's arm and standing behind a family of four, two teenage daughters who looked like twins and their parents, who appeared to be about the same age as Hans and Marta.

Guards stood over all of the groups with their guns pointed. Esther would've liked to have sat down on the grass. Her knee was throbbing. But she knew better than to ask.

A stern-looking guard stood at the front of the group of worn prisoners.

"You are about to be transported to a location where you will be given food and work," he said. "Don't cause any trouble, and you will not be harmed."

Two hours later, the train pulled into the station. It was a freight train.

"Mach schnell!" the guards yelled as the prisoners were forced onto the train at gunpoint. Esther was loaded into a boxcar that was so filled with people that no one could sit down. She rubbed her aching knee as she stood in the corner. Her eyes were fixed on the one ray of light that filtered through the wooden slats. Somewhere on board a child was crying. It was not an infant; it was able to speak in words so she knew it was older. And she could not determine whether it was a boy or girl. "Mommy, I want to go home," the child whined.

Poor little thing. The little one doesn't understand. How could it when I hardly understand all of this myself, Esther thought.

Every few minutes, Esther heard another boxcar slam shut. Then the train began to rock and move slowly forward. The man beside her had fallen asleep standing up, and the motion of the train pushed him into her. "I'm sorry. Please . . . excuse me," he said.

"It's all right."

Someone began to gag from the motion, and then she heard them vomit. She couldn't see them, but she hoped it was into a bucket. Esther felt sick to her stomach and was afraid she, too, might throw up. Every so often someone would ask, "Where do you think they are taking us?" But no one knew where they were headed. And as the hours passed, some of the prisoners fell into panicked fits of hysteria. Esther began to wish she had died with Ted instead of being here on this train. *Remember, life is God's greatest gift to us,* she told herself. *Hashem,* she called out to God, *if you choose for me to live, then I will embrace your choice. I will live and dream of the day that I can be reunited with Almaleh. But I miss my Ted. Help me, please. Guide me, and give me courage because I am so alone and so afraid. And please, Hashem, help Hans and Marta, and even though I know he did wrong, please guide Erwin. He is going to need guidance with his parents gone.* She sighed. *I must stop feeling so sorry for myself. My mother always told me that when I was wrapped up in self-pity, the best thing to do was to do something to help someone else. When you are helping others, you are doing God's work, she always said. And you will find that when you are helping others, you will forget your own misery. Because you cannot be unhappy when you are doing God's work. Oh, Mama, I will try. I will try.*

The child had begun to cry again.

"Where is the mother with the child who is crying? I want to help. I am a grandmother. I have a lot of experience with little ones. I will try to amuse the child."

"I'm over here," a young woman, who looked worn and very thin, called out.

"I'll come to you," Esther said as she gently eased her way through the people who were tightly packed into that train car.

"I'm Esther Birnbaum," she said when she got close to the young woman.

"Really? The real Esther Birnbaum? Didn't you own the big factory that made women's clothes?"

"Yes, my family did," Esther answered quickly. Then she changed the subject not wanting to talk about the past. So what is your name, and who is this sweet little boy?"

"This is my son, Daniel. I'm Ruth Kleinstein."

"Hello, Ruth, it's a pleasure to meet you both." Esther was trying her best to maintain some semblance of normality in spite of all that she saw around her. The child was still crying. "Have you ever heard the story of Daniel and the lions?" she said, picking the child up into her arms.

"No," the little boy said. He looked at her unsure as to whether he should cry or not, being that she was a stranger and she was holding him. But when he glanced at his mother, Ruth nodded.

"Well, in case you didn't notice, you and Daniel have the same name."

The little boy nodded, but he looked at his mother. Then he reached out his arms for her to take him. She took him into her arms. But Esther could see how tired and weary she was.

"If you'll let me, Daniel, I'll hold you in my arms, and you can look at your mother at the same time. She will be right here. And meanwhile, I will tell you the story of Daniel and how very important he was to God and to the Jewish people. Would you like to hear that story?"

"Yes."

"And may I hold you?"

The child nodded and put his thumb into his mouth.

"All right, then," Esther said, taking the little boy into her arms again. She began rubbing his back. Then she began the story. "A long time ago . . ." Daniel lay his head on her chest. She rocked him gently even though he was very heavy for her to carry.

Someone used the bucket, and the smell of feces filled the tightly packed train car. Esther tried not to gag. Instead she forced herself to continue the story. Within a few minutes Daniel had fallen asleep in Esther's arms. Her arms were tingling, and she wished she could put him down in a clean crib, but in reality, there was not even enough floor space for her to lay him on the floor. So she rocked him, ignoring the pain.

"You are so good with children," Ruth said.

"I was blessed to have a daughter."

Ruth looked down. Then she turned back and asked, "Where is she?"

"She's gone. She passed away."

"Was she ill?"

"Yes, very."

Ruth nodded. "I'm sorry. I hope she didn't suffer," she said quietly. "So many of our people have suffered such great losses." Then she added, "My husband was arrested right after Kristallnacht, and we haven't seen him since. I'm hoping to find him when we arrive at our destination."

Esther nodded. *Our destination. Who knows where they are taking us? And who knows what they have in store. They say they are relocating us so we can work. I hope it's true. But I don't trust them.*

CHAPTER 55

I t had grown dark outside. Esther knew because no light was coming through the opening in the wooden slat. *It must be a new moon. It's so dark.*

"I can take him now. Your arms are trembling," Ruth offered. "I've had a little rest. And I can't thank you enough. I needed it desperately."

"Don't mention it," Esther said.

Ruth reached out, and Esther handed Daniel to her. "He was getting heavy for me even though the little fellow is so light."

"You've been such a great help to me," Ruth said, rocking the boy in her arms.

"You probably don't realize it, but you have helped me too. Little Danny here has taken my mind off my troubles. He's been a bright little star during this harsh journey," Esther said. Her arms were still aching, but she managed to smile. It was too dark in the train car to see Ruth's expression. So she knew Ruth could not see hers either.

"It's good to hear you say that. When we first boarded this train, I was afraid everyone was going to complain when Daniel cried," Ruth said.

"Well, don't you worry. You and I will do the best we can to keep him quiet. I have lots of tricks up my sleeve. I can tell him fairy tales or sing him Yiddish songs." Esther smiled when she remembered her own mother singing Yiddish songs to Goldie when Goldie was little.

"You are truly a godsend."

CHAPTER 56

As dawn broke, beams of light began to filter into the small boxcar. As the hours passed, more people were using the bucket to relieve themselves, and the smells of vomit, urine, feces, and sweat permeated every bit of air in the crowded boxcar. People were crying and complaining of thirst. Esther's throat felt like sandpaper. But she didn't complain. *What good does it do for me to tell all these people how thirsty I am? They don't have any water. They can't help me. So it's pointless.* After holding the little boy for so many hours, her elbows ached. She rubbed her elbows and thought, *But it was worth it to hold him. He is such a warm and tender little soul.*

Then the train began to slow down but not enough because it came to an abrupt halt, sending the prisoners flying forward. The bucket spilled, and its contents ran across the wooden floor. Esther heard someone gag and then vomit. Then the sound of rattling steel sent a shock wave of fear through Esther as the door was flung open. There stood Nazi guards with guns, and beside them were growling dogs with their teeth bared. Ruth looked at Esther. "Be brave," Esther said to Ruth, and she managed an encouraging smile, but Esther was suddenly not feeling brave at all.

"Get out. Move! Schnell!" the guard on the ground said, and the prisoners began to run out of the boxcar.

CHAPTER 57

Some of the people were falling out of the train cars; others came out running. All of them were being forced into a line. Esther's knee almost gave out as she began to walk. Every step was miserable. But she kept going. An old woman who had been walking in front of her fell, and one of the guards shot her dead. Esther could hardly breathe. She wanted to go to the woman, but something told her that if she stopped, she would be shot too. Blood seeped into the soil. Esther had never seen so much blood. She forced herself to look straight ahead, and although she winced from the pain, she kept moving. Then she was shuffled into another line where a few feet in front of her, Daniel was being torn from his mother's arms. His mother would not release him. She held him tightly to her breast. The child was wide eyed and shrieking. And Ruth was begging the guard to let them stay together. "Shut up," the guard warned. "Shut up, or I'll shoot you both."

"Please, let him stay with me. He's very attached to me. He won't cause any trouble," Ruth begged.

"Give me the child," the guard said. "Give it to me now."

"No. I can't," Ruth said bravely. But her voice was trembling. Esther wished she had the courage to go and help Ruth. But the guards were terrifying. And just a few feet away, a dog had attacked a man who refused to get in line. He'd torn through the man's pant leg, and now blood was running down from the man's calf onto the ground. Esther turned away, afraid she would vomit if she continued to look at him.

The guard had lost patience with Ruth. He slapped her face so hard that her head whipped around. Then he kicked her in her shin, and she fell. And when she fell, Daniel rolled out of her arms. The guard grabbed the child, lifting him up by his arm, and carried him away. Ruth was weeping. But Esther could not get out of the line and go to her because a handsome man, an SS officer, with dark, wavy hair was now standing in front of Ruth. Two lines had formed, one on the left side and one on the right side of the dark-haired man.

"Right," he said. And Ruth was sent into a long line of prisoners who were standing on the right. They were all young. Men and women. But no children.

Something akin to snow was falling upon Esther's shoulders. She looked up at the sky. It appeared to be snowing. But it wasn't cold enough to snow. She touched the white flakes that fell on her coat. They weren't cold, and they weren't snowflakes. *Ashes. Why are ashes raining from the sky here at this terrible place?*

The handsome, dark-haired officer continued through the line saying "Left, right, right, right, left."

Then he was standing in front of Esther. "Hello, Grandmother."

"Hello," Esther managed.

"You Jews people call grandmothers bubbies, don't you?"

"Yes," Esther said. The word bubbie coming out of his mouth made Esther's skin crawl.

"I thought so." He smiled. His teeth were as white as parchment paper. They sparkled in the sunlight. But there was something in his eyes, a dark emptiness, that made Esther shiver. "You go to the left, Bubbie," he said.

Esther got into the line on the left. She stood behind an old man with a cane.

"We are in the death line," an old woman, with a hump in her back, said.

"The death line?" the man with the cane asked. "What do you mean?"

"They plan to kill us. You see that building? There are gas chambers in there."

"You're crazy," the man said. "You think they mean to gas us, all of us?"

"I know they do. I have heard stories. When I was in the ghetto in Lodz, I heard plenty of stories from partisans who had been captured. They said that they saw it with their own eyes."

"And you know for certain that these stories are true?"

"Not for certain," she said, "but look at the ashes all over you. Do you know why that is?"

"Why?" he asked skeptically.

"They are burning the bodies. Look, you see that chimney? That's the crematorium."

"Shut up. I don't want to hear any more of your frightening lies," the man said.

Esther was hardly able to breathe. There was something in the old woman's words that rang true. *But is it possible that they would murder and burn all of these people?* she thought. *Dear God. What kind of human beings are these? How could normal, everyday German people have taken jobs like this? I don't care how much they need the money. How do they sleep at night knowing they've spent their days murdering innocent people? I don't understand. Only ten years ago, the German people were our neighbors. Their children played at my home with my daughter. They worked at our factory. My husband was always generous to anyone who needed help. It was our way, German or Jewish. It didn't matter. How did the world come to this? And for heaven's sake, what happened to Luisa? I know she had a difficult childhood, but how could she ever have become so cruel? I only tried to help her when she was growing up. And her hatred and resentment of me and my family is horrifying.*

CHAPTER 58

The line had stopped moving. Everyone looked around wondering what had happened. One of the guards walked up to a man who was obviously in charge. "We are overloaded, Lagerführer," he said respectfully. "They are working frantically at the front to get the line moving again. I am terribly, terribly sorry."

"All right. So wait a few minutes. Let them catch up at the front. Then start the line moving again."

"Yes, Lagerführer. I will go to the front and give them your orders immediately."

"No hurry, Rapportführer Ernst. It's been a while since you and I took a few minutes to have a conversation, and you know how important it is to me to keep up good communication with my men."

"Yes, Lagerführer."

"So I know that you recently got married. I enjoyed your wedding very much," the lagerführer said, "and how are things going?"

"Very good, sir. My wife, Heidi, is a good woman. She's very dedicated to the Reich."

"I like to hear that," the lagerführer said. "However, I've been hearing some things from your in-laws. They say that your son from your previous marriage and your new wife are not getting along well. You know that your wife is a distant cousin of mine, don't you?"

"Yes, I do. And it is an honor to be a part of your family," Heinrich Ernst said. He was nervous in the presence of his superior.

"Isn't your boy from your previous marriage very young? Just a child? I don't remember his age exactly."

"Yes, he is just a boy. He turned twelve last month, and he's very angry that his mother died. He doesn't understand why she was taken from him. He blames Heidi."

"How could he blame Heidi? She wasn't even a part of your life when his mother died."

"Yes, I know this. But he feels like she is trying to take his mother's place. And he resents her."

"That's a terrible shame. I promised my uncle I would help you to make things more pleasant for your wife. Not only that, but I care about my men. Their morale is important to me. It is a difficult and messy but necessary job that we must do here with the undesirables at Auschwitz. And I need my men to remain strong in their dedication to our cause."

"Yes, Lagerführer. That is why the men have so much respect for you. Me included, of course."

"And I've noticed that something is wrong. You are not yourself these days. It's Heidi, isn't it?"

"Yes, my wife is unhappy. She's having a hard time adjusting to life here at Auschwitz. She misses her family in Nuremburg. We've only been married a few months and already she is pregnant. And I am glad that she is, but the smells from the camp bother her. They make her sick to her stomach."

"What good news that she is pregnant already. She is a true German hausfrau. The kind of wife every good German man needs."

"Unfortunately, she has been very ill with her pregnancy. Frankly, she could use help around the house. And I am too busy to do housework."

"Of course you are. I wouldn't expect you to do woman's work. So why don't you choose a Jew and take her home. She can do all the cooking and cleaning until Heidi has the baby and gets back on her feet."

"Are you sure it would be all right if I take one?"

"I am the lagerführer, and I am giving you permission. I have the authority to do that." He smiled. "Besides, what is one Jew more or less? Your wife will be happy. My uncle will be pleased. It's a good idea."

"If I bring a young woman into my home, my wife will go mad with jealousy. She is not herself since she had become pregnant. I suppose some women get very sensitive when they are with child. She should know that I would never look at a Jew, a subhuman. But right now, she is irrational." He shook his head. "I am afraid that if I do anything that might upset her, she will lose the baby."

"I quite agree. We don't want that, now, do we? Another child for Hitler is always welcomed. So why don't you take one of these old women here, in this line. Go through the line, and find one who says she can cook and clean. If she lies to you, you can bring her back. But hopefully she can handle your household until the baby is born or until you no longer need her. Once you are done with her, send her back here to Auschwitz, and we'll dispose of her. Poof, just like that, we'll turn her into ashes. What difference does it make if it's now or later?"

"You are quite brilliant, Lagerführer."

"Go on. Pick one out. You have a whole line to choose from. Try to find one who is fairly healthy. You want her to be able to work hard. Go on, Heinrich, have some fun. Play God today. The old Jew you choose will live for a little bit longer. It can be a rather entertaining game. I enjoy it sometimes."

Esther had overheard the conversation between the rapportführer and his superior. She turned away for a moment and forced herself to bite her tongue. She winced with the pain and tasted the salty liquid. Then she took her finger and spread the blood on her cheeks to make herself appear healthy. Despite the pain in her knee and in her arms, she stood up as straight as she could. *Pick me*, she thought. *Please, Ted, if you are watching, ask God to help me.*

Heinrich Ernst walked up and down the walkway passing the old and weather-beaten Jews who waited in line. He looked them over. *Sorry lot,* he thought. *They are certainly pitiful. Painfully thin. Decrepit. He shook his head.* Then he noticed Esther Birnbaum. She was slender and definitely not young. But there was still something elegant, something proud about her.

"You," he said, pointing to Esther. "Get out of the line and come here."

Esther did as he commanded, but he could see that she was trembling.

"Don't be afraid, old woman. Today is your lucky day. I am taking you to my home. Can you cook? Are you able to clean a home and manage things? Can you do the wash?"

"Yes," Esther said. "I can do all of it."

"How are you with children? Perhaps you are a midwife? I would like to have someone around the house in case my wife needs anything during her pregnancy."

"I have plenty of experience helping pregnant women," Esther said. It was half true. She had experience helping other pregnant women, but she had implied that she was a midwife. And she most certainly was not.

"Well, that's good. So come. Follow me."

CHAPTER 59

E sther followed the Nazi. He did not speak. They walked outside
the gate that read Work Makes You Free. Then down a long path
to a red-brick house. "Come on," he said, opening the door. She
followed him inside. "Stay right here. Don't move from this spot."

Then he left Esther standing in the kitchen shivering. It was a small
kitchen with a stove and wooden table. *I suppose this is where I will cook.
I've never cooked in my life. My family always had a cook. But somehow, I
must learn and learn fast. I lied to him too. I gave him the impression that I
was a midwife. But I had no choice. I believe that this was God's way of saving
my life, so that I can live long enough to see Alma again. I must find a way to
get my hands on some books that at least give me some idea of how to handle
childbirth. Dear God, you brought me this far. Help to find a way to do what
is required of me.*

Just then a surly young boy came into the room. "Who are you,
Jew?" he asked. "And what are you doing here? Stealing?"

"N-no," she stammered. "Your father brought me here to help your
family during your mother's pregnancy."

"She's not my mother," he said. "She isn't half the woman my
mother was."

Esther could sense how angry the boy was. "May I ask you your name?" she said, hoping he would warm up to her.

"You may ask me nothing. That band on your arm tells me everything I want to know about you."

Heinrich Ernst walked back into the kitchen. "I see you have met my son, Rudolf."

"Why did you bring a dirty Jew into our home, Father?" Rudolf asked.

"Don't question my motives. You understand?" Heinrich said threateningly.

The boy immediately backed down, and Esther could see the fear in Rudolf's eyes. "Yes, Father," Rudolf said.

"Now, you, Jew, follow me. I am taking you to meet my wife. And from then on, you will take all of your orders from her."

Esther followed the Nazi into a dimly lit bedroom where a woman sat on a chair. She was folding clothes and putting them into piles on the bed. "This is the Jew I told you about."

The woman nodded. "Do you have a name?" she said to Esther.

"Esther."

"A Jewish name, of course," the woman said sarcastically as she folded a white slip. "Well, never mind. Your name doesn't matter. I am Heidi Ernst. You may call me Frau Ernst. From now on you will do as I say. Is that understood?"

"Yes, Frau Ernst."

"I will write up a list of chores that you'll be expected to perform daily. Can you read?"

"Yes."

"Good. Now, remember, if you fail to please me, I'll throw you out of my home and send you right back to where you came from with the other Jews."

"Yes, Frau Ernst," Esther said as she remembered all the maids who'd worked for her over the years. She'd always tried to treat them kindly and respectfully. But she had a feeling that this would not be the case in this Nazi's home.

"I would prefer that this old Jew stay here at the house with us,

Heinrich. Just during the pregnancy. Just in case I need anything," Heidi said to her husband.

"I think that's wise," Heinrich said. "Besides, it's cleaner here. If she slept in those filthy barracks at the camp, she might bring a disease back to our home, and, of course, it would be a disaster if it spread to the baby you are carrying."

"Yes, that is very true. Every time you go to work at that camp, I am afraid you might bring some disease back with you."

"Don't worry about me. I wash my hands constantly," he said, "and I keep myself immaculate."

CHAPTER 60

Italy, End of October 1943

Alma was sitting up in her hospital bed one afternoon, which was across the aisle from Isabella and Luciana. They spent all day in bed just in case the ward received a surprise visit from the SS. Sometimes Alma's back hurt, and she wished she could go outside and take a long walk. But she never mentioned it to the others, especially the children. Today, as the patients looked out the window at the top of a tree that had begun to shed its leaves, Alma told them all a story. It was a children's tale from an old fairy-tale book she'd read as a child. But everyone was quiet and listening, even the adults. Alma looked around at their faces, old and young. These people had suffered. Many of them had lost everyone they loved. And now all they had to look forward to each day were the stories Alma told. Their eyes were smeared with red lipstick to make them appear as if they were bleeding, another tactic to scare the Germans if they came. No one complained. It was a dull existence, but at least they were alive.

"And so Aurora found the hidden spinning wheel," Alma said as Lory walked into the room. He smiled and winked at his wife. Alma returned his smile. Then she turned to the other patients. "Excuse me.

I'll continue the story in just a little while. I have to take a few minutes to speak with the doctor," Alma said as Lory sat down on the edge of her bed.

She saw the other patients turn away, and she knew they were trying to give her and Lory some privacy. Although she and Lory had never openly declared that they were husband and wife, most of the patients knew it.

"I long to kiss you," he whispered as he looked at her lovingly.

"Even with this war paint around my eyes? I haven't seen a mirror, but if the other patients' faces are any reflection of how I look, I am a fright."

He laughed. "You are beautiful as always. From the first time I saw you, I knew you were the most beautiful woman in the world, and so far, I have not seen a single woman who could outshine you. And to be quite honest, I know I never will."

"Lory, you always say the sweetest things. When we are old, you will be telling me how lovely I am . . ." Alma said. Then out of nowhere she began to cry.

He put his arms around her even though he wasn't supposed to. He was supposed to keep up his appearances as the doctor, not as her husband, just in case the Nazis came by to inspect. But seeing her cry made him forget all the rules. He held her to his breast and whispered, "Shhh, Alma. It will be all right," into her ear.

"I am afraid, Lory. I am afraid we will never get old. We will all die here. This will be the end of our beautiful lives together. And what about these children? They've never even had a chance to live? Look at them. Look at my poor little friend, Isabella, and Vito's sweet young cousin, Luciana. Those two tender young girls will never know love the way I have known it. It breaks my heart," she whispered back as quietly as she could so the others would not hear her.

"Nonsense. That won't happen. All of us will get through this. You'll see," he said, forcing a smile. Then he added, "In fact, I came today because I wanted to speak to you about something."

"Yes," she said, wiping the tears from her face with her blanket.

"Dr. Borromeo wants to start moving the patients out of the ward to safe houses. And from there he wants to get them out of Italy and to safe countries. That will open up the ward and enable us to save more Jewish lives. He is one of the kindest men I've ever met. He wants to save as many Jews as he can."

"I see," Alma said. "How can I help?"

"Well . . ." He hesitated. "I want you to go. I want you to leave here and go."

"Will you be coming with me?"

"No, I must stay here and help the doctors. But as soon as this is over, I will find you."

"No! Absolutely not. I will not leave you."

"You must. More than anything I want you to be somewhere safe."

"Lory, but haven't I been a help with the patients?" She was trembling. "I have been the one who is always keeping everyone calm. Giving everyone hope constantly. Please, Lory, let me stay. You need me here."

"I need you to be safe. I need you to take Isabella and go. I don't know what Vito wants to do about his cousin. But I want you to go." His voice was firm, but she could see the pain in his eyes.

"I can't. I can't, Lory. If you are not with me, then life is not worth living. I must stay here. I will help with patients as I have been doing."

"Alma, if anything happens . . . if things go sour and the Nazis arrest all of us . . . then what? I can't allow you to be here if that happens," he said, his voice cracking.

"I won't leave you, Lory."

"Is everything all right?" an older female patient, a few beds away, asked.

"Yes, everything is fine," Lory answered, forcing a smile. Then he turned back to Alma whispering even more quietly. "Listen to me. We believe that last night the Nazis located the radio we've been keeping here in the basement to communicate with the partisans. As soon as it gets dark tonight, we are going to get rid of it."

"How?"

"Vito is going to take it and throw it in the Tiber."

"But that will cut off all communications with the Allies too, won't it? Without the radio, we won't know what is going on. We won't know who is winning."

"I know that, but if we are caught with that thing, the entire hospital will be shut down. And who knows what those bastards will do, not only to the Jewish patients, but to all the patients."

"Lory, I am afraid for you."

"I know, love. I am afraid for all of us. But we must do this. Please don't worry. I'll be all right. I just wish you would go. If I knew you were safe, I would feel much better."

"Who's to say that it won't be even more dangerous to try and make our way out of Italy with the Nazis on our heels?"

"Yes, I've thought of that too. I just don't know what is best at this point. I am sick with worry for you, my darling."

"I know you are. But please let me stay."

"Alma, Alma," he said, and then he took her in his arms and held her.

She whispered, "I haven't mentioned this, but, Lory, I am worried about my bubbie. She's probably returned from Cuba already. She may have sent me a letter, but I'll never know. It would have gone to our old apartment. And you must never return there, not even to pick up the mail. I can't write to her either because I don't want to tell her that I am sick and in the hospital. She would go mad with worry. And if I tell her the truth, the letter could be censored, and then the Nazis will know that our syndrome is a lie."

"You're right, it is not a good idea for you to write. It's too risky."

"I can't help but think that if the Nazis have rounded up the Jews here and sent them to some hellish place, can you imagine what they have done in Germany? My bubbie is old. She is not strong. I am sick with worry about her."

"All we can do is pray. I pray constantly. I talk to God while I am working on patients. I talk to God when I am alone in my room at night wishing you were there in my arms. I feel closer to God now than I ever have."

"I know. Me too," she said. Then she rubbed his stomach. "You've lost weight. Where is my teddy-bear tummy?"

He smiled at the affectionate term she'd always used for his little roll of fat. "Not enough food for everyone. I have had to make do."

"Well"—she forced a smile—"when this all over, I am going to fatten you up. I am going to prepare such delicious food that you will grow that teddy-bear tummy right back."

He smiled. "My Alma," he said, and he touched her hair. "You are such a joy to me."

They held hands in silence for a few minutes, both of them knowing that he had been there for a long time and should be leaving. "I'll see you tomorrow. Will you at least think about what I said about leaving here?"

"I will think about it, if you'd like. But I am staying."

"Isabella too?"

"Yes."

"Very well. If that's what you really want, I won't argue with you."

"I want to be with you, wherever you are."

He blew her a kiss. She closed her eyes. "I love you." she said.

"I love you too."

Alma watched her husband as he walked out the door of the Syndrome K ward, and then she took a deep breath and turned to the other patients. With a forced smile, she said, "So where did I leave off?"

CHAPTER 61

Two nights later, the patients in the Syndrome K ward finished their light dinner of soup and bread. Alma had just returned from the bathroom where she freshened up and reapplied the lipstick to her eyes when she heard loud voices in the hall. Some of the voices were easy to recognize: Lory; Pietro Borromeo, who was Dr. Borromeo's son; and Gabriella, a nurse who Alma had come to know. But there were also loud and terrifying voices with German accents. Terror shot through Alma. *It's the Nazis. They're here. Dear God, please help Lory. Please protect my husband.*

"Start coughing. Cough, like you're dying," she said just loud enough for the other patients to hear her. "And keep coughing."

They all began to hack as Lory, Pietro, the nurse, and three Nazis walked up to the window.

On the outside of the hospital room, the three hospital employees were trying to remain calm. A visit from the SS was unnerving, and all they could do was pray that Dr. Borromeo was right, and the Nazis would be terrified by the contagious illness they'd created.

"This is the Syndrome K room that you wanted to see. You are more than welcome to go into the room. However, in good conscience, before I let you in, I feel it is my responsibility to inform you that the patients in this ward are inflicted with a very contagious disease. It is a horrifying illness that is both debilitating, and disfiguring. It causes blindness, and it affects the respiratory system as well as resulting in severe coughing and a suffocating inability to breathe. If you take a moment to observe their eyes, you will see dried blood. Victims of this syndrome bleed from the eyes periodically. So far, we have no cure, but, of course, we are working diligently to find one. However, right now, this syndrome is one hundred percent fatal," Pietro Borromeo said.

The patients in the Syndrome K ward were hacking loudly. Alma glanced at Isabella, who winked at her. *Poor thing. She has no idea how serious all this is,* Alma thought, but she nodded at Isabella and kept coughing.

"Disfiguring?" one of the Nazis asked, clearing his throat nervously.

"Yes, very. I am afraid it is."

"And one hundred percent fatal?" another of the Nazis asked.

"Yes, sadly, we have no cure," Lory said.

"They are all Jews in there?" the first Nazi asked.

"Not all, but some, yes," Pietro said.

"Can the germs escape from that room?"

"I don't think so. But who knows? Perhaps they might be carried out on someone's clothing. We aren't quite sure how this is spread yet," Lory said.

The Nazi nodded. Lory could see how nervous the SS officer was.

"Now that you are aware of the dangers, shall we go in?" Pietro asked.

"I don't think that's necessary. They will all die anyway, as you say."

"Yes. Unfortunately," Lory said.

"I think we've seen enough," one of the Nazis said, and the three SS officers began to walk hurriedly away. Pietro, Lory, and Gabriella followed them. As they left the ward, Lory glanced back quickly at Alma, and she saw the relief on his face.

Once they'd gone, she lay in bed and thought, *Thank you, dear God, for protecting my husband, and for Syndrome K, the syndrome that saved us.*

CHAPTER 62

Poland, November 1943

Esther's days at the home of the rapportführer were long and filled with physical labor. At night she slept on a small hard cot in a dark and musty room without a pillow or sheets and only a thin blanket. Each morning after she prepared the family's breakfast, she was expected to scrub the floors and make sure there was not a speck of dust in the entire house. Next, she washed all of the laundry by hand and hung it to dry. And once she'd finished, there was more meal preparation to be done. Esther had very little time to sit and think about the past, and although her body ached, she was glad to be distracted. It was true that she had never worked hard before. All of her life she'd had maids who had taken care of these tasks. But from the time she was a child, her parents had taught her to treat the help with the utmost kindness and respect. And they would never have expected so much from one person. However, that was not the case here at the home of the rapportführer, where she was treated like an animal. She was fed once a day. Heidi was diligent about the small allotment of scraps she gave Esther. Sometimes it was a cup of soup, other times a heel of bread. And she made it clear that if Esther was ever caught taking a single additional morsel, she would be severely punished. One day Esther had tried everything to remove a red wine stain from a white shirt that belonged to the rapportführer. But, try as she might, the stain would not budge. She took the shirt to Heidi and explained the situation. When Heidi saw the dark red stain, she was furious. Esther apologized profusely, but Heidi was livid. She slapped Esther hard across the face, sending the old woman reeling across the floor. *I am so much older than her. How can she strike an old woman? Where did these people grow up? Who raised them? They are sick with cruelty and are the crudest human beings I've ever encountered,* Esther thought as she got up from the floor. But she said nothing as Heidi turned and walked out of the room.

Esther had learned to read as a young child. And since that time, she'd been an avid reader. Books had opened worlds for her. They'd taken her to places she'd never been. And in them she discovered the answers to most of the questions she had as a child. So she gave thanks to God when she found a pile of cookbooks in a box in the crawlspace in the rapportführer's home. She would use these books to teach herself to cook. *Now, if I could only find some literature on childbirth,* she thought, but she knew that was highly unlikely. All she could do was pray that Heidi Ernst didn't have any problems with her delivery and that she wouldn't need a midwife. Esther knew that Heidi preferred to give birth at home because she'd overheard her tell her husband as much. She'd listened, pretending she was cleaning string beans as Heidi went on to say that she would like to have the child delivered by Dr. Mengele. She'd met him at a party and she liked him. She was confident that he was quite capable. From what Esther overhead, she assumed that Dr. Mengele was a doctor who was employed at Auschwitz. On another occasion, Esther heard Heidi talking to one of her friends who had come to visit. While Esther served them their lunch, she heard the two women discussing Dr. Mengele. The visitor and Heidi both agreed that the doctor was devastatingly handsome. But then the visitor went on to tell Heidi that not only was Dr. Mengele good looking, but he was also efficient during the selection process when the trains of Jews arrived at the camp. It was then that Esther learned that she'd already met this Dr. Mengele. He was the handsome man with the evil eyes that she'd met on the first day she'd arrived at Auschwitz. He was the one who had called her bubbie and then had sent her into the death line. It had made her blood run cold that he could so easily sentence a person to death without caring at all. At night when she closed her eyes, she could still see his face, his white teeth sparkling in the sunlight, those empty eyes twinkling, and his voice, almost sincere, with just a hint of sarcasm. *How could a man like that live with himself? He looks so refined, and he's a doctor, which means he is educated. He pretended that he cared. He called me bubbie. And then he turned around and sent me to be killed. If there is a devil, it might just be Dr. Mengele.*

Heinrich Ernst mentioned Dr. Mengele again one evening while Esther was serving the family's dinner. Heinrich was telling his wife that Josef, as he called Dr. Mengele, was doing remarkable work with twins. Esther wondered what that work was. But, of course, she dared not ask.

"This is very good," Heinrich said to his wife about the food Esther served.

"Yes, the Jew is doing well. She cooks and keeps the house immaculate," Heidi said. "I must admit, you were right. She's a big help. And, so far, she hasn't so much as stolen a slice of bread."

"I'm very proud of you. I am impressed with the way you keep your servant in line," the rapportführer said as he smiled at his wife.

I am starving, but I dare not eat a single extra morsel of the food I prepare. I would never treat the people who worked for me this way. I would never treat any living creature this way, Esther thought. But she kept her head down and didn't say a word.

Because she'd been a mother herself, Esther was very observant of the family dynamics. As she watched Rudolf, she could see that he was lonely and discontented. He was cruel to her. But she was certain the insults he threw her way were only reflections of what he'd heard from his parents and their friends. They were offensive comments about Jews. But Esther tried to understand the boy rather than to hate him. Rudolf didn't go to school. Instead, he had a tutor come to teach him. And sometimes Esther could hear the tutor yelling and carrying on about the Aryan race instead of teaching the boy academic subjects.

Once a week, the Nazi officers took turns hosting Hitler Youth meetings at their homes. On the week that the meeting took place at Rudolf's home, Esther was able to see the boys doing their exercises through the kitchen window as she prepared the family's dinner. The first thing she noticed was that Rudolf was a loner. When the other boys were laughing and talking, he stood by himself on the sidelines. He looked skinny and pale in his uniform. And as the boys began their various athletic endeavors, Rudolf proved to be a poor athlete. He was the slowest runner and the worst jumper. The others teased him about it. "You run like a girl," one of the boys said.

"Is that the best you can do?" another said.

The leader of the group, who was an adult, never stopped the boys from taunting Rudolf. In fact, the leader shook his head when Rudolf fell during the long jump. "You are very clumsy," Esther heard him say. The other boys laughed. Then Rudolf hung his head and went to the back of the line.

On another occasion Esther overheard Rudolf begging his father not to send him to a campout with the Hitler Youth. He promised his father he would find ways to make himself useful around the house. Finally, the rapportführer agreed. When Rudolf left the room, Heidi asked her husband why he was not insisting on Rudolf joining the other boys at camp. "It would be good for him to get outside more. He sits in his room all day," Heidi said.

The rapportführer replied, "I know, but Rudolf is still mourning the loss of his mother. And it is hard for him to accept our marriage. This is a lot for a young boy. I don't want to force this on him too. I'll let him return to normal at his own pace. He'll be all right. You'll see."

Esther wasn't sure what normal meant to Rudolf. But he never went to camp with the other boys. Occasionally, on Sundays, Rudolf's cousins came to visit. There were two girls and a boy close to Rudolf's age. But when he was around them, Rudolf was clumsy and awkward. And strangely enough, Esther felt sorry for him. Most of the time he stayed in his room with the door closed. *He's a lonely child. He feels misunderstood, and he doesn't fit in anywhere,* Esther thought. She also noticed his parents frowned upon outward displays of affection. They never hugged Rudolf, and they paid very little attention to him. His father never made time to take him fishing or go on any father-son outings. *Rudolf is expected to be a full-grown adult at twelve.* If there had been any extra bread, Esther would have asked Rudolf if he would like to set up a bird feeder. She thought it might be good for him to have a hobby. But the spare morsels of bread were meant to be her food, and she could hardly afford to spare a single crumb.

The weeks passed, Esther learned more about Rudolf and his family. She knew he was not Heidi's son. He was a child from Heinrich's first marriage, a marriage that ended leaving Heinrich a widower with a boy on the brink of manhood, to raise. Heidi was younger than Heinrich. Esther wasn't sure how much younger, but she assumed at least ten years. She was a plain girl who would have been far more attractive if she smiled every so often, wore a bit of lipstick, and was more vivacious. But Heinrich often lost patience with her and raised his voice to her. When this happened, Heidi would run into her room crying. Eventually, her husband would apologize. But his apologies were not warm. They were matter of fact. Heidi would accept that he was sorry for hollering at her, and then life would return to the cold, distant existence that it had been before. Ted had been a powerful man too. Esther knew that sometimes men in power had trouble showing affection. But this was different. This man was deeply disturbed. He seemed to have inner demons haunting him. And she wondered it if was true that he was involved in the murder of all those people who had arrived on the train with her. She also wondered how many other innocent people had arrived in the same manner and were now dead.

Among the books that Esther found was a book on gardening. She read it eagerly. She wondered if she could grow some vegetables if perhaps the Ernst family would allow her to eat them.

Neither Heidi nor Heinrich were easy to talk to. But she decided she would go directly to Heinrich and ask him for permission to start the garden.

Heinrich Ernst was sitting in the living room when Esther approached him.

"May I speak with you, Rapportführer," she said, trembling.

"What is it?" he said curtly.

"I was wondering if it would be all right if I started a garden behind the house."

"Whatever for?" He was annoyed at having his thoughts disturbed.

"I thought it would be nice to have some fresh vegetables," she said, thinking it had been a mistake to ask him.

"Hmmm," he said, considering her request for a moment. "There is no reason for that. Go away and leave me alone, Jew."

Esther left the room quickly.

That night she lay down to sleep. The cot had begun to cause her constant back pain. In the morning her back and hips were so painful she could hardly walk when she first got out of bed. But she knew if she showed any signs of illness or weakness, the rapportführer would think nothing of sending her back to the camp and replacing her with someone else. So, each morning, in spite of the pain, she stretched her joints until she was able to move. Then she would go about her day, forcing herself to ignore the constant aching while she continued to clean and cook as if she were a younger woman. Tonight, as she lay on her cot, the pain was shooting down her legs, and even though she was exhausted, she couldn't sleep. If her calculations were correct, Heidi should be giving birth to her baby in June. Then, unless she could convince the Ernsts that she was needed to help take care of the baby, she would be sent to the camp and probably executed. From what she'd overheard when coworkers of the rapportführer came to visit him and talked about Auschwitz, it sounded horrific. And she was afraid that even if they didn't murder her immediately, at her age she would not survive the filth, disease, and cruelty anyway. Esther was constantly thinking about Hans and Marta and about the young mother, Ruth, and her son, Daniel, from the transport. And she could not help but worry about what had become of them. Each night she said a prayer for them and for Alma, Lory, Sam, and Chana. And before she closed her eyes, she whispered, "Dear God, please be with them."

The following morning, she tried to stretch. But her back was worse than usual. *She shook her head. How much longer can I do this?* Then, wincing, she went into the kitchen and began to prepare the family's breakfast.

Once they'd eaten, she cleared the dishes and cleaned up the kitchen and dining room. Then when she was alone, she grabbed the leftover scraps and ate them quickly before Heidi saw her and told her to throw them away. She was given a small amount of food each day and forbidden to eat anything that had not been designated specifically for her. Esther had just finished stuffing a few bits of fried egg into her mouth when Heidi walked into the kitchen.

"I have an appointment today. Rudolf will be going with me. I expect the house to be spotless when I return. And make sure dinner is ready before Heinrich comes home," Heidi said to Esther.

"Yes, Frau Ernst."

After Rudolf and Heidi had gone, Esther walked outside the house. Until now, she had never had a moment alone when she could really take in her surroundings. She stood outside and looked at the camp and thought, *I wonder if I can escape.* Her heart pounded in her chest. *But where would I go? What would I do? If I didn't get shot by the armed guards in those overhead towers, and if I didn't fatally cut myself on the barbed wire, I would be free from here. Then I am certain they would send those dogs after me. I can't run very fast. The dogs would tear me to pieces. And if I somehow, by some miracle, I made it through all of that, then I would have to hide, so they wouldn't find me and bring me back. But where? In the forest? I could never find food.* She suddenly felt overwhelmed by the situation. She lay down on the dirt and began to cry. "Ted," she said his name out loud, "how has my life been reduced to this? How?" She wept, and as she did, she called out to God. "Hashem, I have always tried to treat people well, Jews and non-Jews alike. All of your children. So why have you let them do this to me? To us, the Jews? Why, Hashem? What is the meaning of all of this? I am an old woman. I must spend the last years of my life surrounded by enemies. My age makes me weak, and that makes me afraid. Why could you not have let me die in the attic with my husband by my side? Why did you send me here to witness all of this?" She felt her throat tighten. Then she took a deep breath. "Perhaps you want me to prove that my faith in you is strong." She beat her fists on the ground until the anger at God dissipated, and all that she had left was her faith. "I will prove it. I will trust in you. Show me why you have sent me here. I know you must have a reason. Show me what it is that you want me to do. Please, Hashem, walk with me. Take my hand and walk with me. I need your protection from these vicious monsters."

Esther lay there for a few more minutes. Then she forced herself to stand up. She wiped her face with the skirt of her uniform, and she went back inside. While the family was out, she decided to risk everything and take a quick bath. She trembled the entire time, but she felt renewed when it was over. Even her back felt better. As she began to clean the house, she decided that she must think of a way to convince the family to allow her to bathe. The idea of a weekly bath gave her enough hope to do her work. Most days Rudolf was in his room, so she had not had a chance to clean it. She went into his room and looked around. It was a mess. But she wasn't surprised; she'd expected as much. She began to pick up the clothing on the floor when she saw a box that had been hidden under the bed. Something told her to look inside. Esther looked around. Of course no one was there. So she opened the box. Inside, she found articles about Rudolf's father that he'd cut out of the newspaper. But underneath the articles, Esther found out the reason the box was hidden. There were three things inside that she knew his father would never approve of.

CHAPTER 63

E sther's hands were trembling as she sifted through the contents of the box. She lifted the photo of a Black male athlete with a medal around his neck that had been cut out of an American newspaper. She couldn't read the words that were in English. The only thing she could decipher was the year 1936. And the name Jesse Owens. She knew of Jesse Owens. To Hitler's horror he'd won five medals at the Olympics in Germany in 1936. She wondered how Rudolf would have gotten such a thing. He would have been just a young child when this happened. Hitler was appalled that a Black man had defeated the athletes of his superior race. And for this reason, Rudolf's father would not have been happy to see his son keeping this memento. Then beneath the newspaper clipping lay two photos of women, both stark naked. Esther gasped with an initial shock, but when she thought it over, she realized it was no surprise that Rudolf was becoming interested in sex. That was natural. But she had so many questions. *How would this twelve-year-old boy, who was kept secluded from anyone outside of this camp, get his hands on these things?* she wondered. *His father would never have kept this article about Jesse Owens, so he couldn't have stolen it from him. I can't imagine where he got this stuff.*

She heard the front door downstairs rattling and quickly put the box away. Then she went on cleaning. When Rudolf found Esther in his room straightening up, he hollered at her. "Get out of here, you filthy old Jew. What are you doing in my room?"

Heidi heard the commotion and came up the stairs. "What is going on here?"

"This old Jew was trying to steal my things."

"I wasn't, Frau Ernst. I swear it. I was only trying to clean his room. I thought you would want me to."

"Yes, I think this room could use a good cleaning," she said. "Let the Jew clean, Rudolf."

"But I don't want her in my things," he protested.

"Let her clean this room, or I am going to tell your father."

Rudolf glared at Esther. "Go on, Jew. I'll sit right here." He parked himself on the bed.

Heidi nodded and left the room. Esther went back to hanging up the clothes that had been strewn about the floor. Then she got an idea. "Rudolf," she said, closing the door.

"Open that right now, or I am going to scream."

"You can scream if you'd like," Esther said boldly, "but I found your box. The one with the newspaper clipping of Jesse Owens and the naked girls."

He crossed his arms over his chest. "How dare you."

"You wouldn't want me to tell your father about it, now, would you?"

"No," he said quickly.

"I wouldn't want to tell him. So . . ." She took a deep breath. Esther had never done anything this underhanded in her life. But her survival was at stake, so she continued. "If you want to keep me quiet, then you must bring me some extra food every day. You must tell your parents it's for you."

"But you work in the kitchen cooking. Can't you just eat what you want?"

"Your father keeps watch of everything in that kitchen, and he takes an inventory. But if you tell him that you are taking food for yourself, he won't mind at all."

He looked at her, shaking his head. "Why are all of you Jews conniving thieves?"

"Because you Germans are starving us. I don't want your money. I don't want your things. I need food to live. When a person is desperate, they do desperate things, Rudolf. You'll learn that as you get older."

"Hmmm," he said. "I suppose that makes sense. But you Jews are all so greedy. Do you know how I got the pictures of those girls? I got them by trading two apples with a prisoner through the fence. I gave him the fruit; he gave me those pictures."

"And what about Jesse Owens?"

"A friend of mine got it from his father who worked at a POW camp. I guess the American soldier must have died and had it on him. I traded a naked girl picture for it. I used to have three."

"You're quite the businessman," she said with a hint of sarcasm.

"So are you," he answered.

"I suppose you're right."

"You seem so calm, Jew."

"Calm? I am calm because I know what your father would do to you if he had an inkling that you were keeping those things. What can I tell you? It gives me a little bit of leverage, no?"

"Fair enough. So I'll get you some extra food each day."

"Thank you. God will bless you," Esther said.

"I don't believe in God."

"But he believes in you. And he's hoping that you will find the good within yourself. God knows it's there. I know it too."

"Adolf Hitler is my god."

"He is no god, Rudolf. He's a deranged man with a hunger for power."

"I should tell my father you said that."

"And . . . if you do, I'll tell him about the box." Esther was enjoying the power she had. "By the way, my name is Esther, not old Jew. Please use my name from now on."

CHAPTER 64

Poland, January 1944

A week later, on a cold and snowy morning, Heidi awoke feeling sick to her stomach. When she went into the bathroom and sat down on the toilet, she saw that her underwear was covered with blood. Then she stood up, and the bowl was filled with blood; it ran like a red river down her legs. She screamed for Esther, who came immediately.

"There's a lot of blood," Esther said. "I will help you now. But I think it is best if we call for the doctor."

"All right. Have Rudolf go to the camp and find his father. Tell him to come home and bring Dr. Mengele with him."

Esther left the room and knocked on Rudolf's door. "You must go to the camp and tell your father that he and Dr. Mengele must return to your home as soon as possible."

"Why?" he said through the door.

"Heidi needs the doctor right away."

Rudolf emerged and nodded. Then he left and headed for the camp. Esther returned to Heidi's bedroom.

"What if I am losing the baby?" Heidi asked. She was pale and covered in sweat.

"You might well be. But if you are, remember that sometimes women lose babies because the baby is not healthy. It's God's way sometimes. You are young; you will have more children."

"Do you think so?" Heidi was frightened and vulnerable. For the first time she was speaking to Esther like a grandmother.

"I know so. Did you know that most women miscarry their first pregnancy?"

"Are you sure about that?"

Esther wasn't sure. She'd heard it, but she wasn't sure it was a fact. "Of course I am sure. The next one will be perfect."

"You think I am going to lose this baby, don't you?"

"I don't know for certain. That's why I thought it best to have the doctor come," Esther said. "But the most important thing is that you stay strong so you can have another one. Now put some menstrual rags in your panties, and then let me help you get back into your bed, and I'll clean you up."

When they got back to the bed, Heidi had to sit on a chair while Esther changed the sheets. They, too, were covered in blood. Once the bed was clean, Esther lay a pile of towels beneath Heidi, then she helped her into bed.

"I feel so sick," Heidi said.

"I'll warm some blackberry brandy for you."

Dr. Mengele did not arrive right away. He arrived at the house later that evening. He checked Heidi and declared that she'd miscarried. "Wait a couple of weeks and then try again," he said to Heinrich, who was standing outside the door of the bedroom.

Esther heard Heidi crying. She screamed and cursed at her husband as Esther listened trembling. *They are probably going to send me back to the camp, to the death line now,* she thought. *She no longer needs me.*

But that was not the case. Heidi had become accustomed to having her home clean and her food prepared by someone other than herself. So when Heinrich suggested sending Esther back, she was adamant about keeping her on.

CHAPTER 65

Normandy, June 6, 1944

S am sat down at the back of the boat. He wanted privacy. Taking the last letter he'd received from Chana out of the breast pocket of his uniform, he began to read.

Dearest Sam,

Every letter I receive from you is precious to me. And now that we have rekindled our relationship, I can't imagine why we let so much time go by being apart. I realize that the loss we suffered drove a rift between us. But I now know that it shouldn't have. We are each other's strengths, and together we have the power to lift each other up. You have always been my one true love. And . . . I will tell you a secret. I have not washed your pillowcase since the last time you laid your head on it. Even when we were estranged, I would sink my face into it and remember our love. Come home to me safely, my darling. I long to feel your arms around me and to know that we have a lifetime to share.

With all the love I have in my heart, your wife,

Chana

"Chana," he whispered her name aloud, "I love you."

Still holding the letter tightly in his hand, he removed the picture his daughter, Ida, had drawn for him on her first day of school. He ran his dirty fingers over the paper, and tears came to his eyes. Then he kissed both papers and put them back into his shirt next to his heart.

Sam looked out at the black water. A chill ran down his spine. He was afraid. Soon he would be faced with battle. The possibility that he might meet his death was very real. The boat rocked. It had been rocking all night. He heard the sound of men puking from the motion. And he realized that he must write a letter to Chana. There was something about the water and the boat that unnerved him. And even though he wasn't sure how he would get the letter mailed; he knew he must write. Sam took out a piece of paper.

Dear Chana,

I am on a boat, on my way into enemy territory. I won't lie to you and pretend to be brave. I'm terrified. And to make matters worse, I hate the water. This boat ride is reminding me of the first time I took a ship overseas with my father. How hopeful he was. He thought he was going to find a way to win my mother back. But he never returned. He died in Germany. And then Ida. Our dear, sweet Ida. I lost her on that terrible day at the beach. That day will always haunt me. Sometimes I look at the ocean, and I am afraid that there is curse on me and it has to do with water. The only bright memory I have of being near the water is our honeymoon in Niagara Falls. You were the only person I have ever loved who had the strength to survive this curse. But if you remember, when we returned from our honeymoon, our apartment had been robbed. Everything we had was gone. Everything but our love. The curse only took material things that time. And I am truly grateful that it did not take you. As I am writing this letter, I am afraid when you get it, you will think I've lost my mind. Perhaps I have. But because each breath could be my last, my feelings are heightened. And so I am writing this letter to you because there I things that I must tell

you, just in case I don't come home. You already know that I love you.
But I want to tell you again. I want to tell you a million times until
it's burned into your heart. You are loved, Chana. Not a day has gone
by that I haven't felt my heart swell with love for you. You are so damn
loved.

Tears were falling from Sam's eyes. His hands were dirty, and the
wetness of his tears stained the paper with dirt.

I know you won't understand why I am saying this. But it's important
that you listen to me. If I don't make it back home into your arms, I
want you to marry Izzy. He loves you. He's always loved you. And I
know he will take care of you. Izzy is the kind of man who loves you
enough to take our son and raise him as his own. I will rest peacefully
knowing that you and little Irving are safe and cared for.

Now, this could all be just jitters, and I might survive this thing
just fine. It warms my heart to think of you in my arms and the
both of us laughing as we read this note. But, just in case,
remember what I said. The drawing that I am sending to you
with this is the first drawing that Ida made for me on her first
day of school. I know you will cherish it as much as I do.

You are, and have always been, my one true bashert, my one true love,

Yours, Sam

Sam rolled up the letter along with the picture he kept that Ida had
drawn for him and tucked them both into his shirt. Then he wrote
Chana's address on the back of the paper because he didn't have an
envelope. Under the address he wrote, "If I am found dead. Please
mail these two pieces of paper to the above address."

It was four o'clock in the morning as the boat came near to its destination. There was an eerie silence as the moon cast its light over the
ocean. Under the cloak of darkness, the Allies' boats were about to
land at the beach in Normandy, France. Sam Schatzman felt his heart

beating wildly in his chest as the rough waves tossed the boat around like a child's toy. The soldiers had begun to vomit from seasickness and nerves. A dense odor of sweat and fear wafted through the night air.

"Roll down the ramp," someone said.

The men began to line up to disembark and climb aboard the transport boats that would deliver them closer to land.

We're here, Sam thought, not knowing what to expect. But as soon as the boat ramp went down, the machine-gun shooting began. Those in the front of the line were shot dead immediately. Sam saw them fall like rag dolls. Then as the men began to run off the ship and onto the transport boat, a mine exploded, and Sam saw one of the other ships a mile away from them explode. The men left the boat and got on the transport. They were only on the transport a few minutes before they arrived. When the boat stopped, they got off and began to run toward the shore. Sam was among them. The ninety pounds of equipment he carried on his back and the water beneath his feet was slowing him down considerably. He felt trapped as the men all around him were shot down, and the water began to turn red with blood and fill with dead bodies. He climbed over the bodies as the bullets came within inches of his head. *Dear God*, he prayed, *help me. Help me make it through this hell.* Sam shivered as he tripped over a man with half of his face blown off. He fell on top of the man, and brain matter found its way onto Sam's cheek. When he reached up to wipe it away, he felt sick to his stomach and vomited. But there was no time to stop. He had to keep his eye on the beach or he would surely end up lying beside the dead and dying here in the Atlantic Ocean, a world away from home.

"Help me . . ." men were calling out. "Mama . . ."

Sam swallowed hard. He dared not look down. If he stopped, he was certain a bullet or a mine would find him. But then he heard someone call out his name. "Schatzman."

Sam looked around.

"Schatzman. Over here."

Sam looked to his left and recognized the face of a man he hated. It was Tyler Ashurst laying in a pool of blood.

"Help me, Schatzman. I'm dying."

Sam wanted to run. He wanted to protect himself and leave Ashurst there to die. But something inside of him wouldn't allow it. He looked down at Tyler. "Don't be afraid. I'm going to help you."

"God bless you, Schatzman," Tyler said, struggling to speak.

"You're too heavy for me to pick you up. I'm going to have to drag you. I'll try not to hurt you."

Tyler nodded. "Thanks, Schatzman. And, you know . . . I shouldn't have treated you the way I did."

"Quit talking. Save your strength."

"But I didn't realize that you would risk your own life to . . ."

"Quiet. I understand what you're trying to tell me. You didn't realize that a Jew would be the man who would save your life."

"Yeah."

"God works in mysterious ways," Sam said.

Hooking his hand into Tyler's belt, Sam began to pull Tyler toward the beach when he saw a boat with a red cross printed on its side.

Sam turned and began to lug Tyler toward the hospital boat. When they reached the boat, two men came down to help carry Tyler aboard. "Before they take you on that boat, I have a favor to ask of you," Sam said.

"What is it, Schatzman? I'll do whatever you want. I am so sorry . . ."

"Here," Sam said. "Put this letter in your shirt, and if you survive, make sure that you get it to my wife. The address is on the back. Mail it to her or take it to her. Will you do that?"

"If I live, you can bank on it."

"Thanks," Sam said.

As they lifted Tyler out of the water, Sam saw Tyler had been severely wounded in the stomach. "Good luck to you," he yelled as the Red Cross medics carried Tyler up the ladder.

"Good luck, and long life to you, Schatzman. May God be with you," Tyler managed to say.

Sam's attention was redirected when a mine blew up, and an arm that had been torn from its body came flying at him, hitting him in the jaw. Pain shot through his face. Then Sam turned and began to make his way to the beach. He thought of Chana. *I have to get home to my bashert. I must make it back. I can't die here.*

Sam began trying to run toward the shore. His jaw ached. There was a salty taste of blood in his mouth. Two of his teeth floated in his mouth. He spit them into the water. It was so dark he couldn't see anything below the surface. The sounds of bombs and guns made him jump. *I don't see anyone from my troop,* Sam thought as he looked around him. Then there was a pain in his side. A pain like none he'd ever felt before. It was sharp and penetrating, and it burned as if a dagger of fire had been shot through his body. He gripped his side and then looked at his hand; it was covered in blood. *I am hit. I am dying.* He thought of Chana, and he began to cry. I will never see her face again. The dark water was sucking him under. It had taken hold of his ankles and was pulling him down. His heart pounded with fear. And then he closed his eyes for a second. When he opened them again, he was no longer on a beach far away from his home surrounded by blood and death. He was on Coney Island on a beautiful, hot summer day. The beach was crowded with sunbathers. Children were laughing and building sandcastles along the shore. In the distance he could see the Ferris wheel. Then he heard her voice. "Daddy."

"Ida?"

"Yes, Daddy, it's me, Ida." She was walking toward him in the same pink-and-white bathing suit she'd been wearing that day he'd lost her.

His pain was gone. In fact, he felt nothing but pure bliss. She came out of the blue water and walked toward him, her red-gold hair sparkling in the sunshine.

"Give me your hand, Daddy."

He reached out for her. He felt her hand in his. "I should never have left you alone on that beach," he said.

"It's all right. Please, Daddy, you must forgive yourself. You and I will be together."

"What about Mommy? Will she be all right without me?"

"She'll be all right. We'll watch over Mommy. I have been watching over both of you. I saw that you kept the picture I drew for you."

"You saw that?"

"Yes, Daddy, I did. I always felt your love. And we'll make sure Mommy feels our love."

"Ida . . ." Tears fell down his cheeks. "I am dying, aren't I?"

"Yes, Daddy. But don't be afraid. It isn't so bad, is it? You don't have any pain anymore, do you?"

"No."

She was bathed in a blinding-white light, but it didn't hurt his eyes. It warmed him, and then she smiled at him. "Now, come on, Daddy, let's go and get some ice cream."

CHAPTER 66

Poland, August 2, 1944

The entire week had been hot. Hotter than usual even for August. Esther pushed the hair back from her forehead as she stood in the kitchen preparing an extensive meal for the rapportführer and ten special dinner guests who would be coming tonight. Heidi had woken her early because there was so much to do. After serving the family their breakfast, Esther began kneading dough to bake a bread. And despite the heat, she'd turned the oven on high and roasted several chickens until they were golden brown. Steam rose from two large pots on the stove where turnips and bunches of bright green asparagus rolled around in the boiling water. On the table were rows of apple tarts that Esther had assembled for the evening's desert. They were next to go into the oven. Sweat ran down Esther's cheeks and soaked the front of her uniform. But the smells of wonderful food filled the house. Esther's mouth watered. She was so hungry; she would give anything to taste some of the food she was preparing. But she dared not. If she were caught shaving even a thin slice from one of the chickens, she would face severe punishment, even death. She knew this because she saw the rapportführer shoot a young man for stealing two turnips. They were standing right outside the kitchen door. The prisoner had come to deliver the vegetables to the house for the dinner tonight. As he stood waiting to be dismissed, the rapportführer counted the turnips. When he found the basket to be short, he asked the prisoner where the two turnips had gone. Esther saw the prisoner trembling. At first the young man denied ever seeing the extra turnips. But when the rapportführer hit him on the cheek, cracking his cheekbone, and breaking his nose, and said, "I hate liars. Now, if you tell me the truth, I will let you go without any further punishment. But if you continue to lie to me, I will see to it you are sorry."

The prisoner was terrified. Blood was pouring down his face. "I ate them," he admitted, his voice cracking.

"You see, you were a liar all along. Now that I know you can't be trusted, I must do away with you." The rapportführer pulled out his gun.

"Please, don't kill me. I was hungry. I am sorry. I didn't think they'd be missed." The man was crying. Esther felt sick, but she couldn't look away. Then the rapportführer shot the man in the face. And there was silence. But inside of Esther's head, she was screaming.

She forced herself to continue working, lest the rapportführer see her watching him and become angry at her. As she took the breads out of the oven, Heidi came into the kitchen. "I brought you a fresh uniform. I would like you to go outside and bathe with a bucket of water, so you don't smell when you serve our dinner," Heidi said.

"Yes, Frau Ernst," Esther said. *I am happy for the opportunity to bathe myself and put on clean clothes.*

Then Heidi walked outside. When she saw the dead prisoner lying in a pool of blood, she screamed. Then she called for her husband. He walked through the kitchen ignoring Esther and went outside. "Heinrich, look at this. Do you know what happened?"

"Never mind," he said. "It's nothing. I'll have a prisoner sent over from the camp to clean it up." Then he smiled at her. "Please don't let it upset you, dear. I'll take care of it. Before the party tonight. After all, we don't want any of our guests to lose their appetite."

Esther looked away. She couldn't stand to see that young man lying dead in a pool of blood. It not only made her want to vomit, but it hurt her heart. She was a mother, and a grandmother. This young man had a mother somewhere, a grandmother too. His mother had held him when he was a baby and rocked him to sleep. She'd heard him speak his first words and take his first steps. She'd held him when he cried and read to him before bed. Esther knew for certain that his poor mother had never anticipated that her precious child's life would end in such a hideous way.

Two young male prisoners came to take the young man's body away. Esther could not watch them. She forced herself to focus on her work. Once the yard was cleaned up, she went outside to bathe.

Esther found a private corner where she washed entire body thoroughly. Then she dressed in the clean uniform and went back in and set the tables for the dinner party.

The guests began to arrive at seven that evening. She recognized some of them from the newspapers she'd read before she'd gone into hiding. These were some important men in the Nazi Party. They had well-dressed women at their sides, and they drank and talked as if they were ordinary successful businessmen. But Esther knew that their business was anything but ordinary. Their business was the murder of innocent people. She thought of that young man who died needlessly earlier that day. And although her face never betrayed her inner feelings, she hated them.

After everyone was seated, Heidi walked into the kitchen. "Start serving now," she commanded.

Esther nodded and began bringing out large platters of food. Then as she was laying a steaming plate of asparagus on one of the tables, she overheard a conversation.

"Yes, I think it's best we get it over with tonight. We've indulged them with that family camp far too long. They have begun to think they are important," the rapportführer said.

"I have to agree. But still, I did enjoy their violin music," the hauptsturmführer said. "And their children can be delightful. Sometimes I feel it's such a shame that we must destroy them. However, it is for the best. The greater good, shall we say."

"Yes, I quite agree. There is no doubt that they are good musicians, but they are also filthy scum, and so it is our responsibility to eliminate them. I have scheduled for the liquidation of the gypsy camp to take place while we are dining. I'd rather not be involved in the mess of it all as I am sure the rest of you would prefer not to be there either," the lagerführer said.

"When we return to work tomorrow, that dirty place will be empty. We'll have to have it deloused," the rapportführer said.

"Yes! It will be over. The gypsies will be gone," the lagerführer said. He raised his glass and yelled, "Prost." And then all of them raised their glasses.

"Dr. Mengele won't be happy about all of this. He enjoys toying with the gypsy children. He makes them call him uncle," the hauptstrumführer said.

"Yes, I've seen him do it. He tells them to call him uncle, then he empties his pockets of candy, giving them each a piece. But when he leaves the room, he goes to the guard and tells the guard to send the children to the gas."

"It's a game he plays."

"Well, it's time for that game to end. We must get rid of them all, and tonight it will be done."

Esther went back into the kitchen and gagged. *Demons, all of them.* But when she returned to the table with a pitcher of water, her face betrayed nothing. She refilled their glasses.

CHAPTER 67

Italy, August 1944

Vito went to visit Lucinda in the Syndrome K ward one afternoon. He brought a few cookies for Alma, Isabella, and Lucinda.

"How are you?" he asked Alma.

"I am doing the best I can, considering the circumstances. How are you?"

"The same," Vito said. "We had a terrible setback last week. Did Lory tell you anything about it?"

"No, he tries to keep things from me because he doesn't want to upset me. But I must know. What happened?"

"I don't want to do anything that would anger your husband."

"Please, Vito, just tell me. What happened?"

"Last week, fifteen partisans were captured by the Germans. Three of them were men who were working with us. All of them were executed, and then their bodies were hung up in a village square."

"I heard about this. Was it the Square of the Martyrs?"

"Yes."

"One of the new patients told me. I didn't know that the men involved were men who were working with us to transport the Jews."

"Yes, three of them were."

"Dear God. What are we going to do?"

"What we always do, Alma. We are going to keep trying to save the people who need us."

CHAPTER 68

Manhattan, December 1944

E ven though Chana had told Izzy that she and Sam were back together, Izzy came to visit her at least once a week. He promised Chana that he accepted that she belonged to Sam, and all he wanted from her now was her friendship. He explained to Chana that he had been rejected by the army because of a medical condition, and since he was at home, he wanted to be there in case she needed anything while Sam was away. Izzy even went so far as to praise Sam for his bravery for joining the army. Chana wasn't sure what sort of medical condition Izzy could possibly have. He seemed healthy in every way. Still, she never asked him any questions about his medical condition. She assumed he'd found a way out of serving his country. Since Izzy had taken over the Jewish syndicate in Manhattan, it was obvious he'd grown very wealthy. He purchased a new automobile and moved to a beautiful apartment. It wasn't that he wasn't patriotic, but Izzy had always been the type of man to put his own needs before the greater good. Still, he had always been nice to her. He came by one Saturday to visit her. When he saw she was busy cleaning, he moved all of her furniture for her so she could sweep underneath. Another time when he dropped by her apartment, he noticed her lamp was broken. He took it home and repaired it for her. As he had promised, Izzy was always a gentleman. He never once tried to kiss her or act inappropriately in any way. But what Chana enjoyed the most was that whenever he dropped by, he always brought his dog, who Chana adored. One afternoon Izzy came by without his dog. Instead, he brought a little golden-haired puppy. She was a straggly female mutt that looked like she might have had some retriever in her, with big kind eyes.

"You want her?" Izzy said, pulling the dog inside Chana's apartment by her leash.

Chana looked at the little creature. *She certainly is cute.* "Oh, I don't know. I'd have to walk her and take care of her . . ." Chana protested. But then the dog nuzzled up to her and rubbed her head on Chana's calf.

"She likes you already." Izzy smiled.

"I can see that," Chana said, petting the puppy's soft head. "All right."

"All right! You'll take her?"

"Yep. She sold herself to me." Chana laughed. "So what shall we name her?"

"Why don't we grab some lunch and talk about it?" Izzy said.

"I just made myself a quick lunch. Would you like some? It's nothing fancy, just a grilled cheese sandwich and some tomato soup. I have plenty of soup, and I can easily fix another sandwich."

"Now . . . how could I turn down a grilled cheese? Did I ever tell you that grilled cheese sandwiches were my absolute favorite?"

"You're kidding, right?"

He laughed. "Nope. I love them. My mama, God rest her soul, used to make them for me when we were kids. Do you remember my mother?"

"Sure. How could I forget Mrs. Reznick? She was always nice to us kids in the neighborhood."

"Yeah, she tried. She was so young when she lost my dad, yet she never remarried."

"Yeah, I remember so much about the old neighborhood," Chana said, sighing. She and Izzy had grown up in the tenements around Delancey Street. They knew each other well.

"Remember that kid Mick with those firecrackers? He was nuts," Izzy said, smiling.

"Yes, I remember I was afraid of him. He was always playing with dangerous things. I even remember the time you protected me from him." She felt a smile come over her face, and it had been a long time since she'd smiled at anyone but her baby son.

"When was that?" Izzy asked, but she knew he remembered.

"When he was throwing those snowballs packed with ice at the girls as we were walking to school. He aimed a few at me. One hit my coat, and you went running over there and punched him in the nose. He never bothered me again."

"I know you don't want to hear this, but I always loved you, Chana. I always will. I know you belong to Sam, and I won't ever try to get in the way of that, but I can't help my feelings."

She looked down at the floor. "Oh, Izzy. I often wonder if I am hurting you by allowing you to be a part of my life. Maybe if you stopped coming by, you would meet a girl and get married."

"My friendship with you has nothing to do with my meeting anyone. I am dating. I promise you that. Please let me remain in your life, Chana."

She looked into his eyes. She didn't think he was dating anyone seriously. *But maybe I am wrong. Maybe he is,* she thought.

"Enough talk about all this serious stuff. I'd love to stay for lunch. Let me take this little girl outside for a quick walk, and I'll be right back." Izzy picked up the leash and led the dog to the door.

"Me too!" Irving said.

Izzy glanced at Chana. "Can Irving come with us?" he asked.

She nodded.

"All right, kid. Your mom said yes, so you can go."

"You two go on and take the dog out. I'll make your favorite sand-wiches, and they will be ready when you get back." Chana shook her head as Izzy took Irving's hand. Then he grabbed the puppy's leash, and the three of them left the apartment. *Sometimes Izzy makes me laugh. Everyone thinks he is such a big, scary mob boss, but he's really just a softy for puppies and kids. And, of course, I don't believe him that he loves grilled cheese. Poor fella, he would do anything just to spend the time with me. I feel guilty sometimes about his visits. But nothing ever happens that Sam should be jealous of. We just sit and talk and sometimes play cards. I don't know if I should put a stop to it or if it's all right as long as we keep it on a platonic level.*

There was a knock at the door. "Come in, Izzy. It's still unlocked," she called out.

A young man entered. He looked uncomfortable. "I have a telegram for Mrs. Schatzman," he said, his voice cracking.

Chana stood up. She looked at him. He was young, perhaps eighteen or nineteen. His hand that was holding the telegram was trembling. She felt weak, like her knees might collapse. *A telegram. Dear God, no. Not the dreaded telegram. I've heard horrible stories of women receiving this and never seeing their beloved husbands or sons again.*

"This is for Mrs. Schatzman," the boy repeated, bringing Chana's attention back to the moment at hand.

She trembled, terrified to admit that she was the recipient of whatever news was inside that letter. "I'm Mrs. Schatzman," she said as she signed for the telegram. Then she took a few coins out of her purse and handed them to the man. He thanked her and left.

Fear washed over her. Her hands were cold but clammy. She could hardly catch her breath. The telegram burned in her fingers. Chana was shaking so hard that her knees grew weak. And then the room went black. She felt as if she were spinning on a wild ride. The noises of the street were muffled in her ears. She could not make out the sounds. Then as she fell to the ground, the letter slipped from her hand, and she fainted.

CHAPTER 69

When Chana awoke, Izzy was holding a wet washrag on her head, and the puppy was licking her hand. She saw the yellow paper that the telegram had been written on laying on the table. Izzy saw her open her eyes, and said, "Irving is in his room with the puppy. He's all right."

"Izzy, did you read it?" she asked.

"Of course." He gently wiped her face.

"Was it about Sam?" she asked, her voice cracking. "Is it about Sam?" she repeated.

"Yes, I am so sorry, honey. I am so sorry," Izzy said, cradling her in his arms.

She began to cry softly. "Read it to me," she said.

"Are you sure you want me to?" Izzy asked.

"Yes, I have to know what it says."

He stood up and got the letter, then he sat down beside her and cradled her again. Izzy glanced at Chana. "Are you sure?" he repeated.

She nodded.

He began to read.

"The Secretary of War sends his deepest regret that your husband,

Private Samuel B. Schatzman, was killed in action. He died a hero in the service of his country. A letter will follow."

"Oh God, how could this happen? Sam and I finally fixed our problems, and now Sam is gone forever. How am I going to live without him?" She began to weep with uncontrollable sobs. He held her gently and rocked her like a baby.

"Well," Izzy said gently, "at least you worked things out before he left. At least you told him that you loved him. It could have been worse. He could have died never knowing."

"This is all my fault. If he and I hadn't fought, he would never have joined the army."

"It's not your fault, honey. Shatzy always did what he wanted to do. He had his own mind. And even if you had been together, he might have joined or been called up. But at least he knew you still loved him before this happened . . ."

She was crying so hard that she was choking.

"It's all right, Chana. Cry, if you need to. I'm here. I'll help you. You're not alone," Izzy said.

CHAPTER 70

Rome, Italy December 1944

Every few days the doctors would smuggle a small group of Jewish people out of the Syndrome K ward. They would take the backstairs and leave by night on a small boat that took them across the Tiber River. A guide would go along with them and lead them to a safe house that the doctors had secured. From there they would begin their perilous journey out of Italy.

As soon as one group left, another group would be admitted into the hospital diagnosed with the dreaded Syndrome K. There was always the danger of being caught as these poor, desperate people made their way out of Italy. But so far, the guides had all been successful.

One night, very late, Lory came into the Syndrome K ward. Everyone was asleep. He sat down on the edge of Alma's bed. He longed to look at her. He longed for just a few moments to watch her sleep. But she awakened, and, in the darkness, she was startled.

"It's all right. It's only me," Lory whispered.

"What are you doing here? Is everything all right?"

"Yes, it's fine. I just had to see you. I know it's not safe, but will you come to my room with me? I want to hold you. I need to hold you. I need it as badly as I need food and water."

She reached up and touched his face. Then she whispered, "Yes." Quietly, they left the Syndrome K ward and went down the hall to Lory's small room. As soon as he closed the door, she fell into his arms and they embraced. He buried his face in her hair, and she could hear him inhaling deeply.

"I love the smell of your hair," he said. "I think I've told you that."

"Yes," she laughed, "you have. But I love hearing it."

He began kissing her. She felt herself become lost in the moment. His kisses made her forget all the terror that she faced every day. They made love; it was quick and full of passion, but it was also filled with love. When it was over, he held her so tightly that she was afraid her ribs would crack.

Gently, she pushed him away.

"Did I hurt you?" he asked. "I'm so sorry."

"You didn't hurt me. You were just holding me so tightly that . . ."

"Oh, Alma, I am sorry. I held you that way because I never want to let you go. When we are apart all I think of is you. I don't know if we will survive this, but I don't want to survive unless you do. My life is worthless without you."

"Lory, I know. I feel the same way."

He held her tightly again but more carefully.

"If we make it through this," she said, "would you consider adopting Isabella?"

"Of course, I would do anything for you."

"She's a good little girl, and I've grown very fond of her," Alma said.

"I know you have. I hardly know her, but I am sure she is a wonderful child."

"You will love her once you have time to spend with her."

"And she will need a family because the Nazis killed her parents."

"Terrible."

"Yes, it is. And I know you have no answers for me, but I can't stop thinking about my bubbie. I hope she and my zede are all right, but I am so afraid that she is dead. She wasn't young or strong. And these Germans are so cruel. Dear God, help us."

"I love your bubbie too. She is a kind and good-hearted lady. We will search for her together as soon as we can."

"What if this never ends," Alma said, "or worse . . . what if the Germans win?"

"They are already losing. The Americans have joined the war, and now Germany is fighting Russia, Great Britain, and America. It doesn't look good for the Nazis. Thank God."

"I hope it will end soon."

"Yes, we all do," he said. Then he kissed her again.

They lay in each other's arms until the sun began to rise. Then Lory walked Alma back to the Syndrome K ward. He tucked her into her bed.

"What would we have said if one of the nurses, who doesn't know the truth about Syndrome K, had caught us?" Alma asked.

"I would have said I was taking you out for some additional testing. No one knows that you're my wife. They might suspect, but no one knows for certain."

"Brilliant," she said. "You always have the right answer."

"I love you, my Alma."

"I love you."

CHAPTER 71

The following week, two more SS officers came to inspect the Syndrome K ward. They stood at the window looking into the room with skeptical looks on their faces while the patients inside coughed.

"Why don't you just euthanize them?" one of the Nazis asked Lory.

He could hardly contain the disgust he felt toward this horrible man. "We don't do that sort of thing in a hospital. We try to save lives," Lory said boldly, and for a moment he forgot the power this man held over him and the danger he had just put himself in.

"But all of you doctors said these patients are bound to die anyway. You did say there was no cure, and the disease is fatal. So why not make it easier for them? Euthanize them. You could do it with a hypodermic needle. It would be fast and efficient. Then have the bodies incinerated and rid this hospital of this germ-infested ward."

"As a medical doctor, I have taken an oath. Killing patients clearly goes against everything I learned and everything I stand for."

Now the SS officers had begun to lose patience. His face was turning red, and his hands were clenched. "I don't care what you stand for. You are under the rule of the Third Reich. You no longer serve that weak Italian government of yours. If I say you will do this, then you will. Or . . . I could have you arrested."

"Yes, you could," Lory said. Then he forced himself to control his anger. He had to think, to use logic instead. For if he didn't, this entire ward would be euthanized. He cared about these people, but his beloved was also among them, and that made the stakes even higher. Lory took a deep breath, then he said, "I can see your point when you say that we should have them euthanized. However, we need to use these patients who are already infected, to experiment on. That is the only way we will find a cure. And, of course, we must be sure that we have a cure, just in case the disease spreads. Can you imagine what would happen if it spread all over Europe? To France? To Austria? To Switzerland? To *Germany?* We would be faced with another plague." If this weren't so serious, and if so many people were not in danger, Lory could have burst out laughing when he saw the look on the Nazi's face when he said Germany.

The Nazi stared at him. "So? Are you close to finding a cure?"

"We hope so. We are working on it day and night. However, I am not sure you want to get any closer to me than you already have. I was going to warn you when you got here, but you started speaking so quickly that I didn't have an opportunity."

"Warn me of what?"

"I've been exhibiting symptoms of Syndrome K. You see, I am one of the doctors who directly works with these patients. I draw their blood samples to use in the experiments. And I started to feel ill this morning, just before you arrived. I was about to quarantine myself, but there was no one else to meet with you."

The SS officer backed away.

"Yes, I am sorry to say that I vomited blood this morning. That is a pretty distinctive sign of the syndrome. But if you would like me to, I will accompany you to the police headquarters."

"I could shoot you right here," the Nazi said, his hand trembling.

"And you'd better hope that no blood splattered on you, or you will be in this ward next week."

"No, no," the Nazi said, shaking his head. Then he and the other SS officer who was with him, walked very quickly down the hall and out the door.

Lory looked at Alma who had been watching. He saw the fear in her eyes, and although he was terrified at how close he'd just come to being arrested, or shot, he winked at her and smiled.

CHAPTER 72

The following day, Lory came into the ward carrying a stuffed animal. It was a brown bear that looked as if it had been a companion to many children. The bear was missing an eye, and there was a food stain on its tummy. But when Lory gave it to Isabella, she smiled brightly.

"For me?"

"Yes it is," he said.

"I love him. What's his name?"

"What would you like it to be?"

"Aldo. That was my brother's name. He died of the flu last year."

"Oh dear. I'm sorry."

"It's all right, Dr. Bellinelli. Don't feel bad. I am getting used to people I love, disappearing. They always do," she said.

Lory shot a glance at Alma. She shook her head.

"Aldo it is, then," Lory said with a smile. Then he turned to Luciana, who was standing right beside Isabella and said, "I'll bet you think I had forgotten you, didn't you?" he asked.

She shrugged. But he could see by looking at her face that she was feeling left out.

"How could I ever forget a girl as sweet as you?" Lory said as he took a pink sweater out of his doctor bag. The same little girl who died and left the teddy bear also left the sweater behind. "Now, because you are a little older, and, as far as I can see, you are very grown up, I thought you would much prefer a pretty sweater to a stuffed animal. And from the looks of this one, I think it should fit you perfectly." It wasn't the truth. It would be a little too big. And he knew she would have loved to have been given a stuffed bear. But he only had one, and of the two children, Isabella was the more fragile child.

"It's very pretty," Luciana said, smiling. "Thank you. I like it very much."

"We can share Aldo," Isabella offered. "He looks like he has enough love for both of us."

Luciana's face brightened. "Really?"

"Of course. Then you can wear my sweater too. We'll share everything just like sisters," Luciana said.

Isabella took Luciana's hand, and together they went to get the crayons Lory had brought them.

Lory watched as Luciana folded the sweater carefully and put it on the table beside her bed. She seemed to like it. He hoped she did.

While Isabella was drawing a picture of Aldo, and Luciana was sitting beside her drawing too, Alma whispered in Lory's ear, "Where did you get that stuff?"

"A little girl died here at the hospital last night. It was terrible. She was just a child. You know how hard I take it when children die."

"Of course I know. I feel the same way."

"The poor thing fell out of a window. When the ambulance brought her in, she was wearing the sweater, and she had the bear clutched in her arms. Sadly, there was nothing I could do. She was dead on arrival. I felt so helpless. Her mother was heartbroken. I wished I could help her, but, again, I had nothing to say. She wept in my arms. And before she left, she told me to take the bear and all of her clothes and throw them away. She couldn't bear to look at them. I understood. I was going to dispose of them, but then I thought these two little girls might like to have these things. I washed them as best as I could."

Alma squeezed Lory's hand. "That was scary yesterday with the SS officers. I know what you told them."

"How could you possibly hear our conversation through the glass?"

"When I was at the hospital in Berlin where we met, I worked with a deaf patient. She taught me to read lips," Alma said.

"Aren't you the clever one. God is so good to me. He sent me a wife who is not only beautiful, but she never ceases to amaze me with her brilliant mind."

Alma smiled, but a single tear ran down her cheek. She quickly wiped it away with the back of her hand.

"How long do you think we can keep fooling them? I am so afraid that some nasty SS officer will catch on. Then what?" Alma asked.

"I don't know. I've thought about it myself. Every night I pray for another day. I realize that at any time this could all be over, and then they will take us all away. I have selfishly thought of taking you and Isabella and trying to get across the border into Switzerland, just the three of us. But I can't. I can't abandon these people. I must do whatever I can to help them. And no matter what the consequences may be, I must keep trying. All of these precious lives depend on it."

CHAPTER 73

Poland, January 1945

At first Esther felt guilty and underhanded for blackmailing Rudolf. In normal circumstances she would never have held someone's secrets over their head. If she would have met a young man like Rudolf before all of this and found out he was keeping things from his family, she would have talked to him. She would have assured him that she didn't think what he'd done was as terrible as it seemed. It is only natural for a boy his age to be curious about women and sex. So his looking at those pictures of naked girls was not as great a sin as Rudolf thought it was. As far as Rudolf's fascination with Jesse Owens was concerned, that, too, was understandable. Jesse Owens was an amazing athlete who had proven his astounding abilities as the world watched stunned.

But, of course, Esther knew that the rapportführer would be unforgiving. He would be appalled at his son for his hero worship of a Black man, especially because Jesse Owens had embarrassed Hitler at the Olympics. Hitler had been outraged when Jesse Owens had won so many medals against Germany's Aryan athletes who Hitler had sworn would prove their superiority. And as far as the naked girls were concerned, she knew Rudolf was embarrassed by his emerging sexuality. She was also certain that Rudolf was concerned because the naked girls in the pictures had dark hair and dark eyes. Esther assumed that Rudolf was probably afraid his father would believe the girls were Jewish. Whether they were or not, Rudolf was scared his father would somehow know he'd gotten them from a Jew in the camp, and he would be angry and repulsed by his son's attraction to them. So even though it went against her moral character, Esther used this as leverage to get what she needed. Rudolf did not disappoint her. He brought more food than she could eat, and she knew it was because he feared his father.

"Be careful when you take this food. Make sure you don't get caught," Esther told him.

"I won't. My parents don't pay any attention to what I do. I could eat all day long, and they wouldn't care. They would just say I was having a growth spurt," he said, laying two loaves of bread and a bunch of apples on the floor by her cot.

She looked at him. "Rudy," she said, "does anyone call you Rudy?"

"No. My name is Rudolf."

"I'd like to call you Rudy."

"Is that part of this bargain?"

"No. If you prefer Rudolf, then I will call you Rudolf."

"I do."

She gave him a quick smile. "All right, Rudolf. I just want to say thank you."

He shrugged.

As Esther studied him, she saw an angry child. *I should not get involved. But I have never been one to back away when a young person needed help. Still, I made such a terrible mistake when I tried to help Luisa. It cost me and my family dearly. Even so, I can't let this boy suffer alone in silence. He needs help, and I must help him.*

"Rudolf, if you ever need to talk, I will listen. I will help you if I can."

"Shut up, Jew. Don't pretend you are nice. You have tricked me by going through my private things."

"I only did this because I need food to live. I don't want to hurt you. I don't want your mother's jewels or your family's expensive things. I need food, and I wasn't getting enough."

He looked at her. His eyes were blank. Then he said, "I'll bring more tomorrow."

That night when the family fell asleep, Esther snuck out of the house. She carried a loaf of bread and half of the apples Rudolf had given her, which she'd wrapped in a towel. She was shivering as she hid from the lights in the overhead towers. *The guards have guns up there. If they see me, they'll shoot. But I must do what I can to help the other prisoners. I remember when I first got off the train and I saw the prisoners at this terrible place. They were walking skeletons. I must share this food with the others. God has been generous with me. I have more than I need. Please protect me, Hashem.*

It was bitter cold. She felt the frigid wind penetrate the thin fabric of her uniform. But she forced herself to be brave and kept walking. Her breath was white. It looked like a cloud that preceded her as she walked forward.

When she got to the fence that surrounded the camp, she looked around. There was no one in sight inside the camp. Esther picked up a tree branch. It was cold and scratchy in her hand. She ran it along the fence, so it made a scraping sound. She did it for a few moments hoping someone would hear her. But no one came. *What if a guard comes instead of one of the prisoners? I tried my best. I think I should go back to the house before anything happens.*

She put the stick on the ground and began to walk back. Then she heard an odd whistle, like a birdcall. Her head whipped around, and she saw a man wearing a striped uniform. He was peeking out from the side of the building.

She ran back to the fence. The man met her on the other side. In a whispered voice, she said, "I'm Esther Birnbaum. I am a Jew. I work at the home of the rapportführer as his housekeeper. I have food for you."

The man wasn't a man at all; he was a boy, a teenager fifteen or sixteen, perhaps. He was thin and pale. As her eyes traveled over his body, she thought, *He is nothing more than a bag of bones trembling in the cold winter air.*

"I'm Isaac Klugman."

"Here. Share this food with the others," Esther said. "I have to go. I'll come back again when I have more food. Listen for that sound of the scratching on the fence. When you hear it, come out and meet me back here."

"This is very kind of you. How did you get this food?" he said, stuffing his mouth with bread.

"Never mind. Just eat it and give thanks to God. God has provided it for both of us."

"Thank you. Thank you so much." The boy was crying.

"Don't eat it all at once. You will get sick. Now get back to your barracks and don't get caught," Esther said. "I must go now." Then she walked away quickly and headed back to the house.

CHAPTER 74

Two days later, Rudolf brought Esther another loaf of bread and two oranges. It was not as much as the first time, but she still felt compelled to share it with that boy she'd met at the fence. *Poor child. Isaac Klugman. He is so young. He should be getting married and starting his life. Instead, he's starving to death as a prisoner here at Auschwitz. I must help him if I can.*

That night a sliver of a new moon hung in a starless sky. Hidden by the darkness, Esther walked quickly to the fence. It had snowed, and the ground was blanketed in white powder. Before she left the house, she'd torn the single loaf in half that Rudolf had brought her. She hid her half under her bed and put the other half under her shirt along with one of the oranges. When she arrived at the fence, she looked around quickly. There was no one in sight. She picked up a tree branch and slowly raked it across the fence. The sound was ever so slight. But loud enough to bring Isaac and another boy out to meet her.

"I brought what I could. It's not as much as the first time," Esther said.

"Thank you," Isaac said.

Then the other boy whispered, "I'm Harry Finkelstein. I wanted to come out with Isaac to thank you personally. He gave me some of the bread and apples you brought. You have no idea what a mitzvah you have performed."

"God bless you. I am happy to help. Now take this food. I have to go." She handed them the bread and the orange. "I wish it were more, but it's all I could spare today. I will bring more when I can."

"Thank you. Thank you," they both said. "God bless you."

Esther began to slip back into the darkness when she heard another voice. It didn't sound like a Nazi guard. The accent was not German. It was Polish. "What are you two swine doing out here in the middle of the night?"

The boys didn't answer.

"What is it you have there? Show me."

Esther ran behind a tree and lay down on the ground. Then she watched in horror.

"You've stolen food, and you haven't given me any?"

"Here, take half," Isaac said.

"I should turn you both in. I'm the kappo here. You have defied me."

"Take the orange too. Come on, Hornstein. You are a Jew yourself. Take what we can give you and shut your mouth. If you cooperate with us, we'll give you more."

"Hmmm. All right. But you'd better not try to hide your food from me. Anything you steal is half mine. Understand?"

"Yes," Isaac said.

"And if you should get caught, be sure you don't mention my name."

Esther crawled on her belly all the way back to the house. When she got to the back door, she stood up and shook off her uniform. It was wet from the snow and filthy. So were her nails from clawing through the dirty snow. *Please God, let them all still be asleep in this house.*

Her body tingled. Her nerves were on high alert. She looked in every direction and listened like a deer being hunted. When she felt certain that she was safe, she slipped into her room and quietly closed the door. Then she took out her hairbrush and began to brush her uniform frantically. The door to her room creaked open, and for a second her heart stopped.

"What are you doing?" It was Rudolf.

She looked at him but didn't say a word.

He continued, "How did you get so dirty?"

"Rudolf, I am going to tell you the truth. Because I can't think of a lie. I am too old to start lying now." She was almost in tears as she was raking the brush across the fabric. It was not getting cleaner. The dirt was only spreading. Finally, she gave up and dropped the brush. Then she looked at Rudolf and said, "I shared the food you gave me with two boys who are prisoners in the camp."

"Whatever for?"

"Rudolf" she said with frustration in her voice, "because it was the right thing to do. There are starving people in that camp. How can you stand by and watch another person suffer?"

He shrugged. "Did you know them?"

"No, I didn't have to know them to help them. They are human beings. It is part of being human to help others."

He studied her as if she'd said something completely foreign to him.

"Rudolf, you have it in you to help others too. You have it in you to be a great man someday. God did not put you on earth to be cruel."

"You confuse me," he said.

"That is because you have been taught some things that are just not right. But these ideas are not yours. You have the free will to make your own decisions about everything. And you know what?"

"What?"

"If you should ever decide to help another human being, you will see how good it will make you feel. And then you will know that there is a God, and it is not Adolf Hitler."

"You speak freely to me because you have those things to hold over my head." He looked at her angrily.

"Oh no, Rudolf. You're wrong. I speak this way to you because I see good inside of you. I see a young man who has been taught things that he instinctively knows are not right. And I believe in you. I believe you will find the good inside of yourself."

He studied her for a moment. She could see he was contemplating all she'd said. "Interesting ideas," he said.

"Are you ever happy? Really happy?" she asked.

"No, never."

"Think about what I said. What you decide to do with your life will be your own decision. But the difference between you and those other men who are a part of the Nazi Party is you know the truth. I just told you how to be happy. So now that you know this, you also know that you have a choice."

He didn't answer, but his voice was soft when he asked, "How did your uniform get so dirty?"

"I had to crawl on the ground to get back to the house because the two young men who I gave the food to were caught by another prisoner. The other prisoner was threatening to tell on them. I was afraid he would see me, so I dropped on the ground and crawled."

"Probably a kappo," Rudolf said casually.

"What is that?"

"My father says they are the worst kind of Jews. They turn other Jews in to the guards."

"That is the worst kind of person," Esther said. "For the first time your father and I might just agree on something."

"I hate my father," Rudolf said, suddenly filled with anger.

"Did something happen?"

"Yes. He told me that I must accept Heidi as my mother. He said my mother is dead, and there is no point in crying for her anymore. I don't accept Heidi. I hate her. And I don't know if anyone has told you yet, but she's pregnant again."

"I didn't know."

"I heard my father talking to her. She just found out that she's pregnant again. I hate that baby that is growing inside of her too."

"What happened to your mother is not the baby's fault. It is an innocent child that will be your little brother or sister."

"I don't want a sister or brother. I want my mother."

"I know. I understand. It's hard to lose someone you love. I recently lost my husband."

"He died?"

"Yes."

"How?"

"We were in hiding. We were very scared all of the time. And one night his heart gave out. And . . ."

"That's very sad."

"Yes, it hurts me. But I find comfort in talking to him."

"You talk to him?"

"Sometimes."

"Does he answer you?"

"In my mind sometimes I can hear his voice," Esther said.

"Do you think I could talk to my mother?"

"Of course."

"But she won't answer, will she?"

"Not in words, no. But you'll hear her in your mind sometimes, and you'll know the things that she wants you to know."

"How do I do it?"

"You just call out her name and talk to her."

"Will you help me?"

"I would be glad to. Do you want to try now?"

"I would like that."

"Tell her what you want her to know."

"I don't know if I can." Tears began to fall down his cheeks. "My father says that it is not proper for a man to cry or to show emotions. Men must be strong."

"It's not weak to show emotions. Everyone has them. It's another part of being human."

He nodded, then he said, "What should I say to my mother?"

"Tell her you love her and miss her."

Rudolf looked at Esther. Then he said, "Mutti, I miss you so much. Every day I miss you more. Heidi will never take your place. Never. I love you, and I wish you would come back. Why did you have to die?" Rudolf began to weep.

"It's all right. Cry, you need to. You must get the pain out so that you can go on with our life. Your mother would want that for you."

That night Rudolf talked to Esther for over two hours before he went up to his room. She lay on her cot unable to sleep trying to think of how she would explain her dirty uniform. *I already tried to convince the rapportführer to let me start a garden in the backyard. But he said no. So I can't tell them that I got dirty because I was tilling the soil. Dear God, what am I going to do? What am I going to say when they see my dirty uniform? I am so tried. I can't think anymore. Please help me.*

When she awoke a clean uniform was laying on the floor beside her cot. Esther smiled. *I knew it all along. Rudolf has goodness in him, dear God. I know he was raised by monsters. But there is good in him. I can see it.* Before anyone awoke, Esther changed into the clean uniform. Then she washed her dirty uniform and hid it under her bed to dry just in case she needed it in the future.

Rudolf brought food again that night and stayed to talk for a while. Esther liked having a friend. But she was still afraid to trust him completely.

"I brought two loaves of bread so that you could give some to the boys you mentioned."

"You are a real mensch," she said, winking.

"What is that?" he asked.

"It means a good person."

"I never thought I would say this, but I like you, Jew. You're not a bad person. And you know what? Regardless of what my father says about Jews, I don't believe you're trying to trick me."

Esther smiled dryly. *It wasn't the nicest compliment I've ever received. But I think it's the best he can manage right now.*

That night Esther didn't want to go to meet the two boys at the fence. The last time she had gone, it had been terrifying for her. But she knew the food she brought for them made a big difference in their lives. So she waited until dark and made her way out again. *I've never been an adventurous person,* she thought as she looked around. The sky was filled with stars. *Ted, are you watching me? If you are, I'll bet you're surprised by my chutzpa, huh? I was never so brave or so bold. Strangely enough, I am afraid of getting caught. I shouldn't be because I am not afraid to die. I know that when I die, we will be reunited. And I can finally sit beside you again. I wonder how many of our friends are up there with you, God rest their souls; may their memories be a blessing. But if they are there with you, then we can start our lives over. I will sit beside you each night and tell you all the gossip in the neighborhood. Who is getting married, who is with child, who has started a new business. Remember how I used to do that when we were young? You weren't interested. I knew it. But you always listened. What a good husband you were. I know you thought you failed me sometimes, but you never did, Ted. I knew that you had a hard time telling me how you felt, but I always knew you loved me and Goldie, and later the grandchildren too. As I walk here alone in the dark, I wonder why I am so fearful. I think it's because I am afraid of being tortured. These Nazis are not human. Especially that Luisa girl. I still shudder when I think of her. But have you seen this boy, Rudolf? I like him, Ted. I see things in him that he cannot yet see in himself. He seems to have a good heart. Yes, it's buried under all of the hideous propaganda he's been taught. But it's there. I know, I have seen it.*

Before she knew it, she was standing at the fence holding a stick and gently raking it across the metal.

No one came.

She pulled the stick across the fence again.

No one came.

An eerie feeling came over her. *Run,* a small voice in her head said. *Run and get back to the house before something goes wrong.*

She shivered. Then she began to run. As she did, the lights went on in the overhead tower. They were scanning the grounds. She fell to her knees then lay flat on her belly. Then she realized the lights were focused within the fences, inside of the camp. A group of guards were running around. They were going into the barracks. Again, Esther crawled back to the house. But this time she had a clean uniform under the bed. Quickly she changed and washed the dirty uniform. Then she lay on her cot breathing heavily.

Ted, what have I done? I think I may have caused those two young men more harm than good. I think they may have been caught and are now in trouble because of me. Hashem, please watch over those two young men. Please protect them. And . . . please forgive me, although I cannot forgive myself.

Rudolf continued to bring food. But Esther never tried to go back to the fence to share the food again.

CHAPTER 75

W henever Rudolf brought food for Esther, he stayed to talk for a while. As the months passed, he opened up to her more and more. One night when he came, he brought her a chicken leg wrapped in a kitchen towel.

"My goodness, Rudolf. I can't remember the last time I had meat. Do you mind if I eat it now?"

"No, go on."

Esther took a bite and closed her eyes. Chewing slowly, she was transported back to a Shabbos dinner she'd been invited to at a friend's house before the Nazis rose to power. She wondered how her friend was doing. Had she and her family survived or had they perished? Esther shivered at the thought. Then Rudolf asked Esther a question, bringing her back to the present moment.

"Do you have any children?" he asked.

"I had a daughter. She died. I have two grandchildren."

"My age?"

"A little older."

"I hate my grandparents. My father's parents are strict. They are mean, in fact. They never make me feel like they love me. And we never see my mother's mother, because she is senile, and my mother's father is dead. I can't believe I am going to say this, but you make me feel cared about. I don't know how that is possible because you are only a Jew."

"Rudolf. You don't still believe all that nonsense about Jews being evil, or lesser people than your Aryan race, do you?"

"It's hard to admit it, but I have been questioning it lately."

"Good. I am glad you are questioning. You must make up your own mind. You must not believe what others tell you."

"I like you, Esther," he said. She felt her heart swell. He'd called her Esther instead of old Jew.

"So I'll be your grandmother. In secret, of course."

"Yes, it would have to be in secret. If my father found out, he'd have you executed," he said in a matter-of-fact tone of voice.

For a moment, Esther studied him. Then she asked, "How would that make you feel?"

"How would what make me feel?"

"How would you feel if your father murdered me?"

"I don't know." He seemed puzzled. Confused. "How should I feel?"

"What do you think?"

"I don't know. I mean. The truth is I would feel bad. Very bad. Yet I am not supposed to feel that way. But I would. I am supposed to believe that you are subhuman."

"Do you really believe that?"

"That you are subhuman?"

"Yes, do you believe it?"

He shook his head. "I don't believe it. But with everything I have been told about Jews, it's hard to trust you. I hope you aren't trying to trick me."

"Why would I want to do that? I like you, Rudolf. I think you are a fine boy. A little confused, it's true. But your heart is good."

He hesitated for a moment. Then he said, "You can call me Rudy."

She smiled and nodded her head. "Rudy," she said, "I like that."

CHAPTER 76

Manhattan, January 1945

The sun was rising, but Fannie and her new assistant baker had been busy at work for two hours already. All of the baked goods had to be made fresh each morning. And now that everything was coming out of the oven, it was time to fill the display case. Fannie checked her watch. *Right on time,* she thought. *We'll be open for business in a half hour.*

"It looks like we're winning the war," Ari Kornblatt, Fannie's new assistant baker, said. "I read it in the paper last night."

"Hush up about the war," Fannie said. "Chana will be here in a few minutes. She lost her husband. He was in the army. It's a sore spot for her."

"I'm sorry. I didn't know. I'll watch what I say," Ari said. He sounded worried that he'd rubbed Fannie the wrong way. Ari was a young man with a wife and baby. He wasn't the greatest baker Fannie had ever hired, but Fannie knew he needed the job. So she'd taken him on, and now she was training him.

"It's all right, Ari. You didn't know. I just don't want Chana to feel uncomfortable here. It took me a lot of convincing to get her out of the house. She was living like a mole. I was getting worried about her. She was holed up in that house with the baby for weeks at a time. But she has finally agreed to help me out here at the bakery. If she gets upset for any reason, I'm afraid she'll go back home and lock herself in forever."

Before Ari could answer, Chana opened the door and walked inside. "It's raining," she said, shaking off the rain. "I'm sorry I'm late. I had to drop Irving off at my mother's house."

"Come on in my office. We'll have a sweet roll and some coffee."

"All right," Chana said.

Fannie looked at Chana as she took off her coat. The tragedies that had unfolded throughout Chana's life had taken their toll on her. It was obvious she was still beautiful, but she looked somber in black. Her long, fiery red hair was wrapped in a neat twist at the nape of her neck. She wore no makeup or nail polish.

Chana sat down across from Fannie and sipped the hot coffee. "This is good, thank you."

"Have a sweet roll. I made them myself. Ari is a lousy baker. But I keep him anyway. I'm hoping he'll learn."

"You are so kind. You've always been the kindest person I know," Chana said.

"I don't know. Maybe you're right. I'm a softie. I feel for the kid. He's got a family to support and really nothing to offer anyone as an employee. I mean, no worthwhile skills. Keeping him here costs me money. I can't put the stuff he bakes on the shelves. The customers expect a certain level of quality from this bakery. You know?"

"Yes I do. And that's why I say you're very kind."

Fannie took a bite of a cherry-filled sweet roll. "This is good," she said, "even if I did bake it."

Chana couldn't eat. She hardly ate these days. "So you asked me to come and help you out. How can I help you?"

"I was hoping you'd work the front for me so I could do the baking."

"Of course I will."

"Good. I'll train you this morning as soon as we're done having breakfast. You won't have any trouble learning."

Fannie was right. Chana was a quick learner, and by eleven that morning she was handling the entire front of the store on her own. *Fannie knew that I needed this. It is good for me to get out of the house and to be busy,* she thought as she waited on the crowd of customers who came into Fannie's bakery every day.

At noon, Izzy dropped by to say hello. Chana had told him that she was going to help Fannie out, but she hadn't expected him to come into the bakery.

"Hello, everyone," Izzy said cheerfully. "I went your apartment and walked Lady," he said. Lady was the name that Chana had decided on for the puppy that Izzy had brought her. When she'd decided to go to work for Fannie two days a week, Izzy had insisted she give him a key, so he could drop in and check on the puppy. She had not felt at all uncomfortable giving him a key. After Fannie, he was her best friend. But she told him, "Now only go by the apartment if you're in the neighborhood. No need to make a special trip. I will walk Lady before I leave, and then I'll walk her again as soon as I get home. She should be all right."

But, of course, Chana knew that no matter what she said, Izzy would make time to walk the dog each day. He was always doing nice things for her.

Izzy's voice brought her back to the moment. He was standing at the counter with a large paper bag.

"I brought lunch. Who's hungry?" Izzy said cheerfully.

"Me," Fannie said.

"Nu, so, why is this night different from all other nights?" Izzy made a joke referring to the four questions on Passover. "You're always hungry."

"Hush up, Izzy," Fannie said, looking inside the bag. "What did you bring?"

"All kinds of stuff from Katz's Deli."

"Do we have enough to offer some food to my new baker?"

"Sure. You know me. I brought enough to feed a small country," Izzy said.

Before he left, Izzy told Chana that she need not hurry home. "I'll pick Irving up from your mother's house, then I'll go by the apartment to feed and walk Lady. Irving and I will have dinner together. We get along well. Why don't you and Fannie go out for dinner after work. It would be good for you."

"I don't know, Izzy. It's hard for me to get back to living."

"And that's all the more reason you should do it," Fannie said. "Izzy is right. Let's go out for dinner after work."

"All right."

CHAPTER 77

After the store closed, and Ari had gone for the day, Fannie and Chana went into Fannie's office.

"How about a glass of wine?" Fannie took out a bottle. "To celebrate your first day."

"Sure," Chana said.

"He's not a bad fella."

"Are you talking about Izzy?"

"Yeah. I mean I didn't like him in the past. But lately he's growing on me."

"You just don't want me to be alone," Chana said.

"You're right. Seeing you so sad for so long is hard, Chana. First Ida, God rest her soul. Then Laevsky. And now, Sammy. It's a lot for one person to take."

Chana shrugged. "I wish I loved him. He loves me so much. He always has."

"Yep. I've always known that."

"But, let's face it, Sam was my bashert, and I could never love anyone the way I love him." Chana sighed, taking a sip of wine. "I can't believe he's dead."

"Chana . . ."

"I thought he would make it. I really did. And when Irving was born, I thought that was God's way of promising me that Sam would come home. But now I don't understand what God's plan for me is, and I am so lost, Fannie."

"I know you are, honey. But you can be sure God has a plan for you and for your son too. You just have to have faith."

Chana nodded. "I'll try."

CHAPTER 78

Poland, January 1945

E sther was awakened on a chilly January day by loud voices coming from the living room of the rapportführer's home. She peeked out of her room behind the kitchen to see that several of the guards from the camp had gathered there. They seemed to be jittery, but Esther didn't know why. Heidi was sitting on the sofa weeping. Esther didn't know what to do. She was not certain whether to come out and start breakfast or to lay low and listen. She opted to listen.

"How can this be?" one of the guards said.

"It is. That is all we know."

"He would not do this to us. He would not leave us like this."

"He did it. He is abandoning us. We are losing the war. Germany is losing the war. There is no way we can win now. We must escape from here as soon as possible. The enemy will be arriving any time now. If it's the British or the Americans, it will be bad. But if it's the Russians, it will be even worse. They are mean and heartless, and we can count on being tortured."

What is going on? Who did what? I can't make sense of this conversation, Esther thought.

Just then Rudy came to her door. He put his finger over his lips to tell her to keep quiet. Then he slipped into her room.

"Our führer has abandoned us. He's gone into his bunker, and he refuses to come out. He's abandoned his people. Germany is doomed. We've lost the war. My family is about to leave here and try to escape from the country before the enemies arrive."

Esther stared at him wide eyed. She'd had no idea Germany was losing the war. "Where will you go?"

"I don't know. Wherever my father takes us, I suppose. But I brought these things for you." He handed her a crinkled-up woman's handkerchief embroidered with lilac-colored flowers. She opened it. Inside, she found two rings, one with a large diamond. The other a gold band, a wedding ring.

"Take these. I stole them from Heidi's jewelry box. She won't miss them. She has plenty more."

"Is this her wedding ring?"

"No, these rings were taken from the Jews who came into the camp. My father gave them to her. Heidi was always afraid that she'd be accused of stealing; she was afraid that the Jews would come back for these things. But my father laughed at this. He said the Jews would never be back. But we had to be careful taking these not to get caught by other members of the Nazi Party because we would be considered stealing from the Reich and that was a crime. Heidi got nervous, but then he added that everyone did it. So it was all right. He brought Heidi gifts like this all the time."

"I don't know if I should take these," Esther said.

"Don't be a fool. You are going to need something of value to sell after you are free. You don't have any money, do you?"

"No, I have nothing but the clothes on my back."

"You are going to need money to start your life over. Take these things and sell them. Even if Heidi starts looking for them, she'll think they got lost somehow when we left this house."

Esther looked at him, and tears came to her eyes. "You're a good boy. I always knew you were."

"I hope so. All I know is that you were kind to me when no one else was. You listened to my problems, and even though you're Jewish, you were a friend to me."

She smiled at him. "Yes, maybe you will realize that Jews are not so bad? Maybe you can see that we are people, just like you."

He shook his head, looking confused. Then he said, "I have to go. My family and I will be gone this afternoon. Stay here in the house until you are sure all the guards have left, and then you should probably go over to the camp and wait. My father says that either the Russians, the British, or the Americans will arrive soon. Hopefully they will help you."

"Do you think your father or mother will come looking for me before you go?"

"No. They are too busy trying to save themselves. You'll be all right here. Just don't come out. They aren't even thinking about you. They are trying to figure out what to do and where to go."

"I don't care about them. But I do care about you, Rudy. And I wish you well. May you grow up to be the man I know you can be," Esther said.

He nodded. She could see he was tearing up. Then he walked out of her room and quietly closed the door.

For the next two hours there was chaos in the house. Esther could hear the crying and the shouting. People were coming and going. There were loud noises, and Esther was afraid that the rapportführer would come and shoot her before he left. But Rudy was right. The Ernst family had more pressing issues to deal with. And they'd temporarily forgotten her.

By midday the house was eerily quiet. But to be safe, Esther waited for an additional hour before leaving her room. She walked into the kitchen and found most of the valuable things had been taken. But there was a half loaf of bread and a chunk of moldy cheese. She was starving so she gobbled up the food. Then she looked through the house. There were a few things of value that the family had left behind, a heavy silver serving bowl, a pair of pearl earnings that had fallen under Heidi's bed. The pearls were not large, but they were set in a thick gold setting. Esther wrapped them up with the two rings that Rudy had given her and stuffed all of it into her shirt. Then she went into Rudy's room. There she found the box that had contained his secret pictures. She was surprised he'd left it behind. She opened it. He must have known she would look inside, and that must have been why he left it. Inside the box Rudy had left a clean shirt, a sweater, and a pair of pants all neatly folded. He knew she would need clothes. They were his, and they were big on her. But they were clean, and the sweater was thick and warm. His secret pictures were gone. He'd taken them with him wherever he was going. Esther tried not to think about Rudy. All she could do was hope that if he and his family were caught, that he would not be blamed for his father's crimes. And if they were not caught, she hoped that he would remember her and not be so quick to believe the propaganda he'd grown up with. These were her wishes for him.

Esther ran into the bathroom and quickly showered. The warm water felt good on her tired body. After she dried herself off with a dirty old towel that had been left behind the stove in the kitchen. She dressed in the clothes Rudy left for her. Then she searched for a coat of any kind that might have been discarded. But she found nothing. It was drizzling as she walked outside the house. Esther looked up as she walked toward the camp. The towers that had once held armed guards were now empty. She breathed a sigh of relief. When she arrived at the camp, she found the bodies of two Nazi guards laying in pools of blood on the ground. They were still in uniform. Their bodies had been beaten beyond recognition. There were two sickly looking men standing on the side of the building. Both of them were staring at her. "I'm looking for two young men," Esther said.

"Who are they? I know everyone in this camp," one of the prisoners said.

"Isaac Klugman and Harry Finkelstein," she said, "they were young, maybe in their late teens."

"Yeah, I knew them. They were shot for stealing food along with that kappo, Saul Friedman. The guard caught them with extra food."

The noxious odor of the camp was making Esther feel as if she might vomit. *Those poor boys. I knew it. I knew I had caused them to be killed.* She began gagging. "Excuse me," she managed to say.

The prisoners didn't seem to pay attention to her when she ran away from them and vomited. She was afraid of what she would see if she went to the women's camp to find Ruth and Daniel. But she had to go. So she stepped over the dead bodies of the guards, and without looking down, she continued walking until she found her way to the women's camp. Countless numbers of dead bodies with horrified expressions on their skeletal faces lay piled up against the buildings. Esther shivered. *It was all true. These terrible monsters were murdering innocent people. I didn't want to believe it. But there is the confirmation right there.* She entered one of the barracks. It was empty. There was nothing but long lines of wooden cots with threadbare blankets. She left and went into another of the barracks. There she saw a group of five women shivering. Their heads were shaved, and they were emaciated. Their bones jutted out of their rash-covered faces and arms. They wore filthy striped uniforms and stared at her with blank expressions.

"Excuse me," Esther said to one of the women. She could hardly speak because she was so horrified at what she'd seen. "I am looking for a young woman; her name is Ruth Kleinstein. She had a young son with her. His name was Daniel. Do you know her?"

The woman shook her head.

"I knew her," one of the other prisoners said. "Who are you?"

"I'm Esther Birnbaum. I am Jewish. I was a prisoner at the home of the rapportführer. He and his family fled this morning."

"All the guards fled," someone else said. "God be praised. Germany lost the war, and that son of a bitch, Hitler is hiding. I hope they find him and torture him."

Esther ignored the comment. She turned to the other woman prisoner. "You knew Ruth?"

"Yes, I saw her die. It was during roll call. They were taking all the children away. She wouldn't let go of her son. One of the guards pulled him away from her. He started to cry. She ran after him. The guard told her to get back in line. But she wouldn't listen. She ran to her boy and grabbed him into her arms. The rapportführer came. He saw what was happening and got angry at the guard for not having control of the prisoners. He called him weak. Then the rapportführer shot Ruth's little boy. Ruth fell on her son. He was still alive. The rapportführer aimed at the boy. She started shouting, 'No! Please.' She kept shouting,

'No, please,' over and over. But the rapportführer ignored her. He shot the little boy again. This time the child was dead. I could see that half of his face was gone. Ruth got up and came at the rapportführer. She was wild. Her fists were clenched, and she was punching him. He threw her off and shot her dead."

Esther gasped. She could not speak. *When had this happened? Perhaps if I had poisoned his food, he would never have had the opportunity to kill those poor young people. I should have done it. I thought about it plenty. But I was a coward. I was afraid.*

"Are there any guards left here?" Esther asked.

"Not alive. Not anymore," one of the prisoners said. "The men beat a few of them to death. The others ran away like cowards. They're afraid of the Allies."

"Well, it's good that they are all gone."

"Yes it is, but most of us prisoners are half-dead anyway. Last week the guards rounded up anyone who was fairly healthy and took them away on a march of some kind. Over the last couple of days, the Nazis have been running out of here like frightened rabbits," another one of the women said.

"How many prisoners are left?"

"I don't know. There some who are alive. Some who are sick and barely alive. We do our best to care of the sick ones. But they die every day. There is so much disease here."

Esther nodded. "Can I help?" she asked.

"Yes, of course. You can do what we do. You can make them as comfortable as you can."

One of the other women said, "There is no food left. We are slowly starving to death. If the Allies don't come soon, we will all be dead."

Esther wished she had not eaten the entire chunk of bread and cheese she'd found. But there had not been much left, and she hadn't eaten since the previous morning. *If I had known what I would find here at this camp, I would have brought the little bit of food that was in that house instead of eating it. But I was selfish and greedy.*

Esther helped tend to the sick as much as she could. But the other prisoners were right. Those who had fallen ill were already at death's door. It was a frigid winter, and the Nazis had not left much behind in the way of blankets. The prisoners shivered in their thin uniforms. Esther felt guilty wearing the sweater that Rudolf had left for her when no one else had that luxury. The more she saw of the camp, the more she realized she had been blessed. Her time at Auschwitz had been frightening and difficult. She'd worked hard and had lived under the constant threat of being sent to the camp. But now as she looked around her, she realized she had not suffered nearly as much as these poor souls.

One afternoon Esther was melting snow to make water to drink when a prisoner asked her to help with a woman giving birth.

"I have no experience with this," Esther said.

"None of us do."

Esther thought about the lie she'd told the rapportführer about being a midwife. Today she wished it had been true. The young girl was breathing heavily. There was a lot of blood.

"I am going to die," the girl said. She was shivering from the cold. Her face strained with pain. "Do you know why?"

Esther shook her head.

"Because I am a filthy sinner. That's why. This baby is the child of a Nazi guard. He forced himself on me. And I let him. I let him because I was too weak to fight. And . . ." She began weeping. "Because he gave me a piece of sausage. I was so hungry . . ." Then her face contorted in anger. "I don't want this baby. I hope we both die."

"Stop that," Esther said. "You are blaming an innocent child for the sins of an evil man. And . . . you are blaming yourself for being human. You were starving and afraid. How could anyone blame you?"

"He killed my mother. I was standing right there. He shot her because she begged him to let me be. Then after she was dead, he kicked her, and he raped me right next to her dead body. I just lay there. The next day he came to me with the sausage. I let him do that to me again. I hate myself for what I did."

"Shhhh." Esther massaged the young woman's forehead. "Wherever your mother is, she understands."

"Do you think she does?"

"I know she does," Esther said in a soothing voice, then she added, "What's your name?"

"Alma."

"That's my granddaughter's name," Esther said, still rubbing the woman's forehead. "I love her very much."

"Would you forgive her if she did what I did?"

"Of course. You know why? Because what happened wasn't your fault. It wasn't the baby's fault either."

"I miss my mother every day. When we were arrested and brought here from the ghetto, I was betrothed to a nice boy. I was a virgin. We were going to get married and have a house filled with children. This was not the way my life was supposed to be." She let out a scream of pain.

"You're cold. You're shivering," Esther said as she took off the sweater and laid it on top of the young woman. "There. Does that feel a little better?"

The girl shrugged. "I'm thirsty," she said.

"I'll get you some water. I was melting snow to make water, so I have some ready. I'll be right back."

Esther ran outside to get the bowl. But when she returned, she found that the young girl had stabbed herself in the stomach with a knife that someone had found and brought to cut the umbilical cord.

"Alma," Esther said. It unnerved her to call this dying woman by her granddaughter's name. But she repeated the name twice. The girl did not answer. Esther felt for a pulse. There was none. She took her sweater that was smeared with blood and put it back on. Then she kissed the girl's forehead before she turned and left the room.

A little over a week later on the afternoon of the twenty-seventh of January, a troop of Soviet soldiers marched into Auschwitz. The prisoners came out of their barracks like they were emerging from the darkness into the light for the first time. When they saw the soldiers, some of them wept. Others fell to the ground and kissed the soldiers' boots and hands. Some of the soldiers were crying. Esther saw one of them vomiting on the side of the building by the pile of corpses.

Esther thought of that young girl who died so needlessly, and she wondered what would have happened if the girl had not gone into labor. *If only she had waited a couple of weeks, perhaps these soldiers could have gotten her to a doctor. But God always knows best. The poor thing might never have been able to recover from all she'd been through. Perhaps it happened for the best. Who am I to say?*

"Is the war over?" Esther asked one of the soldiers.

"Yes."

"Is it safe for me to leave this place and try to go home?"

"I don't know what's safe anymore," the soldier admitted, "but those miserable Germans have been defeated. The Nazis are no more."

The soldiers brought food. The Red Cross brought medical help.

Esther stayed at the camp until spring when the weather began to warm up. Then when a couple of young Red Cross workers, a man and a woman, mentioned they were going to Berlin, she asked them if they would give her a ride.

"Are you going back to your hometown?" the woman asked.

"Yes, I grew up in Berlin. My home is there," Esther replied.

"I don't know how to tell you this. But I'd rather you hear it from me than to back and see for yourself."

"What are you talking about?"

"Most of the homes that were evacuated by those who the Nazis imprisoned are now owned by Germans."

"But how is this possible? How can they own my home? It's mine. It belongs to me and my family."

"I understand. But once the houses were empty, the Nazi government gave them to German families."

"I must return and see for myself."

"So you'll ride with us," she said. "By the way, my name is Maria."

"I'm Esther."

The ride to Berlin would take several hours. Esther rode in the back of an open truck with Maria. As they drove through town, Esther saw a group of women who were half-naked. Their heads had been shaven.

"Prisoners?" Esther asked Maria. "They don't look the prisoners from Auschwitz. They are too healthy looking."

"No, they aren't prisoners from camps. They are probably Polish women who were known to have collaborated with the Germans."

"You mean they were spies?"

"Some. But most were just Polish women who slept with German officers to get extra food. Now the Polish people hate them, and this is their punishment. Public humiliation."

"There are so many aimless people wandering around."

"Yes, they are all in search of those they lost during this terrible war. I see that so many of them are wearing camp uniforms."

"Yes, many are. Around here most of these people were prisoners in Auschwitz. But there were so many other camps too. I was involved in the liberation of at least five, and I know there were more."

"My goodness." Esther sighed. "How many people did they murder? It's unbelievable what happened here. How could the German people have allowed this? They were so civilized, so cultured. I don't understand it."

"Well, after the war, the country was in such deep financial trouble, and then the hyperinflation that followed scared everyone. They needed strong leadership. It just so happened that Hitler appeared to be what they were searching for. He promised them a new Germany. A country they could be proud of. Hitler told them that every German would own an automobile. The German people were mesmerized by his promises, which, of course, turned out to be all lies. But they were so swept up in his promises that they never saw it coming. Then it was too late." Maria shrugged. "And now, look what has happened to the world. People are wandering not knowing where their next meal is coming from, not knowing if their loved ones are alive or dead." She shook her head. "It's a terrible situation. You are going to be shocked when you see what the bombings have done to Berlin."

"I was still in Berlin during some of the bombings before I was arrested and sent to Poland. It was horrifying."

"What's left of the city is probably a lot worse than you remember."

CHAPTER 79

Maria was right. The city was in ruins. Esther held her breath until she saw that the home she'd lived in with Ted was still standing unharmed by the bombings.

"This is it," Esther said, "Thank you so much for the ride."

"Pull over, Paul," Maria called from the back of the truck to the driver. "We're letting Esther out here."

Paul pulled the truck over to the side of the street in front of the house. The landscaping was no longer well maintained, but at least the structure was intact, and anyone looking at the house could see that it had once been magnificent.

"This is quite a beautiful home," Maria said. "You must have been very wealthy before the war."

"I was," Esther said wistfully. "My husband and I owned a factory. We had plenty of money. But I had so much more than just money. I had my family. My husband. My daughter. My grandchildren. Now, my husband and daughter are gone, and I don't know what has become of my grandchildren."

"I know that must be very hard on you. This war has left so many people displaced from their loved ones and their homes."

"I don't care so much about losing the money. I could live without it. Before the war I never even realized how little I needed to survive. But now that I have survived with almost nothing, I know that you just don't need all the material things to be happy. The greatest loss I have endured is losing everyone I loved. If you have your loved ones with you, then you have real wealth."

"Are you sure that you are going to be all right if we let you off here?"

"I'll be all right," Esther said.

"With God's help, maybe your grandchildren are alive."

"I pray that they are. The last time I heard from my granddaughter she was in Italy. And I have a grandson in America. But I haven't heard from either of them for a long time."

"I hate to break up this conversation, but we have to get moving," Paul said, getting out of the truck and walking around the back. "They expect us back before dinner." He put down the truck bed so Esther could climb out.

"I'm sorry to have kept you," Esther said. "I do appreciate your giving me a ride."

"Good luck to you," Maria said, waving.

The truck pulled away, leaving Esther standing in front of the house. She suddenly felt very alone as all of the memories of her life came rushing back to her. Memories of Goldie when she was a little girl running through the house with her dolls. *How beautiful my Goldie was. She was such a golden child with golden hair. It is impossible to believe that she is gone. And Ted.* Memories of Ted sprung into her mind. She thought about when they'd first gotten married. *How afraid of him I was. He was so handsome and powerful. I didn't know how to speak to him.* Esther smiled sadly as she remembered the dinners she'd had at the house when her parents and her in-laws were still alive. She'd tried so hard to show them all that she was capable of being a good wife and mother. But at that time she hadn't believed it herself. *I doubted myself so much. I had no idea how much I was capable of. I had cooks and housekeepers. Now I know that I can do anything by myself. That's what this terrible experience has taught me. The woman I am today is no longer the woman I was when I lived in this house. I am so much stronger.*

As she remembered what she'd endured at the rapportführer's

home and then what she'd witnessed at the camp, she found the courage to knock on the door. *I am strong enough to cope with whatever I find behind that door.* The old familiar sound of the knocker made her heart skip a beat. She stood there on the step looking around at the garden. Her rose and lilac bushes were dead. She'd loved them so when they bloomed.

It was a few minutes before a woman came to the door. She appeared to be in her mid-thirties. Her hair was very light brown, almost blonde. She had a neat, slender figure and wore a simple gray dress. From where Esther stood, she could see inside the house through the half-open door. There were two small boys playing on the Persian rug that Ted had purchased as a gift for her on their tenth wedding anniversary. One of the boys showed the other one something, and then he giggled.

"Yes?" the woman said curtly. "Can I help you?"

"Hello, I am Esther Birnbaum." Then Esther took a deep breath and mustered all the courage she could. "You see, this was my home before the war. May I ask who you are and how you came to be living here?"

The woman glared at Esther. She ignored her questions. Instead, she said, "It's not your home anymore, Jew. It's mine. Go away. Get out of here before I call the police." The woman slammed the door.

Esther felt lost. Everyone had told her this might happen. But now that she'd seen her house was gone, she felt a deep emptiness in the pit of her stomach. *This was my home. Those were my things. My rug, my bushes, the home where I slept beside my husband. The home where I raised my daughter. And now, my entire life is gone. I have heard that it is best not to contact the police. They won't help. I know I am strong, but what should I do next? How do I start over? Rudy was right. I am going to need those pieces of jewelry he gave me. The money I get from selling them will help me find a place to live. But how can I trust anyone to buy them and not just steal them? I am an old woman; physically I am unable to fight. If someone wanted to take those pieces of jewelry away from me, they could easily do so. My best bet is to use each piece as a bargaining tool. I'll see if I can't trade the earnings for the price of renting a room in someone's home. And then once I am settled, I'll find a job. Any kind of job, it doesn't matter. I'll do whatever is necessary, but not in this neighborhood. I'll go to a less-expensive area, where a set of pearls might buy a month's rent.*

Then she remembered Hans. She was deeply grateful to him, and she wanted to go and see him before she got settled somewhere. She owed him a thank-you. But she was afraid he had perished. *Still, I must go and face whatever awaits me,* she thought. *And I can probably find lodging somewhere near Hans's home.*

It was a long walk, but Esther didn't have money for transportation. Every street she crossed, every corner store she passed, brought back memories. She felt an overwhelming sadness and began to wish she'd hadn't returned to Berlin. *Some things are best left in the past. Perhaps I should not have come. It's too depressing. I am sure that looking at rooms to rent will be even worse. I'll go to see Hans before I look for a place to stay. Hashem, please let him and Marta be alive.* She felt her chin quiver as if she might cry. But she forced herself to stand straight and tall. *It will be all right,* she told herself. *Once I am settled in somewhere, and I have a job, hopefully things won't look as bleak.* As she walked up to the front door of the small house. She felt she might drown in sadness as she remembered the day she and Ted had first arrived there to go into hiding. *Ted, if only I could feel the strength of your arm on my shoulder, I would know that everything was going to be all right. I am so all alone, and I must admit I am frightened of what I will find at every turn. There is death and misery all around. The war may be over, but the hatred of our people is still burning strong here in Berlin. That woman who is living in our home was so filled with it that it was coming out of her eyes.*

Esther looked around. Someone was maintaining the grounds. The house was taken care of. The tree was beginning to blossom. She sucked in a deep breath and knocked on the door. A tall young man answered. He was handsome. He looked almost exactly like Hans only younger.

"Esther Birnbaum?" he said.

He knows my name. "Yes."

"I'm Erwin. Hans's son. I am sure you must remember me from that terrible day."

"I remember that day, of course. But you've grown a lot since then. How old are you now?"

"Seventeen"

"You're still so young." She sighed.

"Yes, and I've regretted that day ever since it happened. I've been hoping you would come by my house at some time. I've wanted to talk to you. Won't you come in?"

Esther nodded and entered the house. It looked exactly the same. Nothing had changed. "Is your father here?"

"No. My parents didn't survive. They both died in a camp."

"Oh!" Esther gasped. Her hands flew up to her throat. "I am so sorry. I feel responsible."

"It wasn't your fault. It was mine. I didn't see things clearly. I believed in the Nazi Party. I believed everything they told me. Then when I met that woman Luisa from my Hitler Youth group, she tricked me into turning all of you in to the Gestapo. It was her. She killed my family. I don't know how she knew that my father was hiding you and your husband. I didn't even know about it. But she must have been watching us. I have been racking my brain trying to figure out how she knew and why it was so important to her. All I can figure is that someone higher up must have put her up to it."

Esther shook her head. "Luisa," she said the name softly. "It wasn't a higher-up. And it wasn't you she was after. It was me."

"You? Did you know her?"

"Oh yes. She and my daughter were the same age. When she was a young girl, I tried to be kind to her and it backfired on me. She and my daughter went to school together. Luisa came from an extremely poor family. I wanted to help. I gave her my daughter's dresses. How was I to know she would be offended that they were secondhand. How was I ever to know that she would be so hurt by what I did that she would hold a terrible grudge against my family that would destroy so many people who I loved."

"I had no idea that she knew you. But I can't imagine why she hated you so much. You were trying to help her."

"Some people take things the wrong way. I wanted to make her life better. Instead, she made mine a living hell."

"I suppose you won't be so eager to help others anymore," he said.

Esther smiled. "No, Erwin. That's not true. I will always do what I can. I believe that is why God put us on earth. To help each other." She sighed. Then she added, "There was a young boy who I met when I was imprisoned in the home of a Nazi. He was the son of an SS officer. His name was Rudy, and he and I had some wonderful and enlightening conversations. I believe I helped him to see the world in a broader light. I know he helped me. You see, Erwin, whenever you help another person, you benefit as well."

"You have a remarkable way of looking at things," he said. "You were imprisoned, and yet you are not angry."

"What good would anger do me? It would eat me up from the inside. I pray a lot. I must trust that God has a plan."

"Do you have anywhere to go?" he asked.

"No, my house was taken away from me. There is a young German family living there now. I have no home anymore. I was going to rent a room until I can get in contact with my grandchildren."

He smiled. "Why don't you stay here until you get on your feet."

"Here, really?"

"My parents would have wanted that."

She looked at him. *I need a place to stay. I would feel much safer here than in the home of a stranger.* I could make myself useful. "I can do all of the cooking. I'll keep the house clean for you, and I'll do your wash."

"It's not necessary," he said. "I'd like you to stay, regardless." Then he added, "But it certainly would be a help."

"I would want to be useful."

"Come, follow me. You can stay in my parents' old room. My mother had some clothes that I am sure would fit you. Would that be all right?"

"It would be most generous of you, Erwin."

Esther settled into the bedroom Hans had once shared with Marta in the Hubermann's home. She bathed and exchanged the clothes that Rudy had left her for a clean housedress. Then she put up a stew and cleaned the house. It was dustier than it had first appeared. When she finished, she sat down at the kitchen table and wrote two letters: one to Sam, the other to Alma, telling them she was alive and where she was staying. Once she'd mailed them, she returned to the house and began to do the wash.

CHAPTER 80

Manhattan, June 1946

Chana received Esther's letter on an afternoon when the bluebirds were singing in the tree outside her kitchen window. She'd gotten the mail and then went back upstairs to her apartment. Izzy had come over, and he was on the floor playing with her dog, Lady, and her son, Irving.

After Sam died, Chana had written to Esther telling her that Sam had passed away, but the letter had been returned unopened. She'd written to Alma as well, but that letter had never been delivered either. At the time Chana had assumed Sam's entire family had perished. Now, as she held this envelope in her hands, it hurt her heart to see that it had been addressed to Sam Schatzman. Seeing his name made his death all the more real. Izzy looked up at her, and he must have been able to see she was upset.

"What is it?" he asked.

"It's a letter to Sam from Sam's grandmother in Germany. She's alive, but his grandfather passed away. She said she was a prisoner in a camp during the war. I have to write to her. She has no idea that Sam is gone."

"Do you want me to write a letter for you?" Izzy asked.

"No, it's all right. I'll do it," she said. He was so different from Sam. Sam had always needed her to lean on. Izzy was the opposite. Chana could lean on him with anything, and Izzy would handle it.

"Are you sure? I don't mind."

"I'm sure, but thanks," she said.

As she wrote these words she wept:

Dear Esther,

My name is Chana. As you know, I am Sam's wife. I received your letter, and I am so glad to hear that you are alive. I am terribly sorry about your husband. I wish I didn't have to tell you this, but I have some terrible news. Sam didn't make it. I don't know if you were aware that he joined the army. But he did, and he died a hero storming the beach in France. I like to think that he contributed to the defeat of the horrible Nazis. I miss him every day. He was the love of my life. When he left I was pregnant with his son. I wish he could have seen him. It would have made him so happy. Our little boy is named Irving. He is a perfect and beautiful child. I can see Sam in the way he crinkles his eyes when he smiles. It warms my heart to know that Sam's legacy will live on in this special little boy.

I wish I had met you. Maybe someday you will come to America. I would love for you to meet your great-grandson, and I know he would love to meet you. You are always welcome in my home.

With deep affection, Chana.

Izzy put Lady's leash on. He helped Irving to put on his jacket. Then he said, "I am going to take the dog for a walk. Irving is going to help me. Aren't you, Irving?"

The little boy nodded and smiled.

"I'll take the letter and mail it for you."

"Thanks," she said.

Izzy winked at Chana. Then he took the leash and Irving's hand and walked to the post office where he mailed the letter. On his way back, he stopped to pick up a box of cookies which made Irving squeal with joy. He gave the boy one and ate one himself. When they finished, they returned to Chana's apartment.

CHAPTER 81

It was almost a full month later that Chana received another letter addressed to Sam. It was midafternoon and she'd just received the mail. Irving and Lady had gotten into a jar of jelly, which he'd used to paint the wall. She'd finally gotten the wall and the dog cleaned up. Then she gave Irving a bath and put him down for his afternoon nap. Lady lay on the floor at the foot of his crib. Chana smiled when she saw how attached the dog and her son were to each other. *They are the two cutest mischief-makers that I have ever seen,* she thought. Then she went into the living room and opened the letter.

Dear Sam,

I have written several letters to you before this one, but since you haven't answered, I am assuming you haven't received any of them. For a while, all of our mail here in Italy was being censored. I am hoping you get this one. In case you tried to write to me, I am no longer at my former address. In order to survive the war, Lory and I had to move out of our apartment. So if you wrote to me there, that's why I didn't answer your letters. After the Nazis invaded the Jewish Quarter in Rome, Lory and I had to get out. I moved into a hospital ward with a lot of other Jewish people. I dared not attempt to write while I was there. We were being quarantined as patients with a fake disease. Because the Nazis were afraid of catching the illness, they left us alone. It was a brilliant plan that was devised by a group of three wonderful doctors who I will remember for the rest of my life. The disease was called Syndrome K. And I will never forget it because it was that syndrome that saved us.

Since the war has ended, I've tried to write to Bubbie. Lory and I even made a trip to Berlin where we went to her house. Some woman answered the door and said Bubbie and Zede don't live there anymore. Do you know if she is all right? With everything that has happened, I am so afraid that she is dead. I love her so much, and I pray for her constantly.

Lory and I are now working at the hospital where the Syndrome K was invented. It's called the Fatebenefratelli Hospital, and we have rented an apartment that is close to work. I've included our new address so that you can get in touch with me. But even with all the tragedy that all of us have endured, I do have some wonderful news. Lory and I have adopted a little eight-year-old girl. She is the light of our lives. Her name is Isabella. And so, you are an uncle!!!!

I do hope this letter finds you well. I will wait eagerly to hear from you.

With love, your sister, Alma.

Chana sat down at the kitchen table. She sighed. *I must tell her about Sam. I hate to tell her. But I must. At least I have some good news for her too. I can tell her that I heard from her bubbie and that she is alive. And I can give her the address of where her grandmother is staying.*

Dear Alma,

This is Chana. I know we have only spoken through letters and only a handful of times, but we had a mutual love for your brother and because of that I have always felt close to you. So you can imagine how sorry I am to have to tell you that our dear Sam was killed in the army. He died a hero fighting for his country and for what he knew was right. After Sam and I lost our daughter, Ida, things were very hard for us for a while. But we rekindled things before he left, and God blessed us with another baby. I gave birth to a son while Sam was overseas. I wish he could have seen him. Choosing a name for a child is an important part of the Jewish religion. So because I know how close Sam was to your father, I named our son Irving. And I know your father will watch over and love our little Irving for his entire life.

I am happy to tell you that I have some more good news! I received a letter from your bubbie. She is alive! But I am sad to say that she told me that your zede did not survive. I have included the address your bubbie gave me. I know she would love to hear from you.

This war took a terrible toll on all of us. But I am truly happy to know that you and Lory are all right and that you have a beautiful little girl. If the three of you ever come to the States, please come and see me. Sam always talked about you, and I would love to finally meet you.

With love,

Chana

After she mailed the letter, Chana called Izzy.

"I got a letter today from Alma, Sam's sister. I had to write and tell her the bad news. Every time I try to heal, something happens, and the scab gets picked off of the wound in my heart again."

"Oh honey, I am so sorry. Why don't I come over? We can play some cards. Maybe I can finally beat you, huh?"

"Would you?"

"Sure. I'll bring dinner. You want Chinese or Italian?"

"I don't care. You choose."

"Maybe you'd rather get out a little? We can go somewhere and have dinner, have a few drinks. Maybe even go dancing? It would be good for you. Staying home and moping isn't help you."

"I know," she said, "but I can't go dancing. My heart is just not in it."

"All right. We'll stay in. I'll bring Italian food."

"Sounds good," she said. Then she added, "Thanks for coming, Izzy. I hate being alone when I am confronted with all of these memories."

"I know. And like I have always told you, I am here for you whenever you need me."

CHAPTER 82

Izzy took a quick shower and got into his car. As he drove, his mind drifted. He loved Chana. He'd always loved her. They'd known each other as children, growing up in the same poor neighborhood around Delancey Street. When they were growing up, Izzy had been certain that the time would come when he and Chana would get married. But then Sam moved into the neighborhood. And everything changed. Chana was smitten with Sam from the first time she saw him. And when Izzy saw them together for the first time, his heart sank. He knew he'd lost her. In those days Izzy had been young and reckless. He was orphaned at a young age, raised by the older hoodlums on the street, always using his wit to survive. He refused to let Chana go, and so he'd tried everything he could think of to turn Chana away from Sam, but nothing had worked. As the years passed, he became more determined. At one point he'd become so frustrated that he had even tried to have Sam killed. Something he was not proud of. Because he'd never really hated Sam. In fact, had it not been for their mutual love of Chana, he and Sam would have been best friends. He liked Sam; they thought alike; they enjoyed the same things. But Izzy knew that as long as Sam was around, Chana would never return his love. He found that he felt bad that Sam was dead. But now, with Sam gone, he had hope. And he was going to do everything in his power to make sure that he was there to help Chana no matter what she needed from him. He would prove his love to her every day, and perhaps, God would forgive him for his terrible behavior toward poor Sam. In exchange for his cruelty to Sam, he vowed that if he had the opportunity, he would love and care for Sam's son as if he were his own child. And . . . maybe, just maybe God would hear his prayers and know that he was sincere. And then God would grant him the love of this woman, who meant more to him than anything else in the world.

CHAPTER 83

Medina, a small fictitious town in Upstate New York
June 1946

The town of Medina, New York was buzzing with activity on that hot summer morning when Elmer and his son left for the countryside. Women had gone shopping for their family's evening meal early to avoid the summer heat. They smiled at each other as they went to the butcher shop and the fish monger. They tried to remain gracious as they negotiated prices with the local merchants. On the sidewalks, men in suits were wiping the sweat from their brows as they walked to their jobs at the bank or their offices. At the corner of Apple and Vine, Glenda the old-maid librarian was rubbing her arthritic shoulder as she turned the key to open the small library. And all over town groups of children had already begun to gather outside their homes for games of jacks or jump rope.

Elmer Ashurst climbed in the driver's seat of the old truck he'd purchased last year from one of the farmers who bought equipment from him. His son, Tyler, got in beside him. Neither of them spoke. But Elmer stole a glance at his son as he started the vehicle. Slowly maneuvering the old truck through town, Elmer thought what a shame it was that his handsome son, a boy who had shown such promise, had lost an eye. In his youth Tyler had been such a good athlete, and this loss of vision would surely affect the rest of his life. Tyler lost his eye when he was wounded and taken to a hospital ship. He had been bleeding from the gut when a bomb hit the ship, and flying debris took his eye.

With all Tyler had been through, Elmer had to be thankful. At least his son was still alive. The Johnsons' boy, Lester, and the Wilsons' son, Ted, had not been as fortunate. Elmer and his wife had attended the funerals for those two local boys. He could still remember how sorry he felt for their parents. He knew that the Wilsons had endured their share of suffering; their daughter, Evelyn, had committed suicide, and now they lost their boy too. He wouldn't begin to say he knew what they were going through. But since the day Tyler left for boot camp, he and his wife had feared that one day they might receive that dreaded letter that would tell them their son was gone. And it could have happened easily. In fact, the only reason Tyler was with them today was because of some fella who Tyler had known before the war. Tyler mentioned his name, Sam Schatzman. But his father didn't recognize that name. Why would he? Schatzman was a Jewish name. Sam had come from the Jewish part of town, and in Medina, the Jews and Gentiles were polite to each other, but they certainly did not mingle.

Since Tyler's return from the war, he'd told his parents bits and pieces of the story of how he'd survived. But Elmer found that if he tried to ask his son any questions, Tyler just shrugged. He didn't like to talk about that day when he had stormed the beach at Normandy and had come face-to-face with death.

Elmer turned the corner at Main Street and Countryside Avenue.

Ben Ryder was standing outside the general store that his family had owned for decades. Ben waved when he saw the Ashursts drive by. Elmer returned the greeting with a quick wave and smile. Then Elmer turned the corner and continued on his way out of town. As the father and son left the hustle and bustle behind, the countryside exploded with a burst of colors. The grass and trees were magnificent shades of green. In the field, yellow dandelions lifted their golden faces to smile at the sun. The sky was cloudless and as blue as a robin's egg. And suddenly Elmer was filled with gratitude. He was glad his son was alive and sitting beside him and that together they were making this very important journey. Tyler had been waiting six months for this day, but he had finally been chosen to receive a trained seeing-eye dog.

Elmer drove for almost an hour until he reached the road sign that read, "Veterinarian, turn right."

"Well, this is it," he said, glancing over at Tyler. Tyler nodded and smiled. Elmer turned onto a private road and followed the sign. "From what I understand, this fella and his wife are considered the best at training them seeing eye dogs," Elmer said.

Tyler nodded. He'd heard that too. According to his friends at the army hospital, the veterinarian they were about to meet was extremely dedicated to the welfare of these animals. Elmer parked the truck in front of the clinic, and he and Tyler got out and then walked inside. A pretty young blonde, who was just slightly chubby, held a small boy with golden hair, in her arms. At her feet were two big dogs. And on the counter a big ginger cat lounged under a ray of sunshine that filtered through the window. She was playing a game with the boy when they walked in. But when the door opened, she looked up to greet the visitors. When she did, Tyler recognized her immediately.

"Betty?" he said. "Is that you?"

"Tyler," she answered warmly. "Yes, it's me. It's been years. How have you been?"

"All right, I guess," he said, shuffling his feet awkwardly. Just then Roland walked in.

"This is my husband," Betty said. "He's the doctor."

Tyler nodded. He was quiet for a moment. Then he said, "I'm here to pick up a dog. I got an approval notice right here. I'm blind in one eye."

"Oh," Roland said sympathetically. "I understand. Our dogs make wonderful companions. May I have the notice, please."

Tyler handed Roland the paper.

Then Roland said, "I know you are eager to meet your new friend. But first you'll have to fill out this questionnaire. We are very careful who we give our dogs to. We raise them from birth. They are like family to us."

"I understand," Tyler said. He sat quietly and filled out the forms. Then he handed the papers to Betty. "I was stationed overseas during the war. That's how I lost my eye." Tyler was quiet for a moment. Then his voice cracked as he added, "Schatzman saved my life."

Betty tilted her head. "Sam? Sam Schatzman?" The pencil that she'd been holding fell from her hand.

Roland looked at Betty. He knew all about her past, and all about Sam Schatzman. He walked over and put his arm around her. "Are you all right?" he whispered.

She nodded. "You served with Sam?"

Tyler continued, "Yeah, Schatzman saved my life. I was wounded, and he carried me through the water during a fierce battle all the way to a hospital boat. If he hadn't helped me, I'd be dead."

She bit her lower lip. Tears began forming in her eyes. "Is Sam all right?" she asked. Then in a quiet voice, "Did he make it home?"

Tyler shook his head. "No. I'm sorry to say that he died on the beach sometime after he rescued me. But before he left me at that hospital boat, he made me promise him that I would deliver something to his widow."

"He was married?"

"Yes. I don't know much about her. I only know she lives in Manhattan. She's got a strange name. Chana."

"That poor woman," Betty said, clutching her chest.

Roland squeezed her shoulder gently.

Then Betty glared at Tyler. "You hated him," Betty said, suddenly overcome with anger. Her face was red, and tears began running down her cheeks. "You and John and all the rest of you KKK boys. You hated Sam for being Jewish."

"I was wrong. God forgive me. I was wrong. I don't belong to the KKK anymore."

Betty put her hands over her face and began to weep. The little boy put his hand up to wipe her tears. "Don't cry, Mommy."

"Shhh, Son. Mommy is all right," Roland said, picking his son up and holding him in his arms. "Mommy just found out that she lost an old friend. She's sad, but I promise you, she'll be all right."

"If her friend is lost, then she should look for him and find him," the child said.

"It's not like that, Son," Roland answered the boy in a gentle voice. "Mommy's friend passed away. Do you remember when that little kitten was born dead, and you asked me to explain why we couldn't help him?"

"Yes. I wanted you to bring him back to life, but you said that it was God's will and that God took that little kitten to live with him in heaven."

"Well, God took Mommy's friend, the same way he took that kitten. And no one can bring him back. He's with God now."

"Don't be sad, Mommy. Please don't cry. Daddy said that the kitten would be happy living with God. So your friend will too."

Betty touched her little boy's face. "I'm all right," she said, then she smiled through her tears. Then she turned back to Tyler and said, "I'm glad you finally saw Sam for who he was, Tyler. He was a good man. A good person. I cared for him."

"I know that, and I sure am sorry for how I acted back in those days. I was a real jerk."

"I know everything works out just the way it's supposed to. And that Sam and I weren't meant to be together forever. We were just kids when we thought we were in love. My husband is the love of my life and my best friend." She glanced at Roland. "But I will always have fond memories of Sam Schatzman."

"Yeah, me too," Tyler said. "You learn a lot about life as you grow older. I sure do wish I could change the past."

"Everything happens for a reason," Roland said.

Tyler nodded.

Then Roland read the form that Tyler had filled out. He could see by what Tyler wrote that he was a lonely man, badly in need of a companion animal. He knew the story of Sam Schatzman and how these boys from the KKK had tortured Sam and Betty. For many years, Roland had hated them for what they'd put his beloved wife through. But Roland had always been one to forgive, and as he looked at the broken man in front of him, all he could feel was compassion. He smiled at Tyler. "Now, why we don't we all go out back and see if we can't find you a nice puppy. I'm sure we have the perfect little friend for you," Roland said. Then he nodded at his wife.

And Betty wiped the tears from her face and smiled.

CHAPTER 84

Manhattan, July 1946

Chana continued to work for Fannie at the bakery a couple of days a week. She was still mourning, but she had fallen into a routine she could live with. On Saturday night she and Izzy went out for dinner. Wednesday nights he came over to play cards. He would have taken her anywhere. He would have come over to see her every night. But Chana had kept him at a distance. She knew how much he cared for her and she liked him too. But she felt that by allowing him to get too close, she was betraying her love for Sam. So Izzy was not allowed even a quick good-night kiss. He never complained.

During the winter, when the snow was deep and the ice formed on the windshield of her car, Izzy drove Chana to work. He made sure she had plenty of food in her apartment and that her heater was working well. The little bit of money she had saved was running out. But that didn't matter to Izzy. He had plenty of money and more coming in all the time. So he made arrangements to pay all of her bills. She'd protested at first. But she was worn and tired, and he was insistent. And if she had not allowed him to pay her bills, she would have been forced to work full time and move to an inferior apartment. Irving was still a toddler, and she was afraid that if she moved him to a flat where there was not enough heat in the winter, he might get sick. Finally, she gave in to Izzy's generosity, telling him that she felt bad taking all of this from him knowing she had nothing to give him in return. He just smiled and said, "I have no family. I have no one. You are my best friend. Friends help each other, right?"

She nodded, then she said, "Thank you. You know I really appreciate everything you do for me."

And that was the end of it. From then on Izzy paid for everything.

It was on a hot July afternoon, when Chana had just returned from walking Lady, that she saw a man standing outside of her apartment building. Irving was holding his mother's hand tightly.

The strange man was leaning against a tree looking as if he were waiting for someone. She felt a chill run up her spine. Chana studied him. He was a tall, heavyset man with a ruddy complexion and very short hair, cut military style.

"Excuse me," he said, "are you Chana Schatzman?"

She was afraid of him. Lady, sensitive to her mistress's feelings, growled. Irving squeezed his mother's hand. His bottom lip jutted out, and Chana could see that he was ready to cry. She forced herself to smile at him. "It's all right, Irving," she said, then she turned to the stranger and said, "Yes, I am Chana Schatzman. Who are you?" Chana was trying to sound brave. Lady was barking. Irving was looking up at his mother with wide, frightened eyes.

"My name is Tyler Ashurst. I have something for you. It's from Sam."

She felt her mouth go dry. She could hardly swallow. Tyler pulled two sheets of paper out of his pocket. "Your husband and I served together. He saved my life. I checked with the army before I came to find you. I had to see if he made it home. I sure was hoping he would have survived. Anyway, I sure am sorry about Sam. It is a damn shame. He was a real nice fella." He was looking down at his feet shuffling around awkwardly.

"You see, I came here because the last time I saw Sam, he made me promise that if he didn't make it back to you, that I would make sure you got these papers. So . . . here," he said, handing her the papers.

She took the dirty, bloodstained papers. "Thank you," she said. Her hands were trembling.

"I better get going," Tyler said, and then he turned and walked away quickly.

Chana leaned against the tree trying to catch her breath. She was afraid she might faint and leave Irving standing helpless and alone on the sidewalk. So instead of opening the papers right there in front of her building, she took a deep breath, then went upstairs to her apartment.

She walked inside her flat, then closed the door and unleashed Lady. "Mommy, can I have a cookie?" Irving asked. Chana nodded. She gave him a cookie. He sat down on the sofa to eat it. And she plunked down at the kitchen table and unfolded the papers.

When she read the words that Sam had written, she began to sob.

"Mommy?" Irving said in a panic, the cookie falling from his hand onto the floor. "Mommy, why are you crying?"

"It's all right." She tried to soothe her son, but her deep heart-wrenching sobs were unstoppable. Lady tried to jump up on Chana and lick her face, but she gently pushed her away.

Sam knew he was going to die. He says that he wants me to marry Izzy. He says he wants Izzy to be a father to Irving. Her hands were trembling as she looked at the picture Ida had drawn so many years ago. *I need Izzy. I need his strength to help me cope with this,* she thought as she picked up the phone.

"Izzy, come over. I have something I must show you."

CHAPTER 85

Alma was setting the table while her bubbie sang songs with Isabella. They were children's songs in Yiddish that Esther had taught her new great-grandchild.

As soon as Alma had received the letter from Chana telling her where Esther was living, she contacted Esther. Then she and Lory had arranged for Esther to come to Italy. When Esther arrived, they talked. Esther told Alma and Lory how she'd survived the war, and they told Esther about Syndrome K. Then Alma explained how they had met little Isabella and how she had no family, so they had adopted her. And although Isabella wasn't an outgoing child, she was immediately comfortable around Esther. Alma wasn't surprised at how good her bubbie was with Isabella. She knew how warm and wonderful her grandmother could be. After all, when she had first come to Berlin and met Esther for the first time she, like Isabella, had felt close to her bubbie immediately. That night as Alma and Lory lay in bed, Lory asked Alma if she would like to invite Esther to come and live with them.

"Oh, yes I would," Alma said. "We have all been separated from our loved ones for too long. She has no one in Germany anymore. It would be wonderful for her to stay here with us."

"Then it's settled. We'll ask her together tomorrow."

Alma curled up in her husband's warm, safe embrace.

The following day when they asked Esther if she would like to move in with them, she was thrilled. "I love you both, and I love little Isabella. Of course, I want to live here with you."

And so it was that Esther moved in, and they became a family.

Esther proved to be a delightful addition. And Lory loved her as much as if she had been his own grandmother. She did the cooking and cleaning while Alma was at work at the hospital. And at night she helped Isabella with her school assignments.

"Whatever happened to Mussolini?" Esther asked one night when they were having dinner.

"He finally got what he deserved," Lory answered. "He was running away like a coward when he was captured by the partisans and killed by a firing squad, then his body was hung in the Square of the Fifteen Martyrs."

"Oh my goodness, wasn't that the same square where the Germans hung those three men who were helping us to get the Jews from the Syndrome K ward, and out of Italy?"

"Yes, those three wonderful men along with twelve other Italian partisans. That's why it's called the Square of the Fifteen Martyrs."

CHAPTER 86

August 1946

Vito and Lucinda were coming for dinner one night. It had been a few months since they'd all gotten together. And Isabella was excited to see her friend. Esther had offered to teach Isabella how to make a challah to serve that night. And now the two of them were busy cooking.

Esther and Isabella were kneading dough when Alma walked into the kitchen. She was carrying the mail. She took out a knife and opened a letter. There was silence for a moment, then she turned to look at Esther, who stopped kneading the bread and was looking at her. "What is it?" Esther asked.

"It's a letter from Chana. A letter . . . and an invitation."

"What kind of invitation?" Isabella asked.

"An invitation to her wedding. She wants us to come to America. She is marrying a man named Izzy. She says that he was Sam's best friend. And she wants us to be there at the wedding so we can meet Sam's son, Irving."

"Irving?" Isabella asked.

"Yes, you have a cousin in America. He is my brother's son. His name is Irving, like my father's name. Chana wants to send passage for all of us to go to America. What do you think, Bubbie?"

Bubbie took a long, deep breath. Then she sighed. "I think that only a stone should be alone. Our dear Samelah is gone from this world. Olav ha-sholom, he should rest in peace. But Chana is alive, and she is still a young woman. Sam would want her to marry again. I say yes, let's go to the wedding. We have had enough sorrow in our lives. It's time for a little joy."

"We're going to America?" Isabella asked.

"Yep," Alma said, smiling. She took out a bottle of red wine and poured a glass for herself and one for Bubbie. Then she raised the glass and said L'chaim."

"L'chaim," Bubbie said. "To life!"

CHAPTER 87

November 1946

The synagogue was decorated with pink and white tule and large bouquets of white and blush roses. The stained-glass windows poured a rainbow of colors onto the white marble floor.

Esther held little Irving's hand as they walked down the aisle. He was acting so grown-up in his black tuxedo as he carried the rings to the front of the alter. At four he looked so much like Sam that it made Esther smile.

The pews were overflowing with guests. Izzy was a wealthy and important man with lots of friends. But even as important as he was, Izzy trembled as he stood at the front of the alter waiting for Chana. She walked toward him wearing a blush-colored gown. When she reached him, he turned to look at her, then he whispered in her ear, "I wasn't always good to Sam. I was a jealous fool. He was a better man than me by far. But I swear to you that I will fulfill this promise. I will always love you, and I will take care of you and little Irving, and I swear that neither of you will ever want for anything."

Fannie had been standing quietly on the sidelines at the altar. Just before the wedding ceremony began, Fannie walked up to the front where she lit a candle for Sam. Then she turned to the congregation. "This is in memory of Sam Schatzman. He was truly loved by all who knew him. May his memory be a blessing." Then she lit another candle and said, "This is in memory of Ida Schatzman. She was taken from us far too soon."

Alma held Lory's hand, and tears ran down her cheeks.

Next, the rabbi began the wedding service.

"I do," Chana said. Her voice cracked, and tears ran down her cheeks.

"I do," Izzy said. His hands were trembling, and his heart was beating fast.

After the couple spoke their vows, they exchanged rings. Then they both drank wine from the same glass. Once they'd finished, the rabbi wrapped the glass in a white cloth, then he put it on the floor. The room was still as Izzy raised his foot. When he stomped on the glass everyone yelled, "Mazel tov!"

But Chana didn't hear them. All she could hear was Sam's voice whispering in her ear, "Mazel tov, my darling. I will always love you. But now I can rest in peace because I know you will be cared for and loved."

AUTHORS NOTE

I always enjoy hearing from my readers, and your thoughts about my work are very important to me. If you enjoyed my novel, please consider telling your friends and posting a short review on Amazon. Word of mouth is an author's best friend.

Please Click Here to Leave a Review

Also, it would be my honor to have you join my mailing list. As my gift to you for joining, you will receive 3 **free** short stories and my USA Today award-winning novella complimentary in your email! To sign up, just go to my website at www.RobertaKagan.com

I send blessings to each and every one of you,

Roberta

Email: roberta@robertakagan.com

Please turn the page to read the prologue from *The Smallest Crack*, Book One in A Holocaust Story Series...

EXCERPT FROM THE SMALLEST
CRACK

Berlin, Germany Spring 1932

Eli Kaetzel paced on the stone steps outside the yeshiva and took a deep breath. He loved the freshness in the spring air as it filled his lungs. Everything about spring made him feel as if the world around him was born anew. The tiny blades of new grass, the flower buds, the crystal-blue cloudless sky. He sighed and looked around. He felt a sense of well-being wash over him. And to make things even better, it was Tuesday, his favorite day of the week. On Tuesday afternoons, when the weather permitted, he and his best friend, Yousef Schwartz, went to the park to study. Instead of being cramped up inside the yeshiva until late afternoon, they sat on a park bench where they ate potato knishes that Eli's mother packed for them and had stimulating discussions about Talmud stories. But that was not the real reason that Eli was so elated and anxious to get to the park today. The real reason was her, the girl in the park. Since the first time he saw her, three weeks ago, he'd thought of little else. She was playing ball with a group of her friends, and when he saw her for the first time, he thought that she might be the most beautiful girl he'd ever seen. All that week he'd hoped to see her on the following Tuesday, and then he thought his heart would burst with joy, when he and Yousef went to the park the following week, and she was there: then, again, the week after. He was mesmerized by her. And even though he knew for certain, by her clothing, that she was not Hasidic, he hoped that at least she was Jewish. Not that his family would have been pleased with him for being attracted to a girl who was not Hasidic. But in his mind, he began creating all kinds of possible scenarios. *Perhaps, she is Jewish, assimilated, but Jewish.* He thought. *And, if by some wonderful miracle I met her and she decided she liked me, she might be willing to join the Hasidic community.*

Today, Yousef was late, but that was nothing new. Yousef could easily get caught up in a heated conversation with his teacher about a story in the Talmud, and a half hour might pass before he realized he'd left Eli waiting. Eli smiled and shook his head thinking about how absentminded his good friend could be.

"Eli!" Yousef called out as he was coming out of the building. "Were you waiting long? I'm sorry. I got tied up discussing today's lesson with the teacher. And you know how intense he can be. Oy! He gets on a subject, and there is just no stopping him. I am so sorry I kept you waiting."

"Don't worry. I wasn't waiting long. And besides, it's so beautiful outside today that I didn't mind at all," Eli said, but he wasn't telling the truth. Inside he was a trembling nervous wreck. He tried to appear calm in order to hide his deepest secret, his attraction to the girl in the park, from Yousef

Eli had known Yousef since they were young boys, and he knew his friend's shortcomings. If he had to place a bet, he would have wagered it was probably Yousef who had been the one who kept the conversation going with the teacher, which made him late. Yousef loved having discussions about Torah.

"Come on, let's go" Eli said.

"Oy, I forgot one of my books. " Yousef looked down at the pile of books in his hands,

"Leave it, you'll get it tomorrow. Let's get going, We want to have time to study don't we? At this rate we won't get there until it's dark."

"I'm sorry Eli. But, I want to read you an important story from this book. I was hoping we could take some time to discuss it. So, I can't leave without my book. I'll be right back. I promise not to get involved in any long conversations with anyone. If anyone tries to stop me to talk I will tell him that Eli Kaetzel the son of the rebbe is waiting and I can't keep him waiting any longer" Yousef winked.

"Stop joking and go and get the book already." Eli said

Eli shook his head. *Yousef should have been my father's son. He's so dedicated to studying. Sometimes I wish I were more like him.*

The two boys, Yousef and Eli, met as seven-year-old children in the yeshiva, their religious school. When they turned thirteen, their bar mitzvahs were a week apart. Even now, memories of Yousef and himself sitting on the hard chairs in the rabbi's study, trying hard to memorize the Torah portions they would recite for their bar mitzvahs, could make Eli smile. The three of them had been so young and so nervous. They knew that everyone in the entire shul would be watching them when they stood up to read their portion of the Torah. Everyone would know if they made a mistake. For Eli, the son of a very well-respected rebbe, making a mistake was just unacceptable. He had to study extra hard so as not to embarrass his father. Each boy would have his own special bar mitzvah day. Following the service, there would be a big celebration, because after all, on the day of their bar mitzvahs, they would become men within their community. It was a very important day indeed. And soon, very soon, they would be expected to take their places in the community as husbands and fathers.

"Come on, let's go," Eli said when he saw Yousef strolling casually out of the building.

"All right, I'm coming." Yousef said, straightening his kippah, the little head covering he wore out of respect for God, and although he pinned it, was always sliding around on his fine hair. He put on his customary black hat and twisted his long payot around his finger, forming curls.

The two boys walked together toward the park, each carrying a pile of books, their identical, long black coats flapping in the warm breeze. The park was on the outskirts of their neighborhood. Dressed as they were, anyone could easily see they were very religious and came from the Jewish side of town. As they entered the park, a scrappy, young man with blond hair and a strong jawline, wearing a brown leather jacket, was leaning against a tree. He sneered at Eli and Yousef. Then he said loudly, "Dirty Jews."

Yousef and Eli shot each other a quick glance but kept walking. They were not permitted to start a fight even if someone insulted them. The Hasidic way was one of nonviolence. Since he was a child, Eli was taught that even if he were attacked, he was not to fight back. Eli's father would have been furious if Eli came home with evidence that he'd been fighting.

"Eli, perhaps we should leave. It's been getting more and more dangerous at this park for us. They used to whisper the insults about Jews under their breath. They are not hiding their hatred of our people anymore. Maybe we should just go home and stop coming here."

Eli's heart sank. Leave, now? He couldn't leave. He had to see her. He'd waited all week to see her. A wave of guilt came over him. He knew Yousef was right. They should probably go but he couldn't. "Yousef, don't worry so much. It will be all right. Come," Eli said smiling. "Sit down; it will be fine. You'll see. Now, let's eat."

Yousef gave Eli a look of concern, but he nodded and followed his friend.

The two boys sat on the bench under the tree and took off their coats. Underneath, they wore white shirts and black pants. They lay their piles of books on the bench beside them. Eli took out the grease-stained paper bag that held the knishes and handed it to Yousef. Yousef took one then gave the bag back to Eli. Eli bit into the knish and closed his eyes. It was delicious—the crispy dough, the soft potato insides. Taking a deep breath, he opened his eyes and glanced across the park and saw a group of girls playing kickball. Eli quickly lost interest in the food as his eyes searched frantically for the girl. Yousef was speaking to him, but he couldn't hear what Yousef was saying. *Where is she? Is she here?* And then he saw her. She was tall and slender with hair the color of rose gold that was blowing in the wind like the mane of a wild lion. As she was running after the ball, he felt dizzy with desire as he caught a glimpse of her thigh. It was as white as his mother's porcelain china, and in that instant, his heart skipped a beat.

She laughed, and he heard her laughter twinkle in the spring air. He thought if the stars in the sky could talk that is how they would sound.

Eli's heart was beating loudly in his throat. He felt had never seen such a free-spirited creature, and her natural beauty left him breathless. Her body was slender and agile, not womanly. She had very small breasts, and her hips were straight rather than curvy. As he watched her playing kickball, he realized that she could run faster and kick harder than any of her teammates.

"What are you looking at?" Yousef asked. "You haven't heard a word I've said since we sat down."

"Nothing."

"Good, and make sure you are not looking over there." Yousef indicated toward the girls playing ball. "You know better than to be looking at them. That is forbidden."

Eli nodded as Yousef handed him his book on Talmud. "Come on, open your book, and let's do some studying," Yousef insisted.

Eli opened his book halfheartedly, then when he was sure Yousef was busy turning pages, he glanced back up at the girl.

"She's pretty, don't you think?" Eli asked. He hadn't meant to say it. Somehow he just blurted it out.

"Prost," Yousef said. "She's prost. Not at all refined."

"She's not prost, not vulgar or cheap. She's lovely and graceful."

"Eli, what's the matter with you? Have you lost your mind looking at a shiksa? Are you looking for trouble? If your father knew, he'd be furious."

"How do you know she's a shiksa?"

"It doesn't matter. She's not one of us. She's not Hasidic. So, she's not for you."

"I'm sorry, Yousef. You're right; we came here to study. And we should stick to strictly business, isn't that right?"

"No, of course not. We're best friends. We can talk about anything. So, since we are taking a little break from studying, I do have to tell you something," Yousef said. "My father wants me to meet this girl. Her name is Miriam Shulman. Do you know her?"

"She's a prospective bride for you, I assume?" Eli asked.

"Yes, why?"

"I met her."

"Your father was considering her for you?"

"Yes."

"And you said no?"

Eli nodded.

"Why? Is she ugly?"

"No, not at all. She's very pretty. And she was nice and refined," Eli said. "I am just not ready to get married, Yousef. It's not that there is anything wrong with Miriam Shulman. She's modest and from a good family. It's just me. I can't see myself as a husband and father yet."

"When, then, will you be ready, Eli? You're seventeen. You're a man. It's time to start your family. And I hate to say it, but if you were married and had a wife to go home to, you wouldn't be so tempted to look over there at the wrong girls."

"But the truth is, I would. I would be looking over there and thinking things I should not think. I would be sinning, committing adultery in my heart. And that's why I should not get married yet. It would be worse," Eli said, feeling a wave of guilt come over him. *Why can't I be more like Yousef? He should have been the son of a rebbe not me. He would have made my father proud.*

"What am I going to do with you? Oy, if you don't stop yearning for forbidden things, you are going to get into trouble for sure."

"Nu? So what should I do? I can't change the way I feel. I try, but I can't," Eli said.

"And it's worse for you because your papa is so important in the community. So, of course, everyone is watching everything you do. Everyone wants you to marry his daughter."

"Yes, I suppose that's true. Not only is my father a rebbe, but we are Kohanes. So, yes, all the old women want me to marry into their families."

"Maybe you should talk to a rabbi. Not your papa, of course. Maybe a rabbi could give you some advice that would help you."

"I doubt it. He'll tell me to follow the rules, and everything else will fall into place. I know because that's what my father tells everyone who comes to see him about their problems."

"Then maybe that's the answer. Maybe it's what you should do," Yousef said.

"Maybe it is. But I can't. I can't just marry some girl and spend the rest of my life with her. I'm just not ready."

They sat in silence for several moments. Yousef put the food down on the bench and stared out looking at nothing. Then he turned a serious face to Eli, and said, "You know that fellow who called us dirty Jews outside the gate to the park today?"

"Yes, what about him?"

"Well, that sort of thing has been happening to me more and more often. And I am quite sure that this Jew-hating sentiment is getting stronger in Germany."

"It'll pass. My father says it will pass."

"You believe him? You think he's right?" Yousef asked.

"I don't know. If it doesn't pass, what are they going to do to us?"

"Who knows? But it scares me. They hate us," Yousef said.

"My father says that pogroms have been going on since the beginning of time, and Jews have always been targeted. This is nothing new; they've always hated us."

"Does he say why?"

"He thinks it's because we are the chosen people."

"Chosen for what?" Yousef said sarcastically.

"I don't know. It's just the way it is, and the way it's always been."

"That doesn't make it right."

"No, it doesn't, but he says you can't change it either."

"How bad do you think it will get?"

"Probably some destruction of our homes and shops and, of course, looting. Then it will be over. It's always been this way for Jews. I hate it too, but I don't know what we can do to stop it," Eli said, shrugging his shoulders.

"I hope you're right. I hope it will be mild and then be over," Yousef answered. "Sometimes, I wish my family would leave Germany but they won't."

"I know. I have felt the same way. I've talked to my father, but he too refuses to leave. He says Germany is as much our country as it is theirs. He was born here, and his father was born here. He says he won't be driven from his home by a bunch of hoodlums."

"The rioting and fighting that is going on in the streets terrifies me, and the rise of that National Socialist party isn't good for us at all," Yousef moaned.

"I agree with you. But what can we do? Our parents have all our family money. You and I have nothing. We can't possibly leave Germany without their consent. And so far, they aren't consenting. Anyway, if you could leave, where would you go?"

"I don't know." Yousef shook his head.

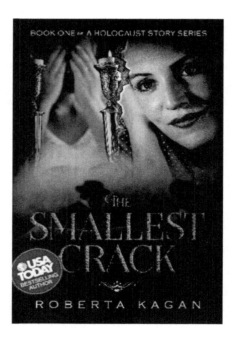

Click Here To Purchase The Smallest Crack By Roberta Kagan

ALSO BY ROBERTA KAGAN

Available on Amazon

A Jewish Family Saga

Not In America

They Never Saw It Coming

When The Dust Settled

The Syndrome That Saved Us

A Holocaust Story Series

The Smallest Crack

The Darkest Canyon

Millions Of Pebbles

Sarah and Solomon

All My Love, Detrick Series

All My Love, Detrick

You Are My Sunshine

The Promised Land

Michal's Destiny Series

Michal's Destiny

A Family Shattered

Watch Over My Child

Another Breath, Another Sunrise

Eidel's Story Series

Who Is The Real Mother?

Secrets Revealed

New Life, New Land

Another Generation

The Wrath of Eden Series

The Wrath Of Eden

The Angels Song

Stand Alone Novels

One Last Hope

A Flicker Of Light

The Heart Of A Gypsy

ACKNOWLEDGMENTS

I would also like to thank my editor, proofreader, and developmental editor for all their help with this project. I couldn't have done it without them.

Paula Grundy of Paula Proofreader

Terrance Grundy of Editerry

Carli Kagan, Developmental Editor

Printed in Great Britain
by Amazon

82575606R00202